Sophie!

Jake's heart stopped, and his mouth went dry. All he could do was stare down at the woman inches from his bare chest, her face tipped up toward him.

He would know those stormy gray eyes anywhere.

It was *her.* The woman—the angel?—who had led him back from the brink of death. She'd called his name when he was slipping away.

The sound of her voice saying his name now, softly, sent a jolt through him. Oh, God, she was beautiful. Beautiful . . . and real.

Kiss her!

The thought jump started Jake's heart and sent it racing.

The idea was strongly tempting. . . .

But it wasn't *his!*

Dear Reader:

Romance readers have been enthusiastic about the Silhouette Special Editions for years. And that's not by accident: Special Editions were the first of their kind and continue to feature realistic stories with heightened romantic tension.

The longer stories, sophisticated style, greater sensual detail and variety that made Special Editions popular are the same elements that will make you want to read book after book.

We hope that you enjoy this Special Edition today, and will enjoy many more.

Please write to us:

Jane Nicholls
Silhouette Books
PO Box 236
Thornton Road
Croydon
Surrey
CR9 3RU

Jake's Angel

KATE FREIMAN

SPECIAL EDITION

All the characters in this book have no existence outside the imagination of the Author, and have no relation whatsoever to anyone bearing the same name or names. They are not even distantly inspired by any individual known or unknown to the Author, and all the incidents are pure invention.

First published in Great Britain in 1994
by Silhouette Books, Eton House, 18-24 Paradise Road,
Richmond, Surrey TW9 1SR

ISBN 0 373 59278 7

23-9408

Made and printed in Great Britain

With gratitude to: my intrepid critique partner,
Doretta Thompson, for her invaluable help;
my "computer guy," Scott Walker, of Avenue Road
Videoflicks, for the information and the inspiration;
my agent, Alice Orr; and my editor, Tara Gavin, for
sharing my vision; and to Mark and Ben for the love.

KATE FREIMAN

says she began creating stories with happy endings even before she could write, after the old movie *Frankenstein* gave her nightmares. Kate credits her late mother, Rose Carlin, for her love of reading. As a teenager, Kate worked in the Windsor, Connecticut, public library, just to be surrounded by books, and may have set a world record for rereading Louisa May Alcott's *Little Women*.

A casual meeting with one of Kate's graduate English professors—to discuss a book, of course!—turned into true love, marriage and immigration from Connecticut to Toronto, Canada. Her husband, Mark, became a lawyer, and they have one teenaged son, Ben, who can usually be found with an open book in one hand.

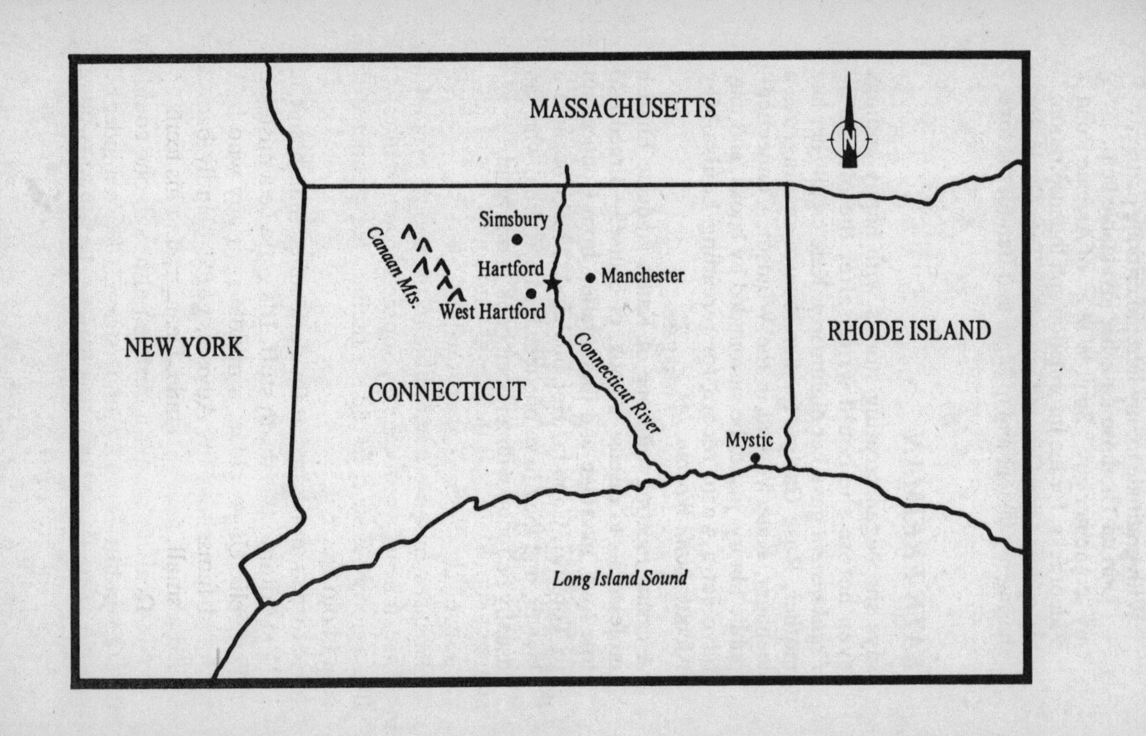
MASSACHUSETTS
N
Simsbury
Canaan Mts.
Hartford
Manchester
West Hartford
NEW YORK
RHODE ISLAND
CONNECTICUT
Connecticut River
Mystic
Long Island Sound

Prologue

"Oh, Dean! Why did you die?" Sophie Quinn whispered through her tears. Looking very alone in the crowd of mourners, she stood with her head bowed under the bright summer sun, staring at the freshly mounded earth.

"I love you, Dean. I always will."

Her last words were inaudible to the people around her, but Dean heard them clearly. Sophie's love had always felt like a noose. Now it felt like a lifeline. He wondered if he could hold her to it.

He turned and glared at the dark-suited man beside him. "I'm not into this death stuff. It's gotta be a mistake."

The Felix Unger clone, a middle-aged guy who had introduced himself as his Adviser, gazed blandly back and smiled a small, tolerant smile. Dean ground his teeth.

"No, Dean. It wasn't a mistake, although one could say that of windsurfing in a thunderstorm." The reminder of his last moments made Dean itch between his shoulder blades.

"Okay, so it wasn't a stroke of genius, but I had my reasons." Which didn't seem all that compelling, in retrospect, he decided glumly. Proving you could do something stupid always seemed to be a better idea at the time. "Put me back and I won't do it again."

The Adviser gave that irritating little smile again. "You've seen too many movies, I'm afraid."

"But Sophie . . ."

"A very sweet girl. What about her?"

He shrugged, suddenly overcome by a feeling he didn't recognize. "*Too* sweet. Always trying to save me from myself."

"She had a valid point, it would seem."

Dean snorted in disgust. Self-disgust. "I should have just taken her to bed, instead of trying to save her from the big, bad wolf."

The Adviser's left eyebrow rose. "One of your few redeeming deeds."

Dean sneered. Pompous jerk. "Yeah? Well, now I'll never know what I was missing."

"If you don't mind my saying so, Dean, your attitude leaves something to be desired."

"Fat lot of good my minding would do, huh? I can't go back and do things over, can I? I'm stuck here, right?"

The enormity of the situation was beginning to sink into his consciousness, and he didn't like it. He wasn't in Mystic, Connecticut, anymore. He was in some kind of Twilight Zone.

He snuck a look at the Adviser, and found him looking back. "Actually," the Adviser said, "you could have an opportunity to redeem yourself. I believe there will be rather pressing unfinished business regarding Sophie."

"You just told me you can't put me back." He said the words like a challenge, not wanting this Adviser guy to know how scared he was. Never show weakness.

"Not as your former self, no."

"Oh. Like, I could come back as someone else?" As long as it wasn't as some geek, some loser. He might even be able to find Sophie and make up for lost time, if he could get back before she turned into a dried-up old maid. Wasn't there a movie . . . ?

"Oh, Hollywood!" The Adviser gave Dean that smile again. Then he gave him a look that made him feel like a bug under a microscope. "No, my boy, you will not come back as someone else. But you will be given an important task."

The Adviser sighed, as if he were expecting him to screw up. Well, why not? Everyone else did. Except Sophie. Aw, Sophie! He tried to steal another look at her, but the Adviser guy was in the way, still talking.

"I certainly hope you're willing to do what's necessary. Otherwise, well, let's say the consequences could be most unfortunate."

Dean curled his lip. "From where I'm standing, the consequences are already unfortunate. What could be worse?"

The Adviser sighed. "The world does not revolve around you, Dean. There are others to consider. Sophie, in particular."

The thought of anything "unfortunate" happening to Sophie made his insides do an uncomfortable little flip. The Adviser put his hand on Dean's shoulder. Funny, but he didn't feel like shrugging it off. He'd rather die than admit he needed anyone's help—actually, that was how he ended up in this mess—but he was kind of glad the Adviser was around.

"Come, my boy. I'll explain what's to be done as we're traveling. But don't get your hopes up. These things take time, and you have a lot to learn. You aren't exactly an angel, you know.''

Dean took one last look at Sophie. She was alone at his grave now. Tears slid down her cheeks and her nose was pink, but she was still one beautiful girl. More beautiful at eighteen than any of the older, more savvy women he'd had his fun with. But it wasn't just that she was pretty. She was . . . special.

Sophie had the kind of beauty guys like him had trouble talking about. He'd always put the brakes on with Sophie, protecting her, although he'd never quite understood why he felt that way when he really wanted to get her into bed. He'd always figured he was too bad, too wild, too selfish, to mess with her innocence.

Now, of course, he was too dead.

Sophie wiped at her tears and took a deep, shaky breath. Dean hesitated, reluctant to let go of the sight of her. For whatever crazy reasons, Sophie had seen something in him worthy of love and faith. No one else really had. Not his dad, who'd raised him alone, with a heavy fist always ready. Not his teachers or his bosses. Not the string of nameless, faceless girls and women who'd passed through his short life and his bed. Only Sophie had cared; only Sophie believed in him.

He had an awful feeling that wherever he was going, no one would view him so favorably.

Sophie looked down at the handful of deep blue flowers she held. Dean watched her raise them over the mound of fresh dirt.

''Goodbye, Dean,'' she whispered. She opened her fingers to release the flowers.

''Don't forget me, Soph,'' he whispered, closer to tears than he wanted to admit. ''Don't stop loving me, babe. Don't leave me alone.''

Could she hear him? Could she at least *feel* him? Would he know?

When she turned away from his grave, Dean could see she held one blue flower. *Yes!*

"Oh, dear." The Adviser's stuffy voice cut into his thoughts. "I do wish you hadn't done that, Dean."

Chapter One

"I can't get a pulse."

Dean!

Sophie lifted her arms and cried out as she awoke, but the vision was already gone. Shaking, drenched in sweat, she lay gasping for breath. It had seemed so real. Dean, reaching out to her, the surf threatening to pull him under. She couldn't reach him, she couldn't save him. He was slipping away from her.

She didn't want to go back to sleep, but her eyes drifted closed. The dream came again, as she knew it would.

"Still no pulse."

"Keep working on him. Come on, buddy, breathe!"

"Nothing."

* * *

"This is your chance, Dean. Save this young man's life and you'll be taking a major step toward righting a dreadful mistake."

Dean looked at his Adviser in disbelief. He knew enough about the drowning man to make this decision.

"*Moi?* The guy's a nerd. You're asking *me* to become a nerd? A computer genius with the social life of a houseplant? You want *me* to step into a life-style with no style? No can do, my friend."

The Adviser heaved a sigh. Dean wondered how someone could possibly get through eternity with no sense of humor. Or maybe, this was his Adviser's idea of a good joke.

"Haven't you paid any attention in the last twelve years?"

Had it really been that long? Time flew! "Sure. But, hey, a guy has to have standards. Anyway, what's this got to do with Sophie?"

"The paramedics are losing him, Dean. It's up to you."

Dean felt a wave of guilt and fought against it. "Get someone else. He's a genius, man. We're talking Ph.D. I couldn't get into college. Hell, I had to pay guys to take my exams for me in high school. All I can do is tinker with engines. He can make a computer do cartwheels. How am I supposed to be him without getting caught being stupid?"

The Adviser sighed. "If you'd paid more attention, my boy, you'd know that only happens in the movies. Put simply, you'll be rekindling his spiritual pilot light, which is about to flicker out."

"Isn't that like using an acetylene torch to light a birthday candle? I mean, I'm the original party animal, and this guy—"

"To be honest, Dean, you've been upsetting the natural balance around here. This young man can use some of your spark, and you can learn valuable lessons from him."

Dean grinned. He got a charge out of knowing he was disrupting things even in the afterlife. At least he hadn't lost his touch. He looked again at the man lying beside the pool, the paramedics frantically trying to resuscitate him. The guy was in okay shape. Better than okay. Lose the black-framed glasses and he'd be presentable. But two people couldn't be more different. What if he made a mistake?

"Ah, what can I learn from a someone who spends all his time playing with computers? I mean, I know what he could learn from me, but—"

"You'd be surprised what Jake Warren can teach you."

He hated when the Adviser used that snotty tone with him. Like the mothers who wouldn't let their precious sons play with him when he was a rough-and-tumble kid. Like the teachers who told him he should stick to shop and not strain his brain on stuff like English and history. Like the women who told him he was great for a fling, but definitely not to be taken seriously.

Sophie never treated him like that. She always told him to believe in himself. Hah! Without Sophie, he had no reason to believe in himself. Was there some way to get her back? Was that why this was happening?

Sophie fought against the pounding surf, holding her hands out toward Dean. He strode through the swirling waves and called her name over the roaring of the storm, reaching out to grasp her hands....

She woke herself with the struggle to shout clearly to him. Her heart pounded painfully in her chest. Sitting up, she tried to calm her breathing. Her hands tingled as if someone had been gripping them.

"Dean, my boy, I shouldn't tell you this, because you're supposed to make this decision on your own, but you're a special case." The Adviser gave him a grim little smile. "And I don't mean that as a compliment."

"Okay, okay. Cut to the chase."

"If Jake survives this incident, he'll be subletting the apartment below Sophie's for the summer. He's in West Hartford on a computer-security assignment for several banks. Sophie is still single, you know."

So *that* was the connection!

"Sophie." He whispered her name like a prayer. Sweet, innocently sexy Sophie, who insisted on seeing the good in everyone—even him. Hell, it might be worth being a nerd for a while, if he got a chance to find out what he'd missed when he was alive. If he could work on Jake's style, he could—

"I'm appalled," the Adviser declared darkly. Dean shrugged, not a bit guilty about his thoughts. "I can see you're going to require frequent supervision in order to make any progress."

Dean grinned. His Adviser must have forgotten all about pleasure, but Dean sure hadn't. Funny, though, that the one woman he remembered, the one he wanted more than any of them, was the one woman he hadn't had. And he'd wanted Sophie so much, it hurt sometimes. His grin faded.

"Time is running out for Jake, Dean. You have to decide now."

Dean fought down a wave of panic. *Sophie.* Maybe Jake Warren was a nerd, but he probably had more to offer Sophie than Dean Wilde ever had. Maybe...

Beside him, the Adviser sighed. "You'll do it, then?"

Dean nodded, the decision robbing him of words.

"I'll check in with you when Jake sleeps. Good luck, my boy. And, Dean? Try to stay out of trouble."

"We've got a pulse!"

Sophie shivered and drew the covers up to her neck. Again, she had dreamed of Dean, so close this time she could almost touch him. Last night, and again tonight, she'd dreamed that Dean was reaching out to her. Both nights, she'd awakened with her arms raised, reaching toward him as if she could pull him back to her. Tonight she imagined she'd felt him holding on to her hands, fighting to save himself.

Twelve years ago, for three nights after his death, Sophie had dreamed of Dean standing defiantly in the pounding, surging waves as the tide rose higher until the water had claimed him. But twelve years ago, it made sense for her to dream of Dean. She'd been madly, passionately, irrationally in love with him. His death had stunned her and broken her heart.

She'd thought her heart had healed with the passage of time. Maybe she'd never really gotten over him. Certainly, she hadn't fallen head-over-heels, happy-ever-after in love in the past twelve years. Not even close. Maybe it was time to consciously let go of Dean's memory.

All she had to do was somehow get the message to her brain and find someone to give her heart to. Easier said than done.

Whatever could have triggered her old nightmares? She couldn't think of anything, but she had no doubt that the young man in her dreams was Dean. There could be no mistaking the tousled, dark wavy hair, the tall, lean quarterback build, the wicked grin or the electric blue eyes that could tease or seduce with equal ease.

She'd never seen another pair of eyes so brilliantly blue, so unforgettably devilish, except in her dreams. But dreams weren't enough. She needed a real man to love, someone to love her back.

She hugged the covers to her again as a shudder ran through her. "Dean, if you're out there, if you're the reason I can't fall in love, let me go. It's not fair."

The sound of her own words made her grimace at her foolishness. Dean was dead. If she couldn't fall in love, maybe she just hadn't met the right man. And if she kept talking to a dead man, they were going to put her in a rubber room where the only people she'd meet would be wearing white coats or straitjackets!

Heavy-headed from lack of sleep, Sophie fumbled for the delay button on her clock radio. When she couldn't find it on the third try, she groaned and decided she might as well get up. If she fell back to sleep now, she might have another reprise of that dream.

It was probably from eating pizza late at night.

While she dressed for work, muffled thumps and shouts came through the open windows and the floorboards of her third-floor apartment. Jake Warren, the man subletting Diane's apartment for the summer, must be moving in. She had to smile when she remembered her landlady's broad hints about the summer tenant who had rented the apartment. He had arranged the rental through Sophie's best friend's husband.

Craig Gardiner, manager of one of the local bank branches, had hired this reclusive computer-security expert, and his wife Lynne, knowing the middle apartment would be available for two months, had put all the parties together. Now Diane, their mutual friend, could really enjoy her summer studying in Rome.

Letters from several California-based businesses, and a personal phone call had secured the apartment sight unseen. Sophie hoped her widowed landlady's faith hadn't been misplaced.

"His name is Jake Warren, Sophie, and he's a doctor," Mrs. Mandel had told her last week when the apartment had been rented. "Not a *doctor* doctor, but a computer-science doctor. A very polite boy. Excellent references. And single."

To Mrs. Mandel, a youthful seventy, everyone under sixty was a boy or girl. Sophie didn't need much imagination to guess that her landlady had made sure the polite, single computer-science doctor from California knew that the "girl" upstairs was unattached, owned the local video rental store and liked to cook.

Poor guy. Mrs. Mandel had a good heart but she had the subtlety of a tornado. Even if she couldn't marry him off before the end of the summer, she'd make sure he ate well. Feeding people was her other mission in life, and she did it with old-world motherliness.

Sophie didn't have the heart to tell Mrs. Mandel, because her landlady was such a romantic, that she had no intentions of getting involved with a man, no matter how nice he might be, who was due to leave town in two short months. Whirlwind courtships just didn't happen in the safety-conscious, commitment-phobic nineties.

She intended to fall in love forever, not have a brief affair with a temporary neighbor. That would be like driving full speed toward the edge of a cliff. Nope. Nobody had brakes that foolproof.

Taking the back stairs to the small paved parking area behind the house, Sophie missed encountering any of the men tromping in and out of the second floor by the enclosed front stairs. When she maneuvered her compact car down the narrow drive, she saw Mrs. Mandel on the front porch waving two burly men through the door. Jake Warren was probably inside, trying to direct the movers through Diane's maze of furniture.

Later, when the dust had settled, she'd welcome her new neighbor. Right now she had to get to the store before opening time, to enter into the computer the orders for future releases. If she was really lucky, she'd not only finish the job today, she wouldn't upset the computer. Today was Rick's day off, and he was the only member of the staff who could coax the computer out of one of its periodic sulks.

Jake braced his hands on the edge of the metal hospital sink and stared into his reflection in the mirror. The eyes that stared back weren't his. *His* eyes were pale blue and severely myopic. He had the black-framed glasses to prove it. The problem was, he couldn't see anything through them anymore.

The eyes that stared back at him were a bright, almost electric blue, and as sharply focused as an electron microscope.

A smack on the head with a slab of concrete could do a lot of things to a guy's brain bucket, including crash his hard disk for good. But change the color of his eyes and give him twenty-twenty vision? Not a chance.

But there it was, in front of his face. Twenty-twenty, in living color. Even the neurosurgeon and the ophthalmologist he'd talked to had shaken their heads. They'd both advised him to chalk it up to a miracle and toss his glasses. But miracles weren't logical, and he didn't like things that defied logic.

"Mr. Warren!" a nurse called, startling him out of his concentration. He gripped the edge of the sink to get control of the wave of dizziness that hit him when he moved too quickly. "Do you need help getting back to bed?"

"No, thanks," he muttered, even though he knew he wasn't as steady on his feet as he wanted to be. He hated to feel helpless about anything.

"Fine. Hop in, then. I have to take your temperature and blood pressure before lunch."

Honey, I don't hop *anywhere. But you could hop in with me any day.*

Jake heard the unexpected thought as if someone had muttered the words aloud in his ear. He glanced over his shoulder, but he was alone with the nurse in the entry of his hospital room.

He gave her a tight smile and forced himself to shuffle back to the bed without grabbing the walls or the bed rails that silently offered help. Holding the back of the indecent hospital gown closed behind himself, he slid under the covers. He clamped his lips around the thermometer and held out his arm for the blood-pressure cuff.

"It's a little higher than before, but nothing to worry about," she told him with a smile. "You'll be going home today, I'm sure."

He nodded, regretting it when the pain seared his skull. He closed his eyes. A moment later, the nurse took the thermometer from his mouth and held it up to read it.

"Normal!" she announced cheerfully.

But it wasn't normal, he thought. *He* wasn't normal. And some of the thoughts in his head weren't his.

Mrs. Mandel was rocking on the front porch when Sophie drove home. There was no sign of the earlier chaos of boxes. Nor was there another car in the parking area, although a battered red mountain bike stood chained to the post of the back porch. Sophie strolled around to the front of the house, inhaling the sweet scents of night air and blossoms.

"Oh, Sophie! I'm so glad you finally came home! Such terrible news about our poor Jake. He was staying with friends in Manchester, and last night—no, it was the night before—he had a terrible accident and nearly drowned."

Sophie's sense of reality shifted. Oh, *Dean!* Mutely, she stared at her landlady.

"That poor boy! His friend called to explain. They were at a public pool and some hooligans ran into Jake. He hit his head on the side of the pool and the ambulance men almost couldn't save him."

The words poured out of the elderly woman. Her plump, wrinkled face was a mask of concern. All of Mrs. Mandel's tenants were part of her family, even one she hadn't met face-to-face.

Sophie swallowed hard. "Is he... is he going to be all right?" Silently she prayed that he would be. It didn't matter that she'd never met Jake. She could feel the chilling numbness of waiting all night on the beach, praying that Dean would survive, as if it were happening all over again.

Mrs. Mandel nodded vigorously. "Yes, yes. He's been in the hospital for two days, and his friend said he had a nasty bump, but he should be here later tonight."

Sophie bent down and kissed her landlady's soft cheek. "You should get some rest now, Mrs. Mandel. You've had a tiring day."

"I will, darling. But, Sophie, I feel so bad for Jake. And I was too tired to make him something nice. Would you be an angel, Sophie darling, and bake him some of your wonderful chocolate-chip cookies?"

Even in her bemused state, Sophie could recognize a setup. But she could see how tired Mrs. Mandel really was, and the added worry about Jake would only exhaust her further. With a smile, she assured the older woman that she'd make cookies for Jake, then ran up the back stairs to her apartment.

After she had baked four dozen double-chocolate-chip cookies, half for her staff and half for Jake, Sophie got ready for bed. Restless despite the late hour and her own exhaustion, she picked up a thick historical romance, hoping to relax. Her eyes started to drift closed almost immediately, then flew open.

Part of her was afraid to sleep.

She didn't want to dream again about Dean Wilde, especially after hearing about Jake Warren's accident. But she knew she would. Hearing about Jake had brought Dean to the front of her mind again immediately, despite her best efforts all day to suppress the afterimages of her dreams. How did you make a memory go away? Wasn't that the nature of memories, that they were the things you remembered?

Not all those memories were positive, either. Sure, she'd loved Dean with the desperate hope and blind foolishness of a teenager. From age twelve to eighteen, she'd dreamed and schemed to win his love. He was such a mystical, elusive creature: a satyr, untamable, arrogant and so very charming.

Being around Dean Wilde had been exciting in a trembly, daring, this-is-wrong-but-it's-so-much-fun kind of way. And she had been certain that, of all the women who trailed behind him, she was the one who could reform him, the one who could tame him.

Hah! Not in *this* lifetime! She'd cherished every moment, every tiny memento, every compliment, every kiss and caress.... And had watched Dean strut from one one-night stand to another while he dodged her attempts to smother him with her fairy-tale definition of love. He was Prince Charming, but he was also the Beast. He'd teased awake her feminine sexuality, leading her further and further into sensual temptation, then left her unsatisfied and feeling undesirable. Dean had had the unique ability to hurt you at the same time that he could make you feel ecstatic to be alive and with him.

Oh, well. She didn't want to find another Dean, but she could at least spend a while with a fictional long, tall Texan and the feisty Eastern schoolmarm who would civilize him in three hundred and fifty pages.

Again, she started to read. Her eyes grew heavy....

The crunch of tires on the gravel drive pulled Sophie out of her doze. Two car doors shut. Then came the dull thump of a trunk closing. Jake Warren had arrived.

Despite her protests that she wasn't interested in her new neighbor, all her senses came awake. Low male voices floated on the breeze, magnified in the living hush of midnight. Footsteps came closer up the wooden back stairs, then shuffled on the open landing of the second floor. The back screen door below her porch squeaked.

"Thanks, Les."

The deeper of the two voices sounded clearly in the still of the night. Jake's voice. She tried to picture him as either very skinny or very heavy—that was how Rick said most computer experts looked—with black-framed glasses, and a straggly haircut. Lynne had suggested a crew cut. Maybe a bow tie. And, of course, a pocket protector.

But that deep, rich voice didn't suit the picture of the classic nerd. Images of Dean kept taking over instead, which made no sense at all. Dean had sounded young and wild, not mature and mellow.

"Hey, no problem," the other man said. "If you're sure you're okay, I'll take off. It's my turn to get the baby for his middle-of-the-night feeding."

"I'm okay. Go get some sleep. Between me and the little guy, you and Annie haven't had much." Jake's words came out slowly, as if he were almost too tired to speak.

"Man, I'm sorry about—"

"Hey, it wasn't your fault. It was one of those glitches that happen."

"Okay. Here's your other bag. I'll give you a call tomorrow, and see if you're ready to get your terminal up and running."

"Sure."

The screen door squeaked again. One set of footsteps receded down the stairs. The car roared to life, startlingly loud in the quiet, then crunched its way down the gravel drive to the street.

Barely breathing, Sophie lay listening for Jake's presence. Through the open window beside her bed, she heard his steps on the wooden landing below her porch. For a long moment, there was only the silence of the night. Sophie started to drift to sleep once again.

A low groan broke the stillness, a restrained, inarticulate sound that startled her into wakefulness. Like the howl of a lone wolf, the sound made her shiver, yet it also made her ache in sympathy. She wanted to rush down the stairs and offer comfort to the stranger who had narrowly escaped death. But she couldn't. That would be too much of an invasion of his privacy.

Besides, no woman in her right mind flew into the clutches of a stranger in the dark, wearing a nightgown that could pass for Saran Wrap.

Jake peered into the darkness outside the porch of the second-floor apartment and breathed deeply. The air smelled sweet. Above the trees behind the house, he could see stars and the pale glow of the full moon.

He wanted something, but he didn't know what. All he knew was it wasn't something tangible. It was something illusive and elusive. It was a *feeling.* Another illogical occurrence. He never deliberately sought emotions. If anything, he carefully avoided anything to do with feelings. Emotions weren't logical. They had always been his absolutely worst subject. The only thing he'd ever truly failed at was feelings. He'd finally reached the logical conclusion that he didn't have any.

But now he felt so...so...*empty.* It was like a hunger that gnawed at him, but it wasn't physical. It was worse than physical hunger. Much worse. When he was hungry, he could have his fill of junk food or something righteously healthy, depending on whether he was in hack mode or real life. But he didn't know what would satisfy this longing he couldn't identify. And how could he understand it if he couldn't figure out what it was?

He took another breath, closing his eyes to shut out the moon. Inside his head, colors and sounds swirled like a psychedelic movie. Then the chaos cleared and he saw *her* again, the woman he'd seen when he'd been dy ng: pale skin, dark hair and storm-gray eyes in a face of perfect, timeless beauty. She had looked at him and held her hand out to him, a beautiful angel drawing him back from the edge of death.

Who was she? Why was she in his mind? Was he *losing* his mind?

The groan that came from deep inside him sounded like the howl of a lonely wolf in the cool, quiet night.

"How could you do this to me?" Dean's anger made Jake shift in his sleep. Served him right, Dean thought.

"Do what?" the Adviser asked in that mild tone of voice that irritated the hell out of Dean. "Give you a chance to redeem yourself?"

"No, damn it! How could you hook me up with a...a...a damn *monk?*"

The Adviser's eyebrows rose. Dean wished he could rub that phony surprise off the man's face.

"A monk? Jake Warren isn't a member of any religious order of which we know."

"He might as well be."

Dean seethed while the Adviser chewed that over. "You mean...?" Dean grunted. The Adviser smiled. "I see. Well, that isn't all that important, is it?"

"What do you know? You're dead."

The Adviser sighed. "I suppose the irony of that remark will occur to you eventually."

Chapter Two

Jake felt himself waking and groaned at the stiffness that gripped his body. Damage-check time. Could he stretch? The slash of pain from skull to midback made him regret moving at all. He still had the remnants of what felt like the world's worst hangover from smashing his head, and he'd forgotten to draw the shades last night. Just his luck, the window faced east. The sunlight hit his eyes like a laser.

His clock radio was in a box somewhere in another room. His internal clock was somewhere in an alternate universe. He pawed at the nightstand for his watch. 8:34. Morning, obviously. Was that early for him, or late? He sometimes worked long into the night and slept until ten or eleven the next morning, occasionally even until noon. Subtract three hours from eastern time, and he was awake at half past five in the morning, and feeling like hell. Not a promising start.

Then again, neither was getting that crack on the head. A visitation, no doubt, by Eris, the Greek goddess of Chaos and other, mostly inexplicable "bad things." A strange sense of humor that lady had. Whatever he'd done to attract her attention, he'd promise never to do it again if he could get himself back to normal.

He rolled carefully onto his back and stretched, then sniffed the air drifting in through his open window. Nice. Sweet. But heavier than in Los Altos. Different trees, too. Birds twittered outside. Otherwise, the street seemed pretty quiet.

Two motorcycles rumbled by, putting a wrinkle in the peace. *A Honda and a Kawasaki,* he heard himself think, except it couldn't be his thought. Damn, it was happening again! He didn't care about motorcycles, let alone be able to identify them from inside the house simply by sound. *The Kawi needs tuning,* the voice in his head announced.

"*I* need tuning," he muttered out loud.

No argument there.

Jake leapt off the bed, then grabbed the nightstand to stay upright. New pains seared his cranium and yanked at his neck. He indulged in a string of creative, hackerly curses before the clink of china on china caught his attention.

Sophie!

Sophie? Oh, yeah, Sophie Quinn, his upstairs neighbor. She must be having breakfast out on the porch above his. Might be a nice thing to do, to eat in the big room, the one with the blue ceiling and the bright light that hackers seldom saw. There were, however, two small obstacles, only one of them temporary: he didn't have any food in the apartment, and if he went outside, he'd probably have to meet Sophie.

Damn straight you would!

He'd ignore that voice. That's all. Like most things external to his work, if he ignored it long enough, it would go away.

Don't bet on it!

He'd ignore that, too. Back to Sophie. Their landlady, Mrs. Mandel, had really laid it on thick. Beautiful, sweet, generous, intelligent, independent, single and a good cook were only some of the virtues the woman had listed during their phone conversation. Two problems: He found it hard to believe what Mrs. Mandel said about her other tenant. No one that fantastic-sounding was ever unattached.

But even if it were all true, and even if he were remotely interested in meeting a woman in *real life,* instead of at the other end of a terminal—which he most definitely was not—then he and this Sophie would go together like oil and water.

He wandered down the hall, blessing his landlady for making some sense of his things while he was concussed and in the hospital. Waiting for the water to heat up, he rummaged through his toiletry kit for his toothbrush and his razor. When his face was lathered, he started to shave off the three-day growth.

Chicks kinda like stubble, the voice in his head declared. His hand jerked. He felt the sting just under his jawline even before he saw the trickle of red.

"Look, whoever you are," he said, glaring at his reflection in the medicine chest mirror, "I don't care what chicks like. Keep your opinions to yourself."

I'm cut to the quick!

"Yeah? Well, I'm the one who's bleeding. Just butt out."

He finished shaving, determined to ignore the voice and simply freeze it out. If whatever it was couldn't get into his circuits, it couldn't access his thoughts.

The pipes clanked when he turned on the water in the glass-enclosed shower. An answering clang of pipes came from upstairs. Sophie was showering, too. Well, so what? People showered at the same time all over the world. That was no reason to wonder what she looked like with water streaming down her naked body.

Get your mind out of the gutter. That's Sophie, not some bimbo.

So what? Hell, he didn't have a clue what she looked like without water streaming down her body, naked or not. What's more, he didn't care. He was in Connecticut to do a job, not to get involved with some woman. Just because cracking his head had fixed his eyesight, didn't mean it had done anything about his heart. That old dog wasn't going to learn any new tricks at this late date. He was as interested in romance as the average android was—and he liked it that way.

Suddenly, as the hot water poured down onto his knotted shoulders and steamed up the glass door, he saw *her* again, the woman he'd seen when he'd been drowning. Delicate features, skin like cream and soft, full lips smiling sweetly. Her long dark hair floated around her face and drifted down her back. And her eyes . . . Huge, stormy gray and filled with some wisdom he knew he needed. He'd looked into those eyes and reached out for her hand just before it was too late.

What if she were real? If she were, and if he could ever find her . . .

Then what? He yanked the shower control into the off position. Discuss the relative merits of various computer languages? Right.

He wouldn't know what to do, what to say, if he found her. With real, live women, especially nonhackers, he was socially dyslexic at the best of times.

I don't know what dyslexic *is, pal, but if it means backward, you're it.*

Damn! Either he was cracking up, or he was getting some bizarre radio signals through his fillings. Whatever it was that was putting these nonsystem thoughts in his head, he didn't want to know about it. One major unexplainable event was sufficient for this lifetime.

Anyway, he knew better than to speculate on a relationship with the virtually perfect Sophie, or anyone else. He might be in the top one percent of the population in intelligence, but when it came to human relationships, he doubted he'd make it past the bottom one percent. It was that old nurture vs. nature thing; except for him, it had been a double whammy: a born nerd, raised in an emotional vacuum. What he knew about intimacy could fit on one of those learn-to-be-a-rocket-scientist-in-your-free-time matchbook covers.

Jake groped for his towel. He found glass and chrome. Foo! No towel. Growling between clenched teeth, he dripped his way to the linen closet in the hall, where he found a note from Mrs. Mandel telling him he was welcome to use Diane's stuff as long as he laundered it. Diane, the woman who usually lived in the apartment, had thick bath sheets in sherbet colors. He had threadbare utility-grade bath towels in shades of dingy gray. No contest.

With a lime-colored towel wrapped around his hips, he burrowed through carefully jumbled clothes in his battered suitcase. The pair of black sweatpants he pulled out would be rejected by the most destitute street person. The scrunched-up white oxford cloth button-down shirt with the sleeves sliced short had a permanent ink stain on the front pocket. At least his underwear was new. Socks? Did he have socks? Sure. In Los Altos, in one of his drawers. No matter. He didn't need any for now.

Holding his clothes in his hand, he frowned. Before he went to any meetings with the suits at the banks, he'd have to get some real clothes. Nothing too constricting, but conservative enough to inspire confidence. He'd be asking the bank hotshots to entrust him with security for millions of dollars. He had to look the part of a successful computer wizard. New jeans and a couple of white shirts would probably do.

He held his breath for a few seconds, waiting for some snide comment from the mysterious voice in his head. Nothing. Maybe he'd solved whatever glitch it was.

He got into his briefs and sweats, then remembered he'd started a list of things he needed to do for this bank-security contract. But where was the list? Right! In the gym bag in the bedroom. He went back down the hall.

Lost in thought, he scribbled notes on a scrap of paper.

Sophie took another quick look into her mirror, checking her makeup, then frowned. Her heart was racing, and her hands were shaking, but all she planned to do was bring a thermos of coffee and a basket of cookies to her new neighbor. She hadn't been this edgy the time she'd met Paul Newman, and he'd been her favorite actor forever. No doubt she was suffering from simple lack of sleep, after those recurring dreams about Dean.

Well, she had to hurry if she was going to be neighborly and get to the store before ten. Thursdays in the summer were always busy, with people getting ready for long weekends, and she still had to catch up on her accounting. If the computer let her.

At the back door to the second-floor apartment, Sophie hesitated before knocking. What if Jake was sleeping? She'd hate to disturb him. But what if he hadn't recovered from his accident, and would welcome the offer of help or food?

She knocked but heard nothing for a long moment. He probably was asleep, she decided, so she wouldn't knock again. The cookies would wait until—

The back inner door swung open and a large shadowy form appeared on the other side of the screen door. She smiled upward, although she couldn't actually see his face.

"Hi. I'm Sophie Quinn from upstairs. I thought you might like some coffee and cookies."

He didn't move. He didn't speak. She suddenly felt uneasy and wished she could see him through the screen. As the silence lengthened, she lifted the thermos and the basket so he could see them. If he glanced at them, she couldn't tell. He didn't seem to be breathing.

"Soph..." His voice sounded rusty. He cleared his throat. "Sophie!"

"Yes?" She offered what she hoped was an encouraging smile.

He reached out and pushed the screen door open. Sophie had to step back to edge around the door while he held it with his outstretched arm. When she stepped toward the threshold, her eyes finally adjusted to the dimness inside, she found herself staring at a wide, naked male chest barely inches from her face. The scent of cedar soap and clean skin filled her head.

"Oh!" she gasped and nearly stumbled backward. A large, strong hand gripped her shoulder and hauled her over the threshold. She felt the warmth of the hand seep through her blouse and glanced up in surprise at the familiarity of that touch. What she saw made her sense of reality tilt. Was she dreaming again?

"Dean?"

"Jake. Jake Warren."

He couldn't be Dean; she knew that. But something about him . . . Jake Warren was muscular and lean like Dean had been. Like Dean, he was a touch over six feet, although his shoulders were broader. But Jake's sun-kissed dark hair curled wildly, shorter over his forehead, long and loose in back. Dean had kept his hair short in back, out of the motors he worked on, and James Dean-long in front, where it fell over his forehead in a wave no woman seemed able to resist brushing back.

Jake's face lacked the hard angles of Dean's face, although he had the same kind of full, sensual mouth that gave a woman fantasies. The lines around his eyes made Jake look older, wearier than the thirty-four years Mrs. Mandel said he was.

But those eyes . . . The most brilliant, electric blue eyes, framed by thick, black lashes . . . Intense, daring, piercing, a little defensive. That was why she'd thought she was looking at Dean. It was as if a stranger were looking at her through Dean's eyes. And staring at her, saying her name, as if he knew her.

"Jake," she echoed. A tremor slid through her at the way his name felt on her lips.

Sophie!

Jake's heart stopped and his mouth went dry. All he could do was stare down at the woman inches from his bare chest, her face tipped up toward him.

He would know those stormy gray eyes anywhere.

It was *her*. The woman—the angel?—who had led him back from the brink of death. She'd called his name when he was slipping away. The sound of her voice saying his name now, softly, sent a jolt through him. Oh, God, she was beautiful! She was beautiful and she was real. He could still feel the warmth of her shoulder in the palm of his hand.

Kiss her for me, damn it!

The thought jump-started his heart, and sent it racing. It wasn't his thought, but the idea was strongly tempting. Sophie still looked up at him, her lips parted, her eyes wide. She smelled wonderful. A little sweet, a little spicy, oddly familiar. Her skin looked as soft as rose petals. He wanted—no, needed—to know how she felt, how she tasted.

The depth of that unexpected hunger stunned him.

It took him a moment to realize Sophie looked as stunned as he felt. He stepped back, suddenly self-conscious about his naked chest. His shirt hung forgotten from his hand. He lifted it and thrust his arms into the ragged sleeves.

"Sorry," he muttered, embarrassed. "I was thinking. Come in." He gave her room to step inside the kitchen while hastily buttoning his shirt. She handed him the basket and thermos. The scent of chocolate wafted up from under the napkin in the basket. "Thanks. Smells good."

She smiled. "I hope you like chocolate-chip cookies."

He felt himself grinning. "My favorite. Have some with me. I think I can find the cups and plates."

Now that was odd. Even yesterday, if a woman as beautiful as Sophie Quinn had appeared on his doorstep with cookies, he'd have been totally tongue-tied. Or worse, rude from awkwardness, or suspicion that it was a joke. But there was no time to contemplate that improvement to his social skills, because Sophie was saying yes and taking the thermos out of his hand. He set the basket on Diane's wooden kitchen table and opened cabinet doors, finding the mugs and plates on the second and third tries.

The whole time that he was moving around the kitchen, he felt Sophie's eyes on him. What was she seeing when she looked at him? For the first time in his life, it mattered.

Sophie knew she was staring, but she couldn't help it. Jake was worth staring at. Now that she had a better perspective, she could see he wasn't so much like Dean after all, despite some superficial similarities. Certainly, Jake was handsome—okay, he was gorgeous—but, unlike Dean, he seemed unconcerned about his appearance. His sweatpants bagged around his lower body, and the shirt he'd put on so quickly was buttoned wrong, so that one shirttail hung longer than the other. The effect was oddly appealing, and sexy in an unconventional way.

He shot her a self-conscious grin that made her suspect he was shy, and pulled out one of the kitchen chairs. It took her a few seconds to realize he'd pulled the chair out for her. Transfixed again by his brilliant blue eyes, she accepted the chair in a daze. He sat across the table from her and opened the thermos. While he poured steaming coffee into two mugs, she watched his hands.

Her shoulder still tingled with the memory of his hand pulling her into the apartment. His grip had been strong, yet gentle. Now, looking at him holding a mug for her, she wondered how his hands would feel cupping her body in a lover's touch.

Her face burned at the direction of her thoughts. She couldn't meet his eyes when she took the mug he offered her, afraid he'd read her mind through her eyes. Her gaze fell to the opening of his haphazardly buttoned shirt, where soft black hairs curled out of the V of the neckline. A minute ago, she'd stood so close to his bare chest that she could smell his freshly showered skin. She could picture her hands spread on his golden chest, could imagine the feel of his muscles and silky hair under her palms, his heart pounding under her touch.

Her face burned even hotter. This reaction to a total stranger wasn't like her. Lust in general wasn't like her. Sex in real life had been such a letdown from the high expectations Dean had inspired. Probably those dreams about him, and her memories of the feverish desires he had stirred but never satisfied, had her thinking about sex at this hour of the morning, with a man who bore a slight resemblance to Dean. It didn't mean anything. It couldn't mean anything. She simply wouldn't let it.

Jake watched Sophie's cheeks turn pink. Had he done something—

She's probably thinking about sex. That always madeher blush.

Jake nearly spilled the coffee he was pouring for himself. That was definitely not his thought. But it was certainly the thought of someone who knew Sophie. Except there were only the two of them in the room. So—

I'll explain later. Just have a cookie.

He found himself reaching for the basket. He bit into the cookie and the taste of chocolate exploded in his mouth. For once, the voice in his head had offered good advice.

"Mmm!" He swallowed. "These are great. Where do you get cookies like these?" He took another bite. It was cookie heaven.

Sophie reached for a cookie. "They're from scratch."

"Scratch? Is that one of those cookie chains? We have them all over the coast. Californians live on tofu, sprouts and cookies."

She smiled and shook her head, her hair swinging like silk across her shoulders. "No, I mean they're homemade."

He grinned. "For me, homemade means microwaving a convenience food that wasn't frozen first. Sometimes I wonder if I glow in the dark."

Her laugh was soft, low, delicious. He wanted to hear it again, but he couldn't think of anything more to say. He tasted the coffee. It was rich and smooth.

"This is better than doughnut-shop coffee," he heard himself say.

Again, Sophie laughed softly. The sound warmed his heart. It was a world away from the silly, computer bulletin-board ways to post appreciation for wit. Seeing the word *grin* on a monitor screen couldn't match the way Sophie's laugh made him feel.

"I'm flattered," she told him, her smile bright, "but I'm also late for work. I'll get the thermos later."

She stood up. He stood facing her, once again at a loss for words. When she walked by him, he inhaled her scent and felt something inside him quicken in recognition. He followed her to the back door.

"Oh! I almost forgot!" She turned at the door and her shoulder bumped his chest.

Quick as the brush of a flame, her heat seared him, and then she stepped back. Her eyes went dark and wide, and her lips parted. *Kiss her!* the voice urged, in complete synchrony with his own sudden desire to do just that.

Talk about incorrect parameters.... Jake Warren, arch computer nerd, did not go around lusting after women he didn't know, let alone act on his urges. He certainly wasn't going to act on the urges of some inexplicable voice in his head.

Much as he wanted to.

"Sorry," he forced himself to say. "You forgot something?"

Her cheeks turned pink. "I... I have a gift certificate for you, for video rentals. A sort of welcome gesture."

Her words came out rushed, as if she were uncomfortable, but she continued to look up at him. She wasn't particularly short, and he wasn't much over six feet, but the way she looked up at him made him feel... a contrast. A very elemental contrast he hadn't noticed before. Very interesting....

"Diane has a good VCR, so..." Sophie shrugged. "I'm sure she wouldn't mind your using it."

He took the envelope she pulled out of the back pocket of her slacks. That was when he noticed how she looked slender and curved at the same time. After years of equal opportunity intellects, he was reminded of a fact he'd deliberately shoved to the back of his consciousness for a very long time: men and women were different.

Maybe he'd been living like a monk for too long, single-mindedly pursuing his work.

Amen to that, the voice muttered. Jake resisted the impulse to scowl.

"Thanks. I don't usually watch movies, but I'm willing to try," he muttered.

Sophie looked genuinely shocked. Well, he couldn't blame her. She made her living off of people renting movies. He shrugged as if to apologize for being such a philistine. She smiled. It was like the sun coming through the clouds.

"Come in today, then, and get started." She glanced past his shoulder to the clock on the kitchen wall. "Rats! I better go. I'm late, and the computer's been sulking again, so I don't know if we're going to have to do everything by hand."

He frowned. "Sulking? What is it doing?"

"*Not* doing. It sometimes refuses to accept new entries, or it slows way down, and I have payroll and accounts receivable work to do." She wrinkled her nose, which he decided was . . . charming. "I've had a call in for service, but the guy who set it up hasn't called back yet. He's had to adjust it a couple of times already. I'm sure it's something simple I'm doing wrong. I'm so computer illiterate that I can barely turn the thing on."

"I'll come in later and take a look." A computer sulking? He couldn't pass that up.

"Oh, no! I couldn't impose. Besides, it's probably nothing. I wouldn't want you to waste your time."

"If I can fix it, I won't be wasting my time."

"Oh. Well. Thanks." Sophie pushed open the screen door and stepped out onto the porch. "See you later, then."

"Right."

He watched her through the screen until she disappeared down the stairs. A moment later, he heard her car start up and crunch its way out of the parking area.

Good goin', tiger! Maybe you aren't as hopeless as I thought.

His sentiments precisely. But with whom was he sharing them? From the clues he'd already stored away, he wasn't sure he wanted to know.

* * *

"Sophie, there's a man asking for you."

She looked up to see her closest friend, Lynne Gardiner, peering into the back office of the store. Smiling, Sophie got up from behind her paper-strewn desk.

"Hi, Lynne. What are you doing here?"

Lynne chuckled. "You tell me," she teased.

"Don't tell me it's after six already?" Although she'd spent most of the day with half of her attention on the front door, wondering when—or if—Jake would show up, the time had gone quickly. She and Lynne started walking toward the front.

"Okay. I won't tell you. Craig sends his love."

"Send mine back," she replied, linking her arm with Lynne's. Craig, Lynne's husband, managed the bank branch at nearby Bishop's Corner, adjacent to the small, expensive clothes boutique Lynne owned. They made a striking couple, Lynne with her model-perfect cool blond beauty and willowy figure, and Craig, with his chiseled Scandinavian features and athletic physique.

"Who is this guy?" Lynne asked in low voice.

"How should I know? I haven't seen him yet." She grinned. "He could be from the IRS."

"Impossible. No tie," Lynne told her. "Gorgeous blue eyes, though. The kind of eyes even Mel Gibson would kill for. The pile of swooning females at the cash desk is growing by the second."

Suddenly knowing who was at the front desk, Sophie stumbled. "Sorry." She forced a smile, hoping Lynne wouldn't suspect the cause of her reaction.

No such luck. "Sophie, have you been holding out on me? Your best friend of a decade? Come on, 'fess up. Who is he?"

"Probably the guy who's subletting Diane's place for the summer. The computer expert from California. I thought you'd met him through Craig."

"Oh." Lynne forced Sophie to a stop. "Oh, no! He's supposed to be a nerd. Forget his eyes. Don't even speculate about what's under those baggy sweats. You don't need a man who isn't going to be around for more than two months."

Sophie was both touched by Lynne's fierce concern, and a little bothered that her friend thought she needed it. She shook her head and started them walking again.

"Fear not. The very same thought crossed my mind days ago, when Mrs. Mandel went into her matchmaking spiel. I think I finally convinced her that I'm really not interested."

But the moment she saw Jake again, she realized she was lying. The sight of him struck a responsive chord deep within her. He stood by the front counter, deceptively rumpled in the same worn sweatpants he'd had on that morning, and a navy blue T-shirt. He'd tied his wildly curling hair back, which made him look more like a shipwrecked pirate than a mild-mannered doctor of computer science. Definitely *not* a nerd!

Clearly, whatever it was about Jake Warren that made her own heart go pit-a-pat had also affected the woman standing beside him. That woman had the kind of looks that made men suck in their stomachs and whistle tunelessly. From the way she was studying Jake as he listened intently to something Rick was saying, she was clearly speculating about what was under those baggy sweats.

Sophie recognized the nasty twinge she felt as jealousy, which was totally irrational. Not a minute ago, she'd just assured Lynne that she wasn't the slightest bit romantically interested in Jake.

She let go of Lynne's arm. "Hello, Jake. Were you looking for me?"

He turned and the full force of his gaze stole her breath.

"I was hoping you'd have time to recommend a couple of movies. How's the computer acting now? Rick said he didn't have any trouble with it today."

She shook her head. "I got so mad at it yesterday that I turned if off last night. It was fine this morning." She shrugged. "The guy who set up the system said to keep it running all the time, because turning it on and off sent dangerous jolts of electricity through it." Jake nodded. "But maybe it needs a rest."

"If it gives you trouble again, I'll take a poke at it. You don't want the system to crash."

"Thanks." Looking into his eyes, Sophie worried that her computer wasn't the only thing at risk of falling. He met her eyes as if no one else around them existed, as if he were trying to look into her soul. It was disconcerting, and it was just a little too exciting.

Behind her, Lynne cleared her throat. Startled, Sophie felt her cheeks burn. Quickly she introduced Lynne and Jake and watched her friend assessing Jake as they shook hands. Then Lynne excused herself to choose a video and Rick moved away to check out a rental for the woman who'd been eyeing Jake a moment before.

"What do you like?"

His forehead wrinkled. "I don't really know."

"Well, what do you read?"

"Technical and scientific journals, computer manuals." He shrugged. "That sort of thing."

He looked embarrassed by his confession, and brushed at the bridge of his nose as if pushing glasses back in place. Then he glanced at his hand and shrugged.

She smiled, not wanting him to feel she expected an apology from him for not reading novels. "Well, how about science fiction?"

"Sure."

She led Jake to the back corner, where the science fiction videos sat adjacent to the Nintendo games. "There are blurbs on the backs of the cases, so you can get an idea of what the films are about. How about this one? It's about a man who gets trapped in a video game."

Jake took the case she held out to him. His fingers brushed over hers, causing little shocks to her skin. She looked up into his eyes and forgot where she was. His gaze dropped to her lips, then lifted to her eyes again. Her lips parted. She felt as if he'd touched them with his own. And in his eyes, she read his desire to do just that.

Without warning, Sophie was engulfed from behind in a hearty male embrace. Stifling a shriek, she pushed away and glared into the teasing brown eyes of Bob Manetti, who owned an exercise-equipment store near West Hartford Center.

"You idiot!" She gasped for breath. "You scared the daylights out of me!"

Bob chuckled. "Sorry. I figured I'd stop by and ask if there was anything special you wanted to do tonight?" She stared at him blankly, her attention fragmented between Jake and Bob's interruption. "We have a date tonight, Sophie. Dinner. Remember?"

To her dismay, Bob hugged her shoulders and kissed her lightly on the temple. "Honey, you work too hard."

This couldn't be happening. She closed her eyes, wishing she could make herself disappear. When she opened her eyes, Jake was the one who was gone. Well, what would she have done or said if he'd stayed around? Bob was simply a friend she went to dinner with from time to time. There had never been any romantic sparks between them, at least none for her. And Bob had always respected that. But why would Jake want to know that?

Why should she care what Jake thought about her private life? He wasn't going to be part of it.

Chapter Three

"I don't believe this guy's timing," Dean groused to his Adviser while Jake slept that evening.

"I—uh, *he* was all set to ask Sophie to watch the flick with him, and this Bob joker waltzes in yapping about a date."

"Perhaps it's just as well," the Adviser replied stuffily. "If Jake had asked Sophie to join him this evening, she would have had to decline. That would have been awkward for all concerned, don't you think?"

Dean considered that. Grudgingly, he admitted the Adviser had a point. "Yeah, Jake's spooked enough about me. It'd be a real bummer to screw things up now. At least I got him thinking about getting close to Sophie. Come to think of it, that part was a snap. One look and *POW!*"

He frowned. Maybe that was *too* easy. He didn't want Warren trying to steal Sophie for himself.

"You must be judicious about interfering in Jake's emotions."

Again with the three-dollar words! Between the Adviser and Jake, he was going to need a dictionary.

"Hey, man, lighten up. I didn't interfere, did I? Personally, I wouldn't have walked away and let that joker have a second alone with Sophie. I kinda wanted to get Warren to clean that dude's clock."

The Adviser smiled. "I know. The voltage meters here reacted in a highly erratic manner. Just remember whose life this is, Dean. And, please. No fisticuffs."

Fisticuffs? What century was this guy from, anyway?

Thanks to a two-hour nap, Jake had his computers set up and running by 1:00 a.m. He was in the middle of catching up on the latest postings to his favorite bulletin boards when he heard the phone. Usually he'd ignore the phone when he was working, but Diane's answering machine needed a new tape and he hadn't had a chance to pick one up. A call at 2:00 a.m. was probably from someone in California, forgetting about the three-hour time difference. Or ignoring it, figuring he was working.

The dial tone purred in his ear, but the phone rang again anyway. Strange.

Then he realized it was Sophie's phone he was hearing through the open windows. That guy who'd come into her store to remind her about their date had picked her up about eight. He'd heard their voices from the stairs. Wasn't she home yet?

The phone stopped ringing upstairs. Jake shrugged. It wasn't his concern where Sophie was, or with whom, or what she was doing. Just because he'd dreamed that her bright laughter had been for him, that he'd been the one driving away with her— Hell, he didn't even own a car!

He scrolled through some postings that didn't interest him. The sound of footsteps on the back stairs distracted him immediately. Odd. The steps were descending. It could be her date, creeping away in the middle of the night, except he hadn't heard them go upstairs earlier.

Check it out, man.

Hmm. Well, he could use an excuse to stretch his legs. It wasn't exactly spying. He just wanted a breath of fresh air. If he met the guy on the stairs, so what? He had no interest in Sophie. She was just his neighbor. Sure, he'd considered asking her to spend the evening over pizza and beer with his rented movie, but that was just being neighborly. A way to thank her for the free movies. No big deal.

Jake opened the back door. Sophie was just stepping onto his porch landing.

"Oh!" she gasped. "Jake! Did I wake you? I'm sorry."

She was alone, her body sihouetted by the porch light. In a pink T-shirt and jeans, she looked small and appealing. To his chagrin, his pulse surged and his heart began to race. So much for "no big deal."

Down, boy.

He didn't need that.

"You didn't wake me," he told Sophie. "I'm a night owl, especially when I'm hacking. Are you all right?"

"Yes. No. Oh, Jake!" The way she said his name wrenched something inside him. "The police called. Someone tried to break into the store. I've got to go down there."

"Give me a second to find my shoes. I'll go with you."

She looked as surprised by his offer as he felt making it. But she also looked so hurt that someone would try to break into her store. And she looked just the littlest bit like she could use someone to lean on. Apparently, her date wasn't around—or was upstairs sleeping while Sophie coped alone. The thought made him scowl. But why? It wasn't any of his business.

Outside, the air was cool. Sophie shivered and hugged her bare arms. Jake pulled his faded Stanford sweatshirt off over his head and wrapped it around her. She stopped short and looked up at him. He froze, then felt her hands cover his as they rested on her shoulders. Her scent mingled with the soft smells of the summer night, making him feel as if he'd been drinking champagne.

"Thanks," she said softly, then started walking again.

His heart finally started beating again about the time he opened the passenger side door for her. Sophie gave him the keys, then sat quietly beside him while he started the car and drove to her store.

Say something to her.

"Uh-uh."

He understood her silence, and knew he shouldn't intrude. She was upset, and had withdrawn into herself. Until they got to the store and Sophie talked to the police, there was nothing important to say. He wouldn't insult her intelligence by patting her hand and telling her everything would be fine.

"Pardon?"

Sophie's soft question started him. "Nothing." He stopped for a red light. Damn! He talked to himself plenty, especially when he was working, but this time, he'd been talking to that voice in his head. Out loud.

There were two police cars at the small corner group of stores. Sophie leapt out of her car almost before it stopped. Jake set the hand brake and followed her slowly.

From where Jake stood, the damage looked minimal. A lot of glass, but whoever had tried to break in hadn't succeeded. He'd managed to disable the alarm, probably in anger after the thing went off. It didn't look too complicated to rearm.

Sophie answered the cops' questions, her voice thin. A dozen times, Jake had to bite his tongue to keep from telling them to hurry up so she could leave. At one point, his sweatshirt slipped from her shoulders. She fumbled for it, but missed the sleeve. He moved closer and adjusted the shirt. Under his hands, he felt her trembling.

Feeling awkward about the unaccustomed gesture, Jake put his arm around her shoulders. He told himself it was only a way to anchor the sweatshirt and keep her warm. But she leaned into him and sighed, and something deep inside him shifted, as if making room for new feelings.

His impatience with police procedures evaporated. The longer they took to dust for fingerprints and make notes about business hours and Sophie's employees, the longer he had an excuse to stand beside her and hold her close. When the cops closed their notebooks, he was disappointed. He, who had always avoided contact, physical and emotional, didn't want to release Sophie.

He kept his arm around her while they walked to her car. When he reached out to open her door for her, she leaned into him and slipped her arms around his waist. He held his breath as he took her slight weight against his chest and absorbed her shivers. Then he realized she was crying.

Feeling totally out of his depth, he touched her hair. It felt like silk threads under his hand. He continued to stroke her hair and rub her shoulders until he felt her relax. When he sensed she was going to pull away, he held her long enough to touch his lips to the top of her head. From deep inside came the inexplicable urge to kiss away the tears from her cheeks. And to kiss her lips until she forgot about the break-in.

"Okay, now?" he asked, his voice choked.

She nodded against his chest, then backed away. "Thanks, Jake. I'm glad you're here."

"So am I."

Me, too.

He gritted his teeth. They got into the car.

Sophie sniffed softly. "I guess I live in a fantasy world where people are always good, but I can't believe anyone would want to break into my store. It's not like a bank."

He started the engine. "You have a lot of valuable stuff in there. Videotapes, VCRs, games, TVs, computers . . ."

"I know. Still, I hate to think of anyone being so dishonest. Do you think the police will be able to find whoever it was?"

"I doubt it. He couldn't have been there long. There must be hundreds of prints on the back door and walls, most of them unidentifiable, most of them probably legit."

She was silent the rest of the short drive back to Mrs. Mandel's house. Being alone in the dark with her, with hardly another car on the road, and few lights on in any houses, Jake felt overwhelmingly aware of Sophie's physical presence. She was warm and delicately fragrant. He wanted to touch her again. Her hand, her arm, her cheek. Anything to reestablish that contact he'd felt earlier.

But the moment he turned off the engine, she was out of the car. He caught up with her at the porch. With a sad little smile, she exchanged his sweatshirt for her keys and murmured her thanks. Then she ran lightly up the steps and disappeared into her own apartment, leaving him gripping his sweatshirt, breathing in her scent.

And yearning . . . Oh, God, yearning for more.

Sophie sat behind her cluttered desk and watched herself tapping a pen on the bill of lading in the center of the blotter. Then she looked up into the accusing eyes of the policeman.

"Rick's prison record has nothing to do with the incident last night."

"Break and enter was his specialty, ma'am. On one occasion, he was apprehended with a number of stolen videocassettes in his possession."

Sophie sighed. "I know that, Officer. Rick told me himself, before I hired him. But why on earth would he try to break into the store through the back door, knowing he'd set off the alarm, when he has keys to both front and back door and knows the combination of the alarm?"

The officer's pale eyes narrowed. "What if he forgot his keys? Or if someone else locked the doors when he'd planned to leave them unlocked for himself?"

"What if you admit you haven't a clue?" Sophie retorted. "Rick locked up last night."

The officer sighed. "Okay, ma'am. But he's still under suspicion. He's been seen with people we suspect fence electronics, including computers."

For a second—but only a second—her faith in Rick slipped. "Well, they can have the computer for all I care! Rick's the only one who can make it work half the time."

"Is that so, ma'am? He knows computers?"

The policeman made knowing computers sound like a federal offense. Sophie forced herself to relax and to speak politely.

"If you'd looked past his rap sheet and conviction record, Officer, you'd see that Rick studied computer programming in prison, and continued after he got out. He's been working for me for five years, and I've never regretted hiring him."

She stood up, impatient with the skeptical expression on the policeman's face. "No one ever expected Rick to be anything more than a petty criminal. All he needed was a way to believe in himself, and someone who believed in him enough to give him a chance."

The policeman stood across from her and tucked his notebook away. "Yes, ma'am. I hope your faith hasn't been misplaced. But for now, he's still a suspect. Thanks for your time."

Sophie watched the man let himself out of her office and realized she was shaking. Was it anger? Or something else? Fear that he'd been right and she'd been wrong about Rick? No, she wouldn't believe that. It was something else.

It was the echo of the past, of the times she said nearly the same words about Dean: He'd never had a chance. He needed someone to believe in him. Poor Dean. If only he'd listened to her. He'd be alive today.

A light knock on her half-open door pushed it open. The person in the doorway was tall, with dark hair swept back.

"Dean?" she whispered. *Oh, Dean!* A wave of the old pain washed over her. No, Dean was gone.

"Jake." His deep voice corrected her brusquely. Well, she couldn't blame him for being annoyed by her mistake. "Want me to rewire your alarm so it's harder to disarm?"

"Oh! Jake, I'm sorry. I..." No, she shouldn't tell him she'd mistaken him for a dead boyfriend. Not terribly flattering. "Never mind. Yes, if it isn't too much trouble. I'd really appreciate that."

His shoulders moved in a shrug. "No big deal. Rick said you've got a toolbox back here. Mind if I borrow it, and Rick? It'll go faster if someone who knows about circuitry gives me a hand."

For a sickening moment, Sophie hesitated. What if the police were right about Rick? He would know that using his keys would incriminate him. If he helped Jake fix the alarm, he'd know how to disconnect it the next time he tried to—No, she couldn't believe that.

"Of course," she said to Jake. "The tools are in the closet behind my desk."

Jake crossed the room. She looked up at him and swallowed hard. There was something about him that kept drawing her, despite her caution. Something that went way beyond his triggering memories of Dean. Last night he'd been so sweet, so comforting. And so understanding. He seemed to know when she needed to talk, and when she needed to think. He didn't patronize her, but when she needed to lean on him, he'd held her so tenderly. It had taken all her willpower not to tip her face up to kiss him.

And now, the way he was looking at her, she could feel him reading her thoughts, sensing her desires. The only other man who had made her feel this quivering awareness had been Dean, but never with this suddenness, this power. In self-defense, Sophie turned away from the intensity of Jake's gaze. She opened the utility closet door.

An enormous black spider floated down in front of her. With a stifled shriek, Sophie stepped backward into a solid wall of warm muscle. Jake grunted and staggered back, stopping abruptly when he bumped the desk. Sophie heard her pen cup rattle.

Jake's left hand caught her left shoulder, but the impact with his body made her tip forward again. Instinctively, she grabbed for stability just as Jake reached his right arm around her to hold her against him. Her hand closed on his thigh just as his big hand covered her breast.

Sophie gasped and froze. Behind her, Jake stood like a statue, but she could feel his heart pounding against her back. She couldn't breathe. The heat of his palm penetrated the thin fabric of her blouse. Her nipple hardened and pushed into his touch. His heat surrounded her and sparks streaked from her breast to her belly. Under her fingers, his thigh muscles bunched, but she couldn't make herself move.

Jake gritted his teeth and slowly, carefully, released his hold on Sophie. She stepped away, not looking at him. He drew a long, deep breath.

"I'll get rid of the spider," he told her, amazed that his voice sounded steady. His body was tingling as if he'd been cozying up to a live wire. "Give me a paper towel."

"Don't kill it."

Amused at her defense of the spider, he looked at her. She still wouldn't look at him. Well, he couldn't blame her. If their roles were reversed, he wouldn't want to remind her of a faux pas. But the roles weren't reversed, and what he really wanted was the chance to savor the feel of her body against him again.

"What do you want me to do with it?"

"Take it outside, please. I don't like to kill spiders because they eat other bugs, but they give me the willies." She shivered.

Keeping one eye on the spider, Jake picked up a file folder from her desk. Scooping the critter up was easy, but as he turned to take it out to the back door, the spider bailed out. He slid the folder under it again, but it skittered off again, sliding down its thread toward the floor. He scooped it up.

Sophie backed away. "Ohh! Stop! It's not a yo-yo, for pity's sake!" She hugged herself and shuddered, but he couldn't help chuckling. "Jake, please get it out of here!"

He carried the spider out to the back door and let it loose in the alley. When he got back to Sophie's office, she wasn't there. She'd left the red metal toolbox in the center of her desk. The message was pretty clear: she didn't want to face him just now.

Damn! He hadn't grabbed her on purpose. But it had happened, anyway, and he felt as if that simple contact had sparked an explosion of impulses inside him. His hand tingled with the memory of her resilient flesh, her hardening nipple against his palm.

Late that night, long past midnight, he lay in bed thinking about Sophie lying in her own bed above him. He placed his hand flat on his chest. The memory of her heartbeat pulsed through his veins. With no interference from the irritating voice in his head, he relived the moment over and over until sleep finally claimed him.

In his dreams, he turned her into his embrace, taking her soft, willing mouth with his. Sweet. So sweet . . .

Her slender body flowed against him, inviting, offering, igniting. As if by magic, their clothes disappeared. Her skin was hot satin. Her fingers branded him with silken fire. Wherever his lips touched her, she glistened silver in the pale light of the moon. Her voice was the wind sighing his name in release.

"Dean?" the Adviser called. "Dean, where are you?"

"Shh!"

"Dean, what—?"

"Come back later, man," he told his Adviser impatiently. "We're dreaming in Technicolor. I don't want to miss a single rapid eye movement."

Hours after she'd fled her office to escape the impulse to throw herself at Jake, she could still feel the imprint of his hand on her breast, still feel the heat of his chest burning through her shoulder blades.

Sophie raised her arms and let the satin nightie slide down her body, imagining it was Jake's hands whispering over her skin like a summer breeze. She wanted to taste his mouth and feel his hands tighten, drawing her closer. She wanted to wrap herself around him and feel him surge into her again and again until they were hot and slick and sated.

"Oh, Sophie, you fool," she moaned, sinking to the edge of her bed. She buried her face in her hands. "I'm doing it again. Wrong man, wrong time." Threading her fingers through her hair, she pulled.

Thank goodness, Jake had been a gentleman about it. Dean would have pressed his advantage, deliberately ignoring the half-closed door and the busy store beyond it. But if she'd turned into his arms, he would have pushed her away. Not because Dean had been a gentleman. Hardly. But because he was scared stiff she'd try to tie him down and try to change him. And he'd been so right. That's exactly what she would have tried, back when she was young and foolish.

Outside, a cat yowled. Sophie walked to the window and poked aside the shade. A full moon floated about the trees, pale and luminous. A moon for lovers.

She let the shade fall closed. In the dark room, she slid into bed, drawing the light blanket over her. Lying on her back, she let her hand glide up the hollow of her belly to the ridges of her ribs, until her palm covered her breast.

It wasn't the same. A kiss might be just a kiss, as the song in *Casablanca* claimed, but Jake's touch was like no other. Not since Dean had she felt this hunger for a man's touch. It was as if she'd been cursed, like a princess in a fairy tale: she couldn't fall in love, couldn't desire any man. Not until Jake. But falling for Jake—for any temporary man—would be such a mistake.

She thought back to the first time Dean had touched her breasts. She'd been so scared, trying to be so bold. They'd snuck out to one of the last drive-in movies in the area, parking in the back of the lot. She never noticed which B movie had been playing. Slipping into the back seat of Dean's souped-up '57 Chevy had been the only thing that mattered.

A sheltered seventeen, she thought she knew what to expect. Then he taught her how to French-kiss. What an enlightening experience that had been! She hadn't been kissed like that since, with such purity of purpose, such focused pleasure.

Dean's mouth had tasted of the rum-and-colas he'd poured from a thermos bottle. She'd been too drunk on forbidden excitement to bother with drinking. And then, when she was breathless from his kisses, when she was lying across the back seat, half crushed by his weight, feeling strangely restless all over, Dean put his hand on her breast.

Shock had made her bang her head on the car door.

And Dean, the rat, had started to laugh.

He'd avoided her for a month after that. When he started to come around again, he told her he'd needed a break from baby-sitting. How stupid she'd felt for driving him into the arms of other, more experienced women. Like a lovesick puppy, she'd begged for another chance. He'd conceded graciously, taking her parking when she was supposed to be at her best friend's house studying. She'd learned not to leap with shock at his caresses, and he had given her hints of how responsive her body could be. But he'd always left her aching.

She used to wonder, if they'd become lovers, would he have been so dumb about trying to prove he wasn't afraid to windsurf in a raging summer thunderstorm? With the wisdom of age, she'd realized the answer to that was a resounding "yes." Dean had been like a comet, streaking through her life, and her love could never have slowed him down or changed his orbit.

Likewise, with Jake Warren. The fact that she found him very attractive didn't cancel the fact that he was only in town for two months. The smartest thing she could do would be to push him out of her mind. Out of sight, out of mind.

With a sigh, Sophie turned onto her side, letting her eyes drift closed. She started to dream.

Gently, her lover eased her onto her back, his fingers tracing the line of her collarbone to her throat. His lips brushed hers, warm and soft. His hand flowed over her bare shoulder and down to rest on her satin-covered breast. The heat of his touch seeped into her, drugging her. With exquisite tenderness, his fingers teased her. Then he bent over her and caressed her breasts with his mouth, hot and hungry on her sensitized skin.

Desire flared deep inside her. She whimpered and shifted to offer him all of herself, restless beneath his hands and mouth. He pushed her nightgown up over her hips. His breath whispered over the quivering skin of her belly. His lips slid down her body, trailing hot wet kisses. Wave after wave of release flowed through her, drowning her in pleasure.

With a startled cry, Sophie woke up. Her skin was hot and damp. The fading ripples of her climax pulsed through her body. The image of her fantasy lover was gone, but there was only one man he could be.

"Jake," she whispered in the empty darkness.

"You're a nice boy for asking, Jake." Mrs. Mandel set a plate of warm apple strudel in front of him. "Wait until that bump on your head is gone before you start tinkering." She sat across her formica-topped kitchen table from him. "So. You've met my Sophie?"

Jake stuffed a forkful of the heavenly pastry into his mouth so he could get away with only a nod for an answer.

"Such a sweet girl. Have some more milk. It's good for you." She leaned over to top up his glass. "So. When are you going to ask her out?"

Jake choked on the strudel he was swallowing. He reached for the glass of milk. The silence stretched. The ticking of the antique mantel clock in Mrs. Mandel's living room grew louder and louder.

"A smart man could catch Sophie," Mrs. Mandel announced.

He set down his glass. "I don't want to catch anyone, Mrs. Mandel," he managed to get out.

"Nonsense! You're single. She's single. Of course, you have to be clever to interest her. She's very independent, my Sophie is. When I was Sophie's age, I was married already twelve years and had all my four children. But..."

He shoveled another piece of strudel into his mouth while his landlady sighed and traced the handle of the knife on the serving plate. When she gazed at him, the probing expression in her dark eyes made him uncomfortable.

"I'm not saying I wouldn't have married my husband—may he rest in peace—today, if I had a chance to do it over again. But sometimes I think it would be nice to be like Sophie. She has her business, her own money."

He swallowed and reached for the glass of milk. Mrs. Mandel shook her head, her shrewd eyes focused still on him.

"But such a waste. A smart man would romance Sophie, show her what she's missing. Men today don't know this much—" she snapped her fingers "—about romance. They write contracts."

She sniffed. "You can't make a romance out of a contract. You need impulse. Stolen kisses. Dancing in the dark. Hand-holding. Talking. Sharing. Not this business about separate interests. Doing things together."

Mrs. Mandel fixed him with a gaze that made him want to squirm. "A smart man knows what's missing in his life and goes after what he needs."

I couldn't say it better myself.

Ah, hell, now he was feeling outnumbered!

"Thanks for the strudel, Mrs. Mandel." He stood up, ignoring the sudden pain in his head when he did. "And thanks for the advice, but I don't think Sophie needs a man like me in her life."

"Being a genius doesn't make you smart, Jake Warren." She smiled, a sweet, grandmotherly smile that took some of the sting out of her words. "Now, you go rest, and think about what I said. And tomorrow, if you're feeling well enough, you can fix the garage door."

* * *

Sophie parked her car behind the house, thoroughly annoyed with herself. After firmly resolving not to waste a single thought on Jake Warren, she'd spent her entire nine hours at the store thinking about kissing him. Maybe she should just have a fling with him. All the sparks she imagined would fizzle out and she'd be able to get him out of her system.

But flings weren't her style. And Jake might not even be interested. He probably had a significant other waiting for him back in California. As many of her single friends lamented, the best guys always seemed to be taken. And as everyone, herself included, kept pointing out, even if Jake wasn't involved with another woman, he was leaving town soon. So, all things considered, she should be immune to the quiet attractions of Jake Warren.

And she would be, damn it!

Climbing the back stairs, Sophie paused on Jake's landing. She really should thank him for fixing her alarm. Rick had talked about Jake's genius with electronics and computers all day. Apparently, Rick had read about Jake in prison, while he was studying computer programming.

Sophie rapped on the screen door, hoping she wasn't disturbing Jake's work. There was no answer even after a long wait. She was about to go up to her own apartment when she heard footsteps shuffling heavily across Jake's kitchen. A moment later, the screen door opened a few inches, with only Jake's fingers visible on the edge of it.

"Hi. I don't want to interrupt you. I just came by to thank you for taking care of the alarm," she babbled, suddenly feeling very self-conscious. If she wasn't careful, the man would get the idea she was much more interested than she was.

"It was nothing," he said hoarsely. "Glad I could help."

"Jake, what's wrong?" she blurted. When he didn't answer, she gave in to impulse and pulled open the door. Catching sight of his pale, haggard face and slumped posture, she gasped. "You're sick!"

Sophie dropped her purse onto the kitchen floor and grabbed Jake's arm. He looked down at her, pain and weariness in his sapphire eyes. Under her hand, his muscles felt rock hard, but he leaned into her hold as if he lacked the strength to stand.

Fear—the kind of white-hot terror she'd only felt once before, when she'd seen Dean launch his sailboard into the storm—streaked through her. "Oh, Jake! What's wrong?"

"My head," he croaked. "It's going to rain."

"Come to bed, Jake. You look like..." She caught herself before saying *death warmed over.* "...hell."

Frightened that his head injury was worse than anyone knew, she led him toward Diane's bedroom. The large, rumpled bed was an island in a sea of books, computer printouts and clothing. After drawing him to the bed, she flipped the covers aside and guided Jake down to the edge. He sat heavily, head bowed.

"Should I call an ambulance?"

"No. The doctors warned me I could be sensitive to air-pressure changes. It'll pass."

She clenched her hands together to resist the temptation to stroke the silky, dark curls tumbling over his forehead. "Can I get you some aspirin?"

Jake looked up. Fine lines were etched around his beautiful eyes. "Took some ibuprofen already." The lines around his eyes deepened as if it hurt to speak.

She looked at him, feeling utterly helpless. He bowed his head again, and raised one hand to massage the back of his neck.

"Let me," she said softly. "Maybe it will help."

He lifted his head again. "What?"

"A back rub."

He grimaced. "You don't have to."

She smiled. "You didn't have to fix my alarm."

He smiled back weakly. "Touché." His eyelids lowered as if they were too heavy to keep open. His thick, black lashes cast shadows on his pale skin.

Making the offer was one thing. Following through, touching him, was something else entirely. Sophie drew a quick breath. If she was looking for a test of her resolve to stay uninvolved with Jake Warren, this was it.

She reached down and slid his heavy watch off his wrist. His skin felt hot. She put the watch on the cluttered nightstand beside the bed. Then she studied him. He had on jeans that were so faded and worn that they showed the cords of his thigh muscles as if the fabric were molded to his flesh. The knees of his jeans were shredded through, and his feet were bare. His San Francisco Giants T-shirt looked like a goat had been chewing on it.

God, he was attractive! Better than attractive. He was sexy, strong, vulnerable. It was a potent combination.

She might as well make this test of her willpower a real trial by fire. "Take off your shirt and lie down," she ordered softly.

His eyes opened. She met their laser brightness steadily, determined to keep the situation under control. The room seemed to grow warmer as she waited for his reaction. Oh, Lord, would he mistake her words for an invitation...? Worse, would he think she was totally insensitive, trying to seduce him—if that's what he mistakenly thought—when he was in such obvious pain?

She searched his eyes for reassurance that he wasn't thinking the worst of her. Jake's jaw muscles tightened. Oh, God, he was going to take off his shirt right now! Her cheeks burned. Her hands were shaking at the thought of touching his bare skin.

"It's okay, Sophie. I think all I need is sleep."

She smiled past her embarrassment. Really, she should be grateful that he'd saved her—saved them both—from the awkwardness a massage would have caused. After all, she'd just resolved to stifle this attraction she felt for him. There was no reason to feel . . . hurt.

"I'll bring you some soup later, if you'd like." To her relief, her voice sounded perfectly normal. As if her throat didn't ache and her eyes didn't sting just a tiny bit from his rejection. "Spring vegetable soup?"

"Sounds good."

"See you in an hour or so, then," she told him, then fled before she gave in to the impulse to touch him after all.

Chapter Four

"I want a transfer," Dean said through clenched teeth.

The Adviser sighed.

"Aw, c'mon! Sophie was ready to climb into bed with me—him—sorta, and he shut her down! Hell, it was a start, wasn't it? Why does he have to be a hero? Isn't there some college maniac around here whose number is up?"

The Adviser gave him that *look*.

"Okay, okay. Can't blame a guy for trying, can you? This being a good sport is a pain."

An hour after she bolted from Jake's apartment, Sophie steeled herself to bring him a container of homemade vegetable soup and a few oven-ready rolls. She crept barefoot down the stairs, hoping she could sneak in and out of his kitchen before he woke up. Irrational and immature as it was, she still felt the sting of his rejecting her when she was trying to resist him.

It was too ridiculous. Having a crush, albeit unwillingly, turned an independent, mature woman of thirty into a jittery, fluttery sixteen-year-old. Probably that old mystique of the forbidden.

Whatever the reason, her heart pounded as she opened the screen door. The tiny creaking noise echoed in the stillness of the dark apartment. Wind from the threatening storm blew in through the open porch and windows. She shut the door softly, and padded to the stove with the food. There was a microwave oven, but Sophie didn't want to turn the crisp vegetables in the soup to mush, so she poured the contents of the container into one of Diane's heavy sauce pots. Careful not to make noise, she set the pot on a front burner of the old gas stove.

"Sophie?" Jake's voice came from the hallway, startling a yelp out of her.

She gripped the counter to calm herself. A moment later, Jake said her name again, this time from behind her. She turned and gasped again. She'd seen him like this before, and yet, she really hadn't. He'd stripped off the ragged T-shirt and stood facing her, a towel in one hand. He was barefoot, and water dripped onto his chest from the curls around his face.

He was broader than she remembered, his body powerfully yet elegantly developed. A swimmer's body. His smooth pectoral muscles flowed down into firmly rippling abdominal muscles. The black hair across his golden chest was fine and silky-looking. It tapered to a thin line between his ribs, leading her eyes down to the waist of his jeans.

The snap was undone.

His worn jeans hugged every inch of his hips and legs, revealing more muscle. Much more muscle, in fact, than she ever would have expected from a doctor of computer science. Standing with his legs braced, his hair curling onto his shoulders, his eyes watchful, he was the image of a fantasy:

all the power of a superior warrior, and the piercing intelligence of one of the keenest minds.

And then Jake blushed. She knew he had no control over it, but it was the most endearing thing he could have done. And it broke the tension for her. She smiled.

"Hi," she said. "I was hoping not to wake you."

"You didn't. The ibuprofen finally kicked in."

"I brought you the soup and some rolls."

"Thanks." He touched the back of his thumb to the bridge of his nose as if pushing up glasses. "Why don't you join me?" he added, surprising her.

"Oh!" She knew she should refuse, should keep her distance. She also knew there was no use pretending she didn't want to spend time with him. "I... I guess I can. There's plenty of soup. I just have to light the stove and preheat the oven."

She turned to suit actions to words, and to have an excuse to hide her own burning cheeks. The burner refused to flare up. She tried again. Still nothing, except for the telltale odor of gas escaping from the jets.

"I think the pilot light is out," she told Jake. "That happens sometimes when it's windy. If you get me a match..."

Her voice trailed off when his bare arm brushed her shoulder. He reached over the counter to shut the window, then passed her a box of wooden matches from the back of the counter. The fresh, clean scent of his skin enticed her to lean closer.

"That's sort of what happened to me," he told her softly, staring at the oven door. "When I drowned." She caught her breath at the harsh image. "The paramedics said they'd lost me. And then I was breathing again."

He looked into her eyes and she felt the full force of her dreams all over again. Except now, she couldn't have said for sure if the man in her dreams had had Dean's retrogreaser's haircut, or Jake's barely tamed curls. She gripped the counter behind her to keep from reaching out to Jake the way she'd done in her dreams—to Dean? Or to Jake?

"I can remember feeling like I was slipping away, and then I felt some—" he swallowed "—someone pulling me back. Reaching for my hands. Calling my name." He shrugged. "Probably the paramedics and Les."

Or me, she thought. But that was absurd. She'd been dreaming about Dean. She hadn't even known about Jake's accident until after the dreams. It was just a coincidence that Jake had nearly drowned almost twelve years to the day of Dean's death.

Of course! That was why Dean had been on her mind. She hadn't even connected the dates until this very second, but of course, it made sense. Well, at least that was one threat to her sanity that she didn't have to worry about anymore. Now, if only Jake would go put on a shirt....

Sophie's gentle smile made him feel as if some door were being opened. For the first time in his life, he felt like confiding in someone. There was something about her that promised comfort, and for once, he not only needed it, he was willing to seek it.

"I guess visions like that are fairly common," he went on, feeling foolish, hoping she wouldn't think he was blithering.

Anything paranormal was diametrically opposed to the world of logic he inhabited. He felt intensely uncomfortable sounding like he believed in any of it. He tried to clarify what he meant, except he knew that he wasn't telling her the truth. At least, not the whole truth. Hell, he wasn't sure what the whole truth really was.

"It must be like dreams, when you incorporate real things into whatever is going on in your imagination. Like the phone ringing, or a dog barking. Subliminal suggestions."

Sophie nodded. She looked as though she wanted to say something, hesitated, then took a deep breath.

"Sometimes, you don't know what's on your mind until you dream about it," she said softly. "Twelve years ago, someone I, uh, someone I cared about, died. I hadn't thought about him in ages, but I dreamed about him the other night. I must have connected the dates in my mind without realizing it."

The way she stood, gazing up at him with her head tilted, he could see the pulse surging in the base of her throat. A rush of fierce, unfamiliar emotions choked him but he had no trouble recognizing jealousy—and desire. Suddenly, he wanted to press his lips to that soft spot and taste her skin. He was so aroused he could hardly breathe, but...

Touch her, man, that damn voice urged. *You got her all softened up, talking about what happened. Put your arms around her. She won't fight it. Remember how good she felt last night, after the hassle at the store. Let her feel how much you want her. Come on, man, let her feel what she's doing to us.*

He looked into the stormy depths of her eyes and knew the voice—whatever or whoever it was—was right. Sophie wouldn't resist if he reached out for her. The memory of her slender body leaning on him last night, of the silk and fragrance of her hair when he'd kissed her, had played through his dreams all the rest of the night.

They were so close, he could easily bend and kiss her. Oh, God, he wanted to! But last night, he'd offered her comfort, sharing his strength. Tonight, she was feeling sorry for him and nostalgic for someone else.

He wanted her passion, not her pity, not her memories.

"I'm sorry," he muttered. "I shouldn't have said anything. I guess I get a little intense sometimes."

"That's understandable," she said, her smile melting his reserves even more.

"Not just because of the accident. I, uh, I usually don't relate well to people," he found himself confessing, suddenly desperate for her to understand him. It was a totally unique impulse. He'd never cared before if anyone understood him, only whether they understood his work.

"I get lost in space. Hack mode, we call it. I get caught up by ideas. Obsessive, sometimes. Especially when I'm trying to solve a problem or write programs. I'm a perfectionist. Except in real life. Then I'm a slob. Absentminded. I guess I can seem rude and antisocial sometimes, but I'm not really. Just distracted."

Self-consciousness caught up with him. He felt his cheeks flush. "Sorry, but you seem so easy to talk to. I'm not used to opening up like that. Do people often tell you their life stories?"

Her soft laugh reassured him even before she said, "All the time. I'm the keeper of countless deep, dark secrets."

The buzzer on the stove made him flinch. Sophie smiled again and took the rolls out of the oven. The combined aromas of the soup and the fresh bread reminded him that he hadn't eaten since breakfast. He smiled back and went to find dishes.

"Mrs. Mandel was right. You're a good cook," he said after his first heavenly spoonful.

"Thanks. I was lucky my mother loved to cook and started teaching me when I had to stand on a chair to see over the countertop. That was the only way I could pass high school chemistry. I did the mixing and measuring, and my lab partner, Elizabeth Ann, who could burn water, did the calculations."

Her confession charmed him. He smiled at Sophie, and dug back into the soup. "I could have used a partner like you in chem. I was a biohazard with anything caustic." He broke off a piece of warm roll. "What else did you do well in?"

"English and history, especially art history. I hated memorizing dates and battles, but I loved learning about the people. The way they lived, the way they thought. Even in science classes, I was more interested in the scientists than in their work."

She waved her spoon and laughed lightly. "Think about Darwin, with all his theories about evolution, seeing a duckbill platypus for the first time. I wanted to know how he felt about an egg-laying mammal, not how he'd classify or explain it."

He grinned back at her. God, she was beautiful! "I guess we don't usually think about the emotional side of science."

"Well, I think that's a loss. It isn't all facts and numbers. Even computer scientists get passionate, don't they?"

He swallowed hard. When he looked across at her, her cheeks had turned pink. His own face felt pretty warm. And from somewhere in the inner regions of his head, he heard a muffled snicker that definitely wasn't his own.

"I mean, passionate about their work," she added.

He nodded, not trusting himself to speak. Apparently, Sophie felt the same way, because she began to concentrate on her soup. He took his cue from her and attacked his bowl. It really was the best soup he'd ever tasted.

"How are you feeling now?" she asked when he'd finished the last drop of his third helping and the last crumb of his second roll.

"Pretty good. We never got that storm."

"Typical Connecticut weather. I think it was Mark Twain who said, if you don't like the weather here, just wait a few minutes." She smiled and reached for his empty bowl.

"I'll do that." He put his hand out and touched the back of hers. Her skin was unbelievably soft. *Oh, yeah! And the rest of her...*

Ignoring the voice, he let his fingers stay a moment longer. Sophie continued to look at him, but her smile faded. Her eyes were as dark as a storm cloud. He wished he knew what she was thinking, what she was feeling—if anything—about him.

"Are you—" He cleared his throat. "Are you busy for the rest of the evening? I thought we might watch a video."

Way to go, tiger! Oh, no. Was that like coals to Newcastle? "Unless you're sick of seeing movies." *Dumb! Don't give her a way out! I can't stand the suspense.*

She took her hand away from his but her smile came back. "You've just given me the perfect excuse to put off balancing my checkbook. Did you have a film in mind?"

"No. I thought you could recommend something again."

I know what I could recommend.

Jake gritted his teeth to prevent himself from telling the voice in his head to shut up. He was going to have to do something about it before he went stark, raving mad, but what? He couldn't devise a solution when he didn't even understand the problem. Anyway, his immediate concern was Sophie.

Mine, too.

"Hmm," she said, looking thoughtful. "I've got a pretty good collection of classics upstairs. If you don't mind seeing an old movie—"

"It'll be new to me." He gathered the bowls, plates and cutlery, and put them into the sink to wash later. "I can bring up a couple of cold beers, unless you'd rather have wine."

"Beer is fine."

He swung open the refrigerator door, and the blast of cold air on his chest reminded him that he'd forgotten to put on a shirt. Muttering an "excuse me," he hurried into the bedroom and dug through the new shirts he'd bought the day before. Hastily, he ripped off the tags and pulled the dark blue polo shirt over his head.

Back in the kitchen, he grabbed two frosty beers from the fridge, then stood back for Sophie to lead the way. As she climbed the stairs ahead of him, he couldn't help watching the slight sway of her hips in formfitting jeans. At the top landing, she turned and smiled. He grinned back and took the last four steps in two strides.

He followed her through her kitchen to her living room, hardly noticing what the rooms looked like. Every atom of his brain was focused on Sophie. Being with her was so easy, so instinctive. With other women, even ones he'd dated, he'd felt alien, out of sync, awkward. With Sophie, he felt comfortable, connected. She could be his friend. She could be his lover.

The thought sent a jolt of desire through him. He and Sophie, lovers. Making love with Sophie would be like dying and going to heaven. She'd be soft and sweet, shy and gentle, pliant and giving. His awkwardness would dissolve into perfect skill.

Visions formed in his mind, visions of Sophie with her lips moist and swollen from his kisses, her eyes dreamy with desire. The images were so clear, they were almost like memories. He shook his head to clear it.

"How about *Casablanca?*" she asked, standing by a tall bookcase filled with videotapes. He forced himself to pay attention to her words. "It's one of my favorites, but I haven't seen it in a while." She smiled.

"I'm in your hands," he told her.

I wish.

Sophie fed the cassette into the VCR. Jake had said he was in her hands. Well, she'd better sit on her hands, to keep them off him. She sat in the corner of her big, overstuffed couch, as far from Jake as she could get without looking rude, but that didn't help. She could still see him in the dim light. She could hear his breathing in the silence before the movie cued up. She could smell the subtle tang of his aftershave.

Why, oh why, couldn't she feel this attracted to someone *right?* Someone who wasn't just passing through her life? Someone like Bob Manetti, who was sweet and fun—despite his love for horror movies and loaded pizzas—and settled in West Hartford? Or someone like Craig's assistant manager at the bank, Mike Riordan, who was handsome and attentive and sophisticated? Or any of the other perfectly suitable men she met, dated, liked, but just couldn't fall in love with?

"It's in black and white!" Jake sounded vaguely indignant.

Startled, she gaped at him. "Of course! That's the way it was filmed."

"I'm surprised it hasn't been colorized."

She glared at him. "That's like coloring in Leonardo da Vinci's charcoal sketches." He studied her for a moment, making her feel foolish for her outburst. "Sorry. You hit a nerve. Films like *Casablanca* are more subtle, more emotionally intense, because they're in black and white."

Jake looked for a moment as if he hadn't heard her. Then his expression cleared and he nodded. She sat through the film aware of his every shift of position and attention. When it was over, she sniffed back her tears and pressed the rewind button.

"You okay?" His gruff tone made her laugh self-consciously.

"I'm fine. I always cry at the end. What did you think of it?"

"Interesting. But no one said, 'Play it again, Sam.'"

She laughed. "That's another movie."

"For another night, maybe." He gave her a quick smile, then stood up. "I better get going. I've got a meeting at nine with the brass from the banks."

Jake held his hand out to her. She hesitated, afraid that if he tried to kiss her, she wouldn't be able to resist. But when he didn't move away, she put her hand into his and let him pull her slowly up to her feet. His hand wrapped hers in warm strength. The contact reminded her of how quietly he'd offered his support after the break-in, without treating her like a child, without getting all swaggering and macho.

She looked up into Jake's eyes. The rest of the room seemed to fade away. The heat from his hand flowed up her arm to her neck like a lover's caress. Her gaze dropped from the intensity of his brilliant blue eyes to his full, sensual mouth. He ran the tip of his tongue over his lips. Without conscious intent, Sophie mirrored his action, longing for the taste of his lips and tongue, even as she warned herself that she'd never be content with just a taste.

"Good night, Sophie," he said softly. "Thanks for... everything."

He released her hand and disappeared into the darkness of the back of her apartment.

Jake unlocked his bike from the post on the back porch and wheeled it toward the street. He had to do something to get the dust from the bank guys out of his brain. Two days with them, and he was regretting taking the job. Why bother to call in a specialist if you've got your own ideas and don't want to listen to anyone else's? Why hire an expert in computer security, if you're going to insist that your computers are secure?

He'd dealt with all kinds of jerks before, but that Riordan guy took the prize. The guy must memorize slang dictionaries. Dropped hacker vocabulary like a groupie. His conversation had more corporate buzzwords than a garbage pail had flies. To top it off, Riordan made a point of telling him he'd been dating Sophie on and off for a couple of years.

He started pedaling, letting his thoughts drift to the problems of computer security that phone access was causing. The air was hot and humid, but the sky looked clear. Occasionally, he passed other cyclists and joggers. Eventually, he found himself on the paths of the Elizabeth Park rose garden. He took a few minutes to wander, breathing in the sweet scents.

Not as sweet as Sophie, the voice said, making an appearance for the first time since Sunday evening. Jake fought with the bike to keep it on the path. Damn! Whatever it was, it hadn't disappeared.

A half hour later, Jake found himself in front of Sophie's store. Through the window, he could see her talking on the phone and sorting through the drawer of video games kept behind the desk for safekeeping. The sight of her filled him with a pleasure he'd never felt before, except when he was particularly pleased by a program he'd written.

Better than that, his inner voice corrected.

"Back off," he muttered, crouching to lock his bike to the rack in the parking lot. An elderly couple passing by circled around him and exchanged alarmed glances. Jake growled in self-disgust.

Sophie smiled when he caught her eye, making him feel as if all the hassles of the past two days had suddenly evaporated.

"Hi," she said softly. "You must be feeling better if you're riding on such a hot day."

He shrugged, not wanting to be reminded of feeling helpless. "There's a breeze."

A woman with a baby asleep on her shoulder handed Sophie a cassette. Jake glanced up at the movie on the big overhead TV monitor while Sophie typed the woman's phone number into the computer, then ran the light pen over the inventory code strip. He didn't have a clue what the movie was about, but had to chuckle at the phony eastern religious ceremony that didn't seem to be doing whatever it was supposed to do.

When Sophie finished giving the woman her change, she turned back to him. "Where did you ride to?"

"I don't know. All over. I've been out a couple of hours."

"Did you do a lot of biking in California?"

"More than I wanted to."

He moved aside to make room for a tall woman in cutoff shorts and a very brief top. *Nice, but she's not Sophie,* came the thought. *Keep talking.*

"I like to ride when I'm trying to solve a problem. The part of your brain that deals with movement through space also deals with creative problem solving." Sophie and the young woman both stared at him. He felt his cheeks burn. "That's why, when you're driving, you can come up with some fantastic idea and miss your exit. Or just not remember the drive at all."

Sophie laughed. "Oh. That happens to me all the time."

He grinned in relief that she didn't think he was a total flamer. "I used to find myself miles—lots of miles—from home, all problems solved, without a clue where I was."

"That explains those fabulous thighs," the tall woman said in a low, husky voice, then winked at Sophie. Sophie looked at him, then looked away, her cheeks turning bright pink. He knew his own face must be the color of a fire engine.

"Maybe you should see him from this side of the counter, Sophie," the woman added, "although what you can see from there is nice, too." With a wicked chuckle, she took her video and left the store.

"Sorry," Sophie said, still not looking into his eyes. "Carla's a character."

He shrugged. "How's the computer behaving?"

She smiled up at him. "Just fine today. Oh, there's Rick back from his dinner break. He said he wanted to ask you about computer crimes. He said you wrote one of the articles he read."

"Could be." *Ask her, dummy! Come on! I haven't got forever. Neither do you.* "Have you had dinner yet?"

Sophie blushed again and looked away from his face. "I, um, I'm going out to play tennis soon, and have dinner after." The way she spoke told him louder than words that her tennis partner was a man.

Rick arrived talking, saving him from having to say anything. Sophie traded places behind the counter with Rick and offered a weak smile. He forced an answering smile. She moved a step closer and he inhaled her delicate scent. When she tipped her face up toward him, he was stunned to see how uncertain she looked.

"If I can get my new charcoal grill assembled, can I invite you for a cookout tomorrow night?" she said softly.

Jake saw Rick's head snap up at Sophie's invitation, but having Sophie so close made everything around him easy to ignore. "Sure. What can I contribute?"

Her smile touched him like a caress. "Wine, ice cream . . . and any expertise with a wrench?"

"Sounds fair." *Sounds like first base to me, buddy.* He grinned in agreement.

Sophie's smile widened. "I've got to run now. See you tomorrow. About seven?" He nodded. "Good. Rick? Are you okay to close up with Larry? He's never done it before."

"Sure thing, Soph." Rick set the books he was carrying down on the counter.

Absently, Jake noted the titles. He had contributed one of the chapters in the anthology of computer crime detection, and had worked with the author on one of the other books.

Rick shuffled through some papers on the desk. "Want me to leave the system on or off?"

"On, I guess. I wouldn't mind seeing if it can do that rental analysis overnight, the way Dennis promised. If not, I'll have to call his message service again. Can you run it? I haven't a clue how to do it yet."

Her quick smile at him looked apologetic. Jake wanted to reassure her he wasn't offended, but was certainly willing to help her learn about her computer. And not just because it would be a way to spend more time with her.

Uh-huh.

Rick grinned. "Gotcha."

"Well, I've got to run," Sophie said. "Good night."

Unwilling to watch Sophie dash off to meet some other guy, Jake turned his back and looked up at the monitor over the desk. The actor was talking to himself and walking like a puppet being jerked two ways.

Rick interrupted to ask him a couple of fairly technical questions about the computer crimes he'd been reading about in his books, so Jake was on familiar ground answering. Enjoying Rick's company, he lingered awhile to talk with him between customers, mainly about the problems Sophie was having with her computer system.

"Maybe I should do some exploring through your software," Jake offered. "It sounds like Sophie's been waiting a long time for this Dennis guy to pay a service call."

Rick shook his head. "Nah. We haven't lost any data yet, and she'd be mighty ticked if I let you do that without her okay." He shrugged. "Sophie has infinite faith in people doing what they promise. Sometimes she gets burned, but you don't want to be the one to point that out." Then he grinned. "She has a hell of a temper for a saint."

A man with three rambunctious boys approached the desk. While Rick took care of them, Jake looked up again at the TV monitor. The male actor was looking into a mirror, but the image talking back to him was that of a woman. Curious, Jake strained to hear the soundtrack.

From what he could make out, the spirit of a dying woman had mistakenly been transferred into the body of a man who disliked her intensely. Their bickering turned hilarious when they had to use the men's room. Like two cats in a sack, they were fighting for dominance of the man's identity.

Suddenly Jake felt sick.

Bingo!

No. It was impossible. Things like that simply didn't happen in real life.

Yeah, well, that's what I thought, too. Guess the joke's on us.

Sophie tried unsuccessfully to shrug Mike Riordan's arm from across her shoulders. They'd beaten their doubles opponents, friends of Mike's who had just excused themselves to rescue their baby-sitter from their four-year-old son. Mike was clearly elated, but Sophie couldn't keep her thoughts from straying to Jake's expression when she'd had to refuse his invitation. Charming and fun as Mike was, he wasn't Jake.

"We make a good team, Sophie." Mike's arm tightened. "How about coming back to my place?" He leaned closer, his lips just brushing her temple. "We can send out for Chinese food and slip into the hot tub while we wait."

"Thanks, Mike, but I think I'm too tired to stay up much longer. Maybe I can take a rain check on dinner?"

He stiffened but didn't release her. "Sophie, I told you it's over for good between Marsha and me. I never really cared about her. I guess I only got involved with her because you kept putting me off for so long. I was lonely, babe."

Sophie sighed. Here she was again, trying to ease out of a relationship with a perfectly suitable man. Mike was everything she should be looking for in a man: reliable, attentive, honest, intelligent, supportive of her ambitions, more sensitive about emotions than most men she knew. But she just couldn't feel a spark of passion for him.

In all fairness to Mike, she needed to be honest with him. It had nothing, she tried to convince herself, to do with the way Jake Warren made her heart beat like a captured bird.

"Mike, we need to talk."

"We can talk at my place."

"Someplace a little less private?"

His hold on her shoulders slackened just a little. "Oh. Well, we can go to the Chinese place in the Center. It should be quiet now, and they won't care how we're dressed."

At the restaurant, the hostess seated them at a table in a corner as Mike requested. Before Sophie could open her menu, Mike had ordered their meal. He gave her a crooked smile.

"I hope I didn't step on your toes, baby, but I think I'd rather concentrate on us than on the moo goo gai pan."

How could she be annoyed? Sophie shook her head and smiled. "You know all my favorites, anyway." And it didn't matter.

Mike poured cups of green tea for both of them. Sophie reached for hers, but it was too hot to hold. She clasped her hands in her lap instead, and gazed at Mike across the table.

"Why do I get the feeling I'm about to get both barrels between the eyes?" he asked. He held his hand out to her, his expression openly miserable. After a moment of indecision, Sophie put her hand into his.

"Mike, I'm sorry." His hand closed around hers. "You know I like you. But—"

"But not the way I want you to. Right?"

She forced herself to continue meeting his eyes. She owed him that consideration. "I feel awful."

"Good." He grinned crookedly. "Misery loves company." His grin faded. "I'll accept that you don't want to jump into my hot tub tonight, but I'm not going to give up easily. We could be good together, Soph." He turned their hands over and stared down at them for a moment. Then he looked into her eyes again. "Is there someone else?"

"No, of course not." Her hasty denial brought an image of Jake bare-chested with his jeans snap undone. The sting of a blush betrayed her.

Mike's eyebrow rose. He opened his mouth to speak, but the waitress reappeared with their appetizers. Releasing her hand, he smiled ruefully. *"Bon appétit."*

Sophie's spring roll tasted like sawdust. She felt awful, especially because Mike was being so decent.

Mike took a swallow of the beer he'd ordered. "This computer wizard living in your building... Is he as good as he's supposed to be?"

Surprised at the sudden shift of topic, Sophie blinked. "I don't know. Your bank hired him. I'm as computer illiterate as a person can get and still use one."

He smiled. "I think it's cute." Before she could defend herself, he shook his head, telling her he was teasing. "Warren is charging six figures for his services. I want to make sure we're getting our money's worth. Our customers' money's worth."

She hadn't realized computer experts made that much money. Jake certainly didn't spend it on the kinds of imported suits and cars Mike liked. But she shouldn't compare the two men. Mike was obviously dedicated and conscientious, even if he was a bit flashy. She respected his sense of responsibility. Unfortunately, it wasn't enough to make her fall in love with him.

"I understand, Mike, but I'm the last one to ask. I can't even get the man who installed my system to make a service call."

He shook his head again. "That's because you're too nice. You need to be more forceful. Call that jerk and tell him to get his butt over to the store."

Sophie smiled. "Not exactly my first choice of words, but I'll call again tomorrow. It was enough trouble getting this system installed. I'd hate to have to start over with another system, and another support company."

Mike frowned. "I don't get it. He's always available to work on the bank's system. I feel responsible, since I recommended him to you. Let me know if you can't get him out by tomorrow. I can try to light a fire under him."

Sophie thanked him just as their main courses arrived, along with Mike's second beer. The thought of eating made her stomach clench. She poked at her food with her chopsticks and let Mike lead her through a series of lightweight topics. All the while, she wondered why she couldn't fall for a nice man like Mike. Why were her thoughts constantly turning back to Jake, an enigma, a stranger, a man who was going to slip in and out of her life like a comet in its orbit?

Finally the waitress brought their bill. Mike refused to let Sophie pay half. He walked her to his new BMW, his hand resting lightly on her shoulder.

"My place or yours?" he asked after he started the car. Before she could answer, he grinned. "Relax, Sophie. I'm teasing."

Mike drove a little faster than he usually did, but Sophie understood that he was eager to get her home before his pride suffered any more damage. She tried to think of something to say that wouldn't make matters worse, but when Mike parked in front of Mrs. Mandel's house and Sophie saw the glow of Jake's lights, she felt embarrassingly eager for tomorrow night.

Chapter Five

Better pour us a stiff drink, pal. You're gonna need it.

"I don't want a drink, *pal.*"

Oh, hell! Now he was talking to the voice in his head as if it really were someone else. At least he'd waited until he was in the sanctuary of his apartment, where no one else could hear him making an ass of himself.

Suit yourself. But I could use a stiff drink.

"All right! All right!"

A stiff drink was in fact beginning to sound like a good idea. Jake slammed around the kitchen cupboards and grumbled until he found a nearly full bottle of very good Scotch. He'd have to replace it for Diane, since his alter ego probably didn't have any spare change.

Bitter, bitter.

Jake poured several inches of Scotch into a tumbler. He took a deep swallow, then grimaced as the liquor burned its way down to his gut. "Okay. Talk. Who the hell are you and what do you want?"

Who I am is the dead dude who saved your life when you were gasping your last breath last week. And, I'm the guy Sophie really loves.

Jake set the glass down feeling as if he'd been sucker-punched. "What?"

Ask Sophie about Dean Wilde sometime. She's my girl. Always has been. Always will be. She's the reason I'm getting a second chance. And she's the reason I saved your worthless life.

After a brief hesitation, Jake drank most of the rest of the Scotch in the glass, welcoming the searing in his esophagus. He drained the glass in one more gulp, hoping to get too looped to hear the voice.

Dean Wilde. The man Sophie really loves. A dead man. The one she'd said she'd cared about. In his head.

No. It was too bizarre. Too illogical. He was a scientist. He knew this couldn't be happening. It was a figment of his imagination, sparked by hitting his head last week. Like the visions of Sophie calling to him, drawing him back from the darkness, back from death . . .

Yeah. Right. And who do you think had Sophie on the brain?

"Sophie was in *your* thoughts? And I saw her . . . ?" It actually made sense, in a bizarre twist of logic. His mind was beginning to fog from belting back the whiskey on an empty stomach, but not nearly enough to erase the memory of Sophie calling him "Dean."

"How did you die, Wilde?"

Same way, man. Only I did it with style.

"You drowned?"

Yeah. In Long Island Sound, twelve years ago. Some jerk dared me to go windsurfing in a thunderstorm. Ask Sophie. She was there.

"Oh, hell!" He refilled the glass and drank some more Scotch. Poor Sophie, having to listen to him going on about drowning and being called back...

Man, we could have had her in your bed in a flash after she heard that.

"Don't you have a conscience?"

That's what you're for. But you don't have to do such a good job. I've been waiting for Sophie for a long time.

Jake choked on his swallow of whiskey. "Just tell me one more thing. And then I want you to go back to wherever you came from."

I can tell you whatever you want to ask, man, but I don't think I can go back to wherever I came from. You and I are stuck with each other. At least until I figure out how to get out of here. I've got this Adviser, an old guy who sighs a lot, but he doesn't do much advising. Maybe you can talk to him sometime.

Jake swore in his most elaborate hacker manner, but it didn't make him feel any better. He couldn't shake his preoccupation with Wilde's relationship with Sophie. Why on earth should he care? He and Sophie were just casual acquaintances, just temporary neighbors.

The memory of holding Sophie in his arms, comforting her after the break in at her store, flashed through his already overcrowded mind. At the sudden surge of heat, he swore again.

You're pretty good at that. I've never heard some of those words. So, what do you want to know?

Jake drained the glass again, grimacing when it burned its way down. He was getting drunk, but he was still feeling pain. He had to know *why.* Why was this happening?

"What do you want?" he demanded of the spirit of Dean Wilde.

Jake held his breath and waited, suddenly anxious about what he might hear. The possibility that Sophie might be in some danger disturbed him. Could this presence in his head force him to do something to her? Was his own free will at stake, as well as Sophie's safety? He had to know. Impatience hummed in his brain, but Wilde's answer was a long time coming.

What do I want? Wilde's laugh came out arrogant, challenging. *What I want is simple, Warren. I want Sophie. I want Sophie back.*

Jake slammed the glass down on the table so hard that it shattered. Until that moment, he hadn't realized his feelings for Sophie were growing into something beyond detached interest.

"Over my dead body," he growled.

That can probably be arranged.

Sophie heard footsteps on the driveway and paused outside her back door.

"Sophie, wait," Mike called. "Sophie, we need to talk." He took the two flights of stairs at a run and arrived at her side faster than she expected. She took an involuntary step backward when he moved close. "Sophie, I can't let it end like this."

"Oh, Mike! I thought you understood...."

"I do, baby. I just decided I don't like the way things are turning out. I want another chance." He reached for the doorknob. "Come on, Soph."

She put her hand on his. "Mike, please... It's late and—"

He turned suddenly. Her tennis racket and purse clattered to the porch floor. Ignoring them, he caught her shoulders in his hands. His grip tightened until it hurt. Fear and confusion paralyzed her. This was *Mike.* She shouldn't be afraid of him. But this was a Mike she didn't know. Had she underestimated the depth of his feelings for her and provoked this fury?

"Sophie, give us a chance. Invite me in. Let me show you how I feel about you."

His desperate tone sparked her immediate guilt over the rather abrupt way she'd broken off with him. Maybe they hadn't had any stated understanding between them, but she could have been more tactful.

Suddenly his grip tightened and he leaned closer. She gasped in disbelief. Mike had never before acted like this. He'd always asked to kiss her, never pressed her when she'd refused to go further than a few tentative, exploring kisses.

"Let me go, Mike," she demanded far more resolutely than she felt. In the dark silence of the night, her voice seemed to echo.

"I don't want to let you go, baby. I want a chance to change your mind about us."

"She said to let her go, Riordan," Jake's voice growled from the darkness.

Mike swore, but his hold slackened. Behind him, Sophie saw Jake materialize on the landing. With the light from the stairs behind him, he looked big, dark and forbidding—like a fierce warrior. The change was a little unsettling, but she'd never been so happy to see anyone.

"Go home, Riordan," Jake ordered in an uncompromising growl.

Sophie felt the tension between the two men as if it were a living, breathing entity. Mike released her. He stepped away and she could see his fists were clenched at his sides. Jake hadn't moved. Neither one looked like he would give in first.

Just when Sophie was beginning to think they would be spending the night staring each other down on her back porch, Mike made a noise of disgust and dismissal and stormed past Jake. His footsteps pounded on the stairs, then crunched on the gravel. The sound of his BMW starting at the curb tore the silence of the night.

"Thanks," she said softly.

Jake's shoulders rose and fell in the shadows. "N.B.D."

"Pardon me?"

He stepped closer, and she could see him more clearly. His hair was mussed, his dark curls wild around his face and his beautiful eyes gleamed with a strange light. Deep inside, she felt as if there were a hidden chord that vibrated softly only to Jake's presence. Her lips parted at the sudden rush of surprise.

He smiled. "No big deal."

But her awareness of him *was* a big deal. It took her a moment to realize he was referring to his showdown with Mike. His modesty touched her. She wanted him to understand that he'd done something good, something special.

"It might have been a big deal, if you hadn't come upstairs. I've never expected Mike to get so—" she shuddered "—so aggressive."

Jake stepped even closer and studied her face. She couldn't look away from his eyes. "Are you all right? He didn't hurt you?" His expression was so fierce, she was glad Mike was gone.

"He scared me, which upset me, but he didn't hurt me."

"Good." His expression softened. "I, uh, I guess I can leave you now," he said, but he didn't move. Neither did she. She couldn't move, couldn't look away from his face.

Sophie saw the way his eyes darkened and her heart did a little flip. Jake wanted to kiss her! After the slightest hesitation, she stepped toward him, wanting—*needing*—to feel his mouth on hers. It wasn't like her to make the first move with a man, *ever.* But she knew Jake was a little reserved. What would he think—what would he do—if she gave him a hint...?

Before she could reason herself out of the impulse, Sophie rose on her tiptoes, and reached up to touch her lips to his cheek. His skin was warm, smooth as if he'd recently shaved. She breathed in the tantalizing scent of his after-shave and a faint trace of Scotch whiskey. She was tempted to seek his lips with hers, but he stood like a statue, just gazing down at her when she took a half step back.

His rejection stung. She felt her cheeks burn. The need to escape propelled her another half step backward. She swallowed hard.

"Well, good night. And thanks a—"

Suddenly he was holding her shoulders in his hands, startling her into silence. The gesture was the same as Mike's moments ago, but the impact was totally different. Her earlier fear, her impulse to escape, even her sense of rejection evaporated in the heat of his touch. She couldn't take her eyes off Jake's. They glittered in the dim porch light. She gazed up at him, wanting, waiting.

Jake drew her closer so slowly that she began to tremble with anticipation. As his head lowered toward her, her eyes drifted closed. The first brush of his lips on hers felt like the touch of a live wire—hot, electric, dangerous if it ever got out of control. And, heaven help her, she wanted to catch fire with Jake!

He smothered her tiny sigh when his mouth covered hers. His lips were soft, warm, gentle on hers. She wanted to reach up and wind her arms around his neck, not let him stop kissing her until she was thoroughly dizzy from the sensations. But her instincts warned her not to break the fragile moment.

His next kiss rewarded her patience. With slow, sensuous pressure, he caressed her lips with his, mesmerizing her, drawing her under his spell. She felt herself melting, invaded by a languid, intoxicating warmth. When he touched his tongue to her lips, she opened for him as if in a trance.

He tasted darkly sweet, a little smoky from the Scotch lingering on his tongue. Greedy for more despite her resolve to let him take the lead, Sophie met his tongue with her own. His sharp intake of breath told her he was feeling the same jagged rush of desire that surged through her veins.

She longed to feel him holding her close, yearned for the solid strength of his big body against her trembling one. Unable to suppress her need any longer, she slid her arms around his neck and pressed into his chest. His arms went around her back and his low groan vibrated through her.

And then he was easing her away with one last, clinging kiss. Disoriented, Sophie forced her eyes open and looked up into his face. For a fleeting moment, barely a heartbeat long, she thought of the way Dean used to hold her and kiss her, that same fierce yet dreamy expression in his beautiful eyes. And then she blinked away the vision and smiled.

Jake's kisses made Dean's fade into her memory, sweet, bittersweet, but definitely in the past, where they belonged. For better or worse, Jake was very much in the present.

"Good night, Sophie," he murmured huskily.

He released her. Disappointment felt like the sudden drop of an elevator. Then he staggered, as if he'd lost his balance. Immediately, she forgot her sense of rejection in her concern for him. Was he still suffering the aftereffects of his head injury?

"Jake, are you all right?"

He frowned. "No. I'm drunk as a skunk. I didn't mean to kiss you. Good night."

Stunned and hurt, she watched him turn and descend the stairs to his own landing. *Drunk as a skunk* indeed! Just like Dean, he'd been teasing her. Was she the victim of some weird curse? Mike, Bob and all the other men she'd met but not loved had always been perfect gentlemen about her lack of passion for them—Mike's recent lapse notwithstanding. But Jake, like Dean, stirred her to the point of mindless desire, then walked away as if he didn't care.

She let the screen door slap shut behind her, and wished Jake the granddaddy of all hangovers.

* * *

You blew it again.

Jake wrenched on the shower, more cold than warm, and peeled his clothes off. "It was your idea to break out the Scotch."

Touchy, touchy.

"Do me a favor, Wilde. Next time you talk to your Adviser, find out what you have to do to get yourself a pass out of here."

"So, Dean," the Adviser said much too cheerfully. "How are we doing?"

Dean felt his lip curl. "Some of 'we' aren't doing very well at all. For a genius, Warren is pretty slow on the uptake. If I hadn't given him a shove, he'd probably still be upstairs staring at Sophie."

"Magnanimous of you."

Dean glared at his Adviser. "Well, hell, if I leave things up to him, he'll be back in California before I get—"

There went the Adviser's eyebrows again. "Do try to think in more spiritual terms, my boy."

"Yeah, well, in spiritual terms, what happens to Warren and me if we part company?"

The Adviser didn't say anything for so long, Dean started to worry.

"I mean, *can* we go our separate ways? Or will we both go *pfft* like bubbles?"

"Interesting question, Dean. What do you think?"

Dean shrugged. "How am I supposed to know? I'm just working my way back to Sophie one step at a time."

The Adviser's gaze was so sharp, Dean had to look away. "Tell me, Dean. Are you willing to risk finding out what will happen if you desert Jake now?"

"Hey, you know me. Risk is my middle name. But, ah—"

"Yes?"

"I think I'll play this hand a little longer, if that's okay with you. Maybe if I knew more about what would happen... If this is my only chance, I don't want to blow it when I'm so close to Sophie."

"And Jake?"

"Jake's on his own, man. The only reason I'm helping him at all is to help myself."

"I see."

That snotty tone again. Damn! What was wrong now? He was only being honest. Jake was in his way.

"So, what's the next step?" he asked, trying to sound like he had his act together, and hoping the Adviser wouldn't notice he didn't.

There went that *look,* the one that always went with the snotty tone.

"You tell me, Dean. What do *you* think is the next step?"

Suddenly he didn't feel so good. The shiver that ran up his spine shook Jake, too.

She was hurrying down the back steps to get to work early when Jake's screen door creaked opened. Suddenly her heart skipped a beat. She paused on his landing, all the desire, frustration and hurt of last night flooding though her mind.

"Sophie?"

Jake stepped onto his porch. He looked unfairly sexy in new jeans and a white button-down shirt open at the throat. He'd tied his hair back, but it tumbled down his forehead in soft, unruly curls that looked slightly damp. His eyes seemed less brilliant than usual, and the lines around his eyes seemed to be etched deeper. Guiltily, she remembered wishing a hangover on him. Of all the wishes to come true... !

"Hi," she said softly, clutching her purse against her middle.

"About last night, Sophie...?" She waited for him to continue. He swallowed. "I don't remember a lot, but I think I owe you an apology."

Warmth flooded through her. "No, you don't. You were wonderful with Mike."

He nodded, then winced. "I remember that much. But... I meant after. Did I apologize for kissing you?"

His words came back to her, bringing with them the barbs of rejection. "In a manner of speaking."

His quick grin was rueful. "Hoof in mouth, huh?"

Suddenly she couldn't find her anger. All she felt was her growing fondness for this strange man, who could be so shy one minute, so fiercely macho the next, tongue-tied, then charming. Her instincts were humming. She decided to follow them. She smiled.

"Jake, it was very nice kissing you. No apology is necessary."

The brilliance suddenly returned to his eyes. He didn't say anything, but she felt as if his eyes were speaking in a timeless language that transcended words. Recalling the taste of his kisses, the feel of his strong body against hers, she felt heat tingle in her cheeks.

"I better go," she said hurriedly. "Rick promised to run a special program overnight, and he said he'd meet me early with the results. I'll, um, I'll see you tonight. For dinner? About seven?"

He nodded and she flew down the rest of the stairs before she gave in to the impulse to circle the railing and cross the few feet of plank flooring between them to taste his kisses one more time.

Rick was waiting for her in the closed store, pacing and muttering. When she greeted him, he waved a sheaf of fan-folded computer paper at her. His mouth twisted.

"Garbage! The program started to run. It was working fine when I left. Then it started putting out this garbage."

Sophie sighed and rolled her eyes heavenward. "And I thought replacing the old system would make life easier. Maybe we should go back to handwritten records." She reached for the papers Rick had rolled up in his hands. "Might as well put this in the garbage pail where it belongs."

He started to hand them to her, then pulled them back. "No, wait. Maybe I can figure out what went wrong."

It was beyond her limited understanding. She shrugged. "Whatever. I'll try calling Dennis's number one more time. If he doesn't get back to me, I'll have to find someone else who can service the system."

As always, a somewhat dim-sounding young woman took Sophie's message and promised Dennis would call as soon as possible. More than a little skeptical about that, Sophie opened the store and attended to the dozens of things she had to do to keep her business running. Every time the phone rang, she expected it to be Dennis. And every time the door opened, she hoped it would be Jake.

No such luck on either front. Eventually, she lost track of time and got caught up in her work. The sound of a familiar voice at her office door made her look up in surprise, then check her watch.

"Hi, babe! What seems to be the trouble with the system?" Dennis greeted her cheerfully. He sauntered inside without waiting for an invitation.

Peeved at his not bothering to apologize, annoyed at being called "babe" by someone she hardly knew, Sophie barely smiled. She leaned back in her chair and looked across the small room at the small, wiry man with the dull auburn hair and eyes the same red-brown color.

"Rick can explain to you what's been happening. And not happening."

"Brrr! Why the cold shoulder?" Dennis grinned widely, as if prompting her to smile back. She refused to respond. "Hey, I got here as fast as I could make it."

"Two months is as fast as you could make it?"

"Two months?" He shook his head. "Sophie, I only got your call this morning."

"The computer's been a major pain, Dennis. It won't do half of the things you promised it would when you set up the system. It's warranteed through you, so I've been calling once or twice a week for the past two months."

"Aw, Sophie, didn't Cissy tell you I've been away for almost two months? Today was the first time I got a message from you." He flashed a smug grin. "And here I am, to the rescue."

She smiled back, relenting a little, but not happy about Cissy's inefficiency. "Obviously, she didn't tell me, or I would have known. You might pass the word along to her that your business depends on your customers."

"Sure, babe. But I'm getting out of the servicing business, except for a few special people, like you. It's too much of a drag always being on call, you know? So, what's the problem?"

"If there were only one problem, I'd be happy. I'd rather have Rick explain what's been happening. I'm still fumbling with the on/off switch. At least you two speak the same language."

Dennis's grin widened. "Don't worry, babe. It's like broccoli—an acquired taste. We'll teach you to compute with the best of 'em. Where's Rick?"

"He's on the floor. I'll take over for him and the two of you can hide out in the office and take the beast apart if you have to. It's pretty slow so far, so I can use written receipts until you're finished."

She rose and crossed the room to the door. A few steps into the store, she thought of a question to ask Dennis and turned back. He was standing at her window, twisting the lock. She forgot what she wanted to ask him.

"It's secure," she said softly.

He jumped, then turned and flashed her a grin. "Good. There have been a lot of B and E's around here lately. Computers are popular things to steal. I wouldn't want some creep to run off with our beautiful system."

She suppressed a shudder at the memory of the night the police had found evidence that someone had tried to break in. "If you can't get it to run the way it's supposed to, Dennis, I'll leave the back door open for any creep who wants it to take it."

He laughed as if she'd said something highly witty.

Almost two hours after she'd sent Rick into her office to work with Dennis, they emerged. "She's working like a dream now, Sophie," Dennis told her, grinning broadly. He winked at Rick. "But you call me anytime she acts up. I promise I won't desert you, even when I'm not doing service anymore. I've got a line on something better."

She smiled, relieved that she wouldn't have to deal with a cranky computer, regardless of gender. "Thanks, Dennis. But if it isn't possible for you to keep servicing the system, promise me you'll recommend someone who's good—and fast?"

He gave her a Boy Scout salute. "Promise. Hey, Rick tells me you've got Jake Warren living in your building for the summer. He's a legend, you know?"

"No, I didn't know."

"Sure. No one knows more about computer crime than Warren. He was fourteen when he got busted for hacking his way into military computers. I think he got nailed for cracking a couple of bank systems in California."

Sophie thought of Mike Riordan's concern for his bank's customers' security. What if she'd somehow misread that entire scene last night? What if the banks had unknowingly hired a computer criminal instead of a security consultant? No, she didn't believe that for a second. And there was no way she'd misread the scene with Mike—and with Jake—last night.

"Then I think I'll start keeping my money under a mattress," she said lightly, but inside she was fuming that he could make her suspicious of Jake.

Rick snorted. Dennis smiled and squeezed her shoulder, his smile fading into a concerned expression as he gazed into her eyes. "You don't have to go that far, babe, but you probably should think twice about letting Warren get his hands on your system. If you have any more problems, you call me, okay?"

She was too nice to remind him that she'd been calling him for the past eight weeks. Instead, she saw him to the door and sighed with relief when he left. She wasn't sure if it was relief that her system was fixed in time for the evening rush, or relief that Dennis was gone, taking his accusations about Jake with him.

The third time the new grill swayed and tipped on its tripod, Sophie swore under her breath and stood up in disgust. She'd invited Jake to a barbecue to start in fifteen minutes, and she was still in her grubbiest cutoffs, wrestling with the grill.

The crunch of gravel in the drive caught her attention. She turned to see Jake dismounting from his bike beside the porch. The sight of him in black cycling shorts and a light blue T-shirt dissolved her interest in the reluctant charcoal grill. Even the baggy cutoff gray sweat shorts he wore over his cycling shorts couldn't disguise his physique.

No wonder Carla had been so predatory the other day at the store. Hugged by the second-skin black fabric, Jake's long thighs rippled powerfully. Even his calves were roundly muscled.

She swallowed past her suddenly dry throat. Her reaction was absurd. Men had been wearing Lycra cycling shorts for years, and she hadn't felt any outrageous impulses to reach out and... Well, she hadn't felt any outrageous impulses since her last day with Dean. Then, she'd been self-consciously tugging at the skimpy edges of her new bikini and trying not to stare at the way his suit hugged his male contours the way she'd longed to.

"Who's winning?" he asked, grinning.

She grinned back and nodded toward the grill. "The enemy."

"Want a hand?"

Keep it light, she warned herself. He's obviously not feeling the same fascination for your greasy cutoffs that you feel for his shorts. "Only one hand?" she joked. "I could use an octopus."

"You could use a better wrench. What have you got?"

He came closer and crouched to look at the diagram lying on the ground. Several times, he glanced up at the grill, then looked at the vague drawing that claimed to be the instructions.

"Hold this," he told her, handing her one of the legs of the grill. "Keep it steady on the ground and I'll attach the others to it."

She crouched beside him, propping up the black metal grill leg while he fitted the parts together. Several times as he moved, his shoulder brushed hers. He smelled warm and sexy from the sunshine and fresh air. His fingers brushed her knuckles with almost every turn of the wrench, each touch sweet torture. She wanted to stop him, take his face between her hands and kiss him until they were both breathless.

Instead, she avoided meeting his eyes. She didn't know why, but she suspected it had something to do with concealing how deeply he affected her. For the first time since

Dean's death, she was with a man who made her tremble with excitement, made her shiver with anticipation. It felt so special, and so scary. It could only be a mistake, and yet she wanted to love someone.

She could be falling in love with Jake. Whether he was the right man for her or not, she felt some sort of relief at the way her heart was awakening. It was a wonderful feeling, but it also made her feel vaguely disloyal to Dean. Irrational as it was, because Dean was dead and Jake was very much alive, her feelings for Jake made her feel guilty.

"Hold the base steady," Jake warned. He wrapped her hands around the legs where he wanted her to support them. She swallowed, barely breathing because of the implicit sensuality of his fingers guiding hers. "I'm going to set the top on."

She managed to keep control of the grill and her shaking hands until Jake crouched beside her again. His knee bumped hers. She lost her balance and reached out for something to help her regain her stability. His powerful thigh muscles bunched under her palm. She pulled her hand away as if she'd grabbed a burning log, and fell onto her bottom.

"You okay?"

"Fine," she lied. Her face was so hot, they could barbecue dinner on it. To her intense relief, Jake didn't seem to notice.

"All done. Where's the charcoal?"

She brought the bag from the porch. "I feel like a relic of the Dark Ages, using charcoal," she told him as she pulled the drawstring on the bag top. "But I'm petrified of gas grills."

He grunted. "Did you hear about the guy who was taking his first jump from a plane?" Jake asked, pouring a layer of charcoal around the basin of the grill.

She frowned. Had she missed something important in the news? "I don't think so."

"He couldn't get his chute to open. He pulled every cord, but nothing happened. And as he's falling, he sees a guy flying up toward him as if he's going into orbit. So he calls out, 'Hey! Do you know anything about parachutes?' And the other guy yells back, 'No! Do you know anything about gas barbecues?' "

She tried not to laugh, but a giggle burst out of her. "That's awful! I thought you were telling me about a real incident."

He met her eyes with soul-stripping intensity. "You're too trusting," he said quietly. Abruptly, he cleared his throat and looked away. "I need a shower, and the coals need to burn down to get ready. How about we meet back here in fifteen minutes?"

The notion of showering *with* Jake brought the heat back to her cheeks. "You're on," she said and practically ran up the stairs, a most urgent question on her mind.

What should she wear?

Sophie stood back and surveyed the picnic table with satisfaction. The black-and-white-checked vinyl cover looked casual but special under her plain white dishes and black gingham cloth napkins. The salad bowl, platter of steaks and Lucite wine cooler sat waiting to be used. With dusk falling, she lit the low black candles in their white bowls. Then she tugged at the off-the-shoulder neckline of the black cotton knit dress she wore, hoping it wasn't too...whatever.

Jake's door creaked open. A moment later he stepped off the back porch in jeans and a white oxford shirt, his feet bare and his arms full of bowls and a bottle of wine. In the center of the things he carried was a bouquet of wildflowers in a vase he'd borrowed from Diane. The unexpected gesture made her blush.

"I hope you don't mind white wine," he said, slipping the bottle into the cooler. "Red wine gives me headaches."

"Me, too," she assured him. "White is fine."

"Good. The baked potatoes are half-nuked, so they shouldn't take long in the coals. You look nice." He turned away and set two foil-wrapped bundles under the grill. "The ice cream is still in the freezer."

It took her a moment to recognize the compliment buried in the rest of his words. By then, he'd already opened the wine bottle and poured two glasses. He said nothing more. Bemused, she sipped her wine and watched the flames leap whenever fat from the steaks fell onto the coals.

"We can start with salad, if you'd like," she offered. "The steaks will be ready soon."

"Sure."

She passed him the glass bowl of mixed summer greens and the carafe of homemade salad dressing. He served himself, then held the bowl for her. Their eyes met briefly. His gaze slid down to her exposed neckline and she felt heat rise in her cheeks. In silence, she sat across from him and lifted her salad fork.

"This dressing is great," he told her. "Is it a secret recipe?"

"Not really. Just balsamic vinegar, dried mustard, salt and pepper. Oh, and extra-virgin olive oil."

Jake sat bolt upright and coughed.

"Oh, no! Did I use too much vinegar? Can I get you a glass of water?" She half rose from her seat.

Jake coughed again, then shook his head. He cleared his throat several times, then took a deep breath. "I'm okay. I just, uh, swallowed wrong. The dressing is exactly right the way it is." He gave her a crooked half smile that convinced her to sit down again. "How did things go with the program Rick ran for you last night?"

She frowned. "Rick said all we got was garbage, but at least I was finally able to get Dennis in to look at it. He and Rick spent hours on it, and it's allegedly fixed now. I'm not going to bet anything on it, though, until I see for myself."

"Sometimes, you know, there's a fault in the motherboard or somewhere else. I won't bore you with jargon, but you could have a defective part. Until it's taken care of permanently, it can seem fixed, then act up again. If you can't afford lossage, you should get the whole system checked out." He refilled her wineglass. "Who's Dennis?"

The question came out so casually, she almost missed the edge in his voice. "He's the elusive character who set up the system and customized the software, and is supposed to look after it while it's under warranty. Apparently, he was away for two months, and his answering service didn't have the good sense to tell me when I kept leaving messages."

"Hmm. Sounds fishy." Jake stared at a piece of red lettuce dangling off his fork, his expression so distant that Sophie doubted he knew what he was seeing.

She stood up to turn the steaks, debating whether to take a chance. She decided to trust her instincts.

"Oddly enough, Dennis was suspicious about you." Jake blinked and turned to gape at her. "He said you're a legendary wizard of computer crime, and that you were arrested when you were fourteen for breaking into computer systems. And later, you broke into bank systems. He warned me not to let you get near my store computer."

Sophie looked up from the grill and saw that Jake was watching her, his expression guarded, unreadable. Every romantic suspense movie fast-forwarded through her head as she recalled Mike's concern about the security of the banks' computers. Then she replayed the way Jake had come to her rescue, the way he'd kissed her after.

She knew what she wanted to believe. But she wanted to know the truth.

"Is he right, Jake? Are you a criminal?"

Chapter Six

Jake's long, steady stare made her want to fidget. Trying to maintain a casual facade, she set down the barbecue tongs and returned to the table. Her hand hardly shook at all when she lifted her wineglass and took a sip. But the tension was worse—infinitely worse—than when she'd waited for Rick to elaborate on his prison record when she'd interviewed him for the store's assistant manager position.

This time, so much more was at stake.

"In a manner of speaking, he's right," Jake said quietly, finally breaking the silence, but not the way she'd hoped.

The wine she'd sipped slid down her throat the wrong way. She fought not to choke.

"But not what you're thinking. I wasn't arrested for breaking into so-called secure systems. I was hired to."

"When you were *fourteen?*"

He grinned. "Well, no. That's how I got, um, discovered. I was hacking around on Stanford's computers. And, uh, the Pentagon's." Laugh lines deepened around his eyes. "And a few of the better-known alphabet agencies. No sense of humor, those guys."

She didn't see the humor in it, either. It was so much like Dean to push the limits and test the rules. His daring had always frightened her. Rightfully so, it turned out. Was Jake, on a different scale, so similar to Dean?

"But are you a criminal or not?"

Jake chuckled. "Not."

Her relief must have been obvious, because his chuckle turned into a contagious laugh. Sheepishly, she smiled.

"I confess I took a few stupid dares, trying to impress older hackers, but I never broke any laws. It was more a case of proving I could do the impossible." He shrugged one shoulder. "Usually, I could. That's how I ended up in computer security."

Sophie thought of Dean's almost obsessive tinkering with motorcycle engines.

Before she realized it, she was telling Jake, "My, um, friend—the one who died—he was like that with motorcycles. He was determined to make each one he worked on run better, sweeter, than any other mechanic could."

"And did he?"

"Usually," she told him, unable to hold back a tiny smile. "Dean was one of the most sought-after independent motorcycle mechanics in southern Connecticut by the time he'd died at twenty-two."

Jake's eyes narrowed. "Dean?"

She nodded, but she didn't want to think about Dean. She wanted to know more about Jake. "You must have started using computers when you were very young."

He smiled grimly. "I cut my teeth on mainframes. My parents both worked on computers, and they experimented on me, too."

What had his childhood been like? She had a feeling it hadn't been anything like her own stable, loving upbringing. Would he think she was prying if she asked him to tell her? Sophie took the steaks and potatoes off the grill and brought the platter to the table.

"I guess you were a child prodigy," she prompted hesitantly.

He snorted. "Yeah. I was." And he didn't sound at all happy about it.

He looked at her and she smiled, hoping he'd continue. He waited for her to serve herself, then accepted the remaining steak and potato. For another moment, he stared at the food in his plate, then, when she was sure he wouldn't say any more, he spoke again.

"My parents were members of an intellectual commune, so everyone had a hand in raising me. In fact, when I was a kid, I wasn't too clear exactly who my parents were, since I called everyone by their first names. By the time I was three, I was reading in English, Latin and German, but I couldn't catch a ball to save my life. I was taking high school courses in fourth grade, and getting the crap beat out of me on the local playground."

"Oh, Jake!" She twisted her napkin in her lap to keep from reaching across the table to him.

His crooked grin touched her heart. "I can't blame the other kids. I was a skinny little geek in Buddy Holly glasses, always spouting off and correcting their mistakes." Sophie smiled at the image. "And I still couldn't catch a ball to save my life."

Jake topped up her wineglass, then sliced open his potato, an oddly distracted expression on his face. He shook his head slightly, as if dismissing an idea he didn't like. She felt as if she were being left out of a private conversation.

"It's easy to spend ten, twelve, even eighteen hours a day at the computer," he told her. Then he gave her a quick grin.

"Most hackers look like cave dwellers from spending all their time indoors. Some are practically phobic about getting outside. And there's a sort of reverse snobbery that says brains count more than brawn or appearances. I know a few guys who have a pretty medieval attitude about bathing."

Sophie couldn't help wrinkling her nose. Jake chuckled.

"Right. They're brilliant on the nets—the electronic networks, the bulletin boards—but I wouldn't want to get stuck on an elevator with them."

Sophie smiled. "There were a lot of computer-science students around when I was taking some business courses a few years ago. A couple of them were like that, but they kept to themselves. The rest of the computer students did look pretty pale. The jocks called them 'monks.'"

An odd expression crossed his face. He lowered his gaze to sprinkle salt on his potato, but she suspected he was avoiding her eyes.

"Most jocks call hackers more colorful things than that." He shrugged, but Sophie suspected some of the disparaging comments had not rolled off his back.

Suddenly he looked up and caught her watching him. His eyes glowed almost black in the fading daylight. She swallowed, remembering the dark light in his eyes when he'd kissed her last night.

"You..." She cleared her suddenly tight throat. "You don't look like a typical hacker."

Again he shrugged. She knew she was digging herself in deeper, but she couldn't seem to stop her thoughts from becoming words.

"But you aren't wearing the Buddy Holly glasses anymore. And you certainly aren't a skinny little kid." Far from it, she thought, casting a quick glance at his broad shoulders and powerful arms. And then there were his muscular legs... Her boldness made her blush. "I mean, you cycle and swim."

The bleak expression that dulled the light in his eyes for a second made her wish she could take back her thoughtless words. She opened her mouth to apologize, but Jake spoke first.

"I'm as obsessive as any hacker," he said mildly. "I don't just cycle. I pedal for miles, trying to see how far I can go, how fast, up the next higher hill. And I don't—didn't—just swim. I swam an hour every day, trying to do one more lap each time. Some guys run the same way. Or work out with weights. Things you can do alone, competing against yourself, pushing the limits the same way you do with programming."

It was eerie. She could have been hearing Dean talk, if she substituted motorcycles for computers. Dean had died pushing the limits—his, the sailboard's, the storm's. Computers didn't seem as dangerous as motorcycles and sailboards, but that same edginess that had driven Dean obviously drove Jake, too. How could two men apparently so different be so much alike? And why, given the range of men in the world, did she have to be so attracted to the unobtainable, driven ones?

"There's one guy I've worked with a couple of times in telecommunications," Jake said. "He's obsessed with sailing. It's his safety valve. Telecommunications burns out a lot of computer people, because companies tend to sell technology they can't support yet. Then they push the programmers to produce what they need in half the time it should take to do it right. So this guy will go into hack mode for three or four weeks, hardly eating or sleeping, and collapse when he's finished. Then, for a couple of months, all he'll talk about is sailing."

"So he has a release for the intensity of his work."

Jake shook his head. "He's never been on a boat in his life, and is scared to death of water. But he knows more about sailing than any three world-class sailors."

"That's so sad," Sophie said, touched by the emptiness of that kind of existence. She needed to lighten the mood. She wanted to see Jake smile again. "What I want to know is, can you catch a ball now?"

His laugh rang out, rewarding her, warming her. "Not to save my life! Now, tell me about you."

"Not much to tell. I've got an older brother, Alan, who's a doctor and a younger sister, Laura, who's a nurse, and I pass out at the mere mention of blood. They still tease me mercilessly. The family joke was that I was supposed to be a lawyer, but I could never go for the jugular."

He chuckled. "Did you grow up around here?"

"I grew up in Mystic, Connecticut. My dad still has a car dealership, and my mom never worked, but she does a lot of community volunteer projects. We call her Pollyanna." She paused for a bite of steak when he did. "Alan and his wife, Joan, have two boys, six and three, and Laura married Paul, an accountant, two years ago."

He swallowed and reached for his wine. "What about later, when you were older?"

"In high school, I was a cheerleader, a member of the swim team and the film critic for the school paper."

"And the steady girlfriend of the star quarterback?"

The slight barb in his tone hurt her. Did he really see her as a shallow hanger-on? She shook her head. "No, actually, I wasn't allowed to go steady. I think it was because I had a crush on an older guy my parents thought was unsuitable."

Jake's eyebrows rose. She felt her cheeks grow warm. "Was he?"

"Totally."

His wide grin surprised her. It was as if he understood the feeling of pure daring, the exhilaration of the forbidden, that had colored her feelings for Dean.

"I had this dream that I could change Dean, make him grow up and want to marry me. I called my parents snobs for saying a motorcycle mechanic was beneath my expectations. But then Dean died, just a couple of weeks after I graduated high school."

Jake's grin disappeared abruptly. "Sorry. I guess that was pretty distressing."

"Devastating. But I finally decided my parents and friends were right when they kept saying I had my whole life ahead of me."

He nodded, a thoughtful expression in his eyes. "So then . . . ?"

"Then I majored in English literature and minored in communications at the University of Hartford. My grandparents left me some money, so with that and a loan from my dad, I bought the video store I'd been working in part-time through school. I've been living in Mrs. Mandel's house and running my store for eight years. If I can ever afford it, I'd love to buy a house in some place like Avon or Simsbury, in the country but within commuting distance. And maybe open another store. I really love the work."

She shrugged, suddenly self-conscious about babbling. Usually, others bared their souls to her, but she seldom talked so freely about herself. The intensity of Jake's steady gaze made her wonder what he thought of her ordinary life and modest ambitions.

"Were you ever—?"

"Hello? Jake? Are you back there?"

A woman's voice called from the driveway, leaving Sophie wondering what he was going to ask. The grin on Jake's face as he stood up from the table told her the interruption was welcome. She watched him pad barefoot across the lawn to the edge of the parking area. A moment later, a woman in a blue denim sundress and leather sandals, with the most amazing cape of waist-length pale hair, appeared under the floodlight.

And, while Sophie sat there with her dinner cooling on her plate, this unknown woman launched herself into Jake's arms with laughter and kisses.

Annie had to be the most emotional, demonstrative person he knew. She clung to him as if she hadn't seen him in years, when in fact, he'd left her house just the week before. Still, he had to admit, it felt kind of nice to have someone care about him, even if she was married to his best friend.

It'd be even nicer if you could get Sophie to do that, Dean Wilde muttered in his head. *It's been too long since I had her in my arms. Do you some good, too, Warren, as long as you don't get carried away and forget she's mine. You heard her. She still loves me.*

Silently, Jake cursed him and told him to go haunt himself. He'd had his fill of Sophie's obvious attachment to her dead lover, and he sure didn't want to have to contend with the guy in person. Or whatever form he took.

"What brings you here?" he finally managed to ask, when Annie released him. "Where's Les?"

Annie beamed up at him and took his arm. "Les is with Robert, playing show-and-tell with the flowers in the front garden. Rose, peony, ivy, ga, da, ba. It's a deep, male-bonding sort of conversation." She laughed. "We were visiting Les's parents, and figured we'd stop to see how you're doing."

"I'm doing fine."

"You look great. How's the head?"

"The head's fine," he lied. Even Annie, with her eclectic Californian approach to life, wouldn't understand what was really going on in his head. Annie was very no-nonsense about life.

"Jake, are we interrupting something?" Annie whispered. She glanced at Sophie, still sitting at the picnic table, and he felt his face flush.

Before he could answer, Les appeared with his five-month-old son cradled in his arms. Robert gripped the dampened front of Les's shirt with one chubby fist and babbled while he waved the other fist. Jake greeted his friend with a grin, then spoke to the baby, who flashed him a toothless grin and held out his arms.

Aw, Jeez, Wilde muttered when Jake took the baby from Les. It was a strange sensation for him, too, he assured Dean. Even spending a few days with Les and Annie before moving into Mrs. Mandel's house hadn't done much for his appreciation of babies. Before becoming Robert's godfather, he'd never been this close to an infant.

Close enough to get goobered on, man. That's too close for me. Sophie'd never stick a guy with a rug rat.

Jake walked toward the picnic table, holding Robert in one arm as the child happily tugged at his hair. He looked at Sophie and wondered, How well did Wilde know her? She had that expression on her face that he'd noticed on Annie's, whenever there were babies around. And, holding Robert, breathing in that sweet baby scent and absorbing the warmth of that chubby little body, it wasn't such a stretch to imagine holding his own baby.

Wilde's reaction was incoherent. His own was more like surprise that the notion had occurred to him.

"Sophie, these are Les and Annie, two of my oldest friends, and this is Robert," Jake said, perversely enjoying Dean's discomfort despite his own conflicting emotions. "Guys, Sophie Quinn, my upstairs neighbor. She owns Center Video."

Sophie rose and smiled and something moved deep inside Jake, something he couldn't identify, didn't understand, that he couldn't take the time to analyze now.

"Hi, Sophie," Annie said, smiling broadly. Les just grinned and nodded. "I hope we aren't interrupting your dinner."

"We were just finishing," Sophie lied graciously when he would have simply told Annie they were still eating. "Would you like some wine or coffee? I was going to brew decaf."

"Sure. Decaf would be nice."

Sophie stood in front of him and stroked Robert's chubby cheek. The baby chortled and wriggled. Jake looked down at Sophie and felt again that vague stirring inside him. She was so beautiful. . . .

Go for it. Just don't forget she's mine.

Silently, Jake rattled off a string of colorful hacker's curses.

"I have a coffee cake in the freezer," Sophie said. "Why don't I defrost that to go with the coffee?"

She was being so sweet about having their dinner interrupted. He looked into her eyes and hoped she could see his regret as well as his thanks. In the growing darkness, her gray eyes looked smoky, sultry, seductive. He glanced at her mouth, curved into a smile for the baby, and a shaft of desire ripped through him. Next time he tasted her mouth, he vowed, he would be stone-cold sober.

"Cake sounds good. We can have the ice cream on the side," he said, amazed that he could function after thinking about kissing her.

"Why don't I go with you and help carry things?" Annie offered. "The guys probably want to talk about computer things."

Uh-oh!

Seeing the curiosity on Annie's face, Jake silently agreed with Wilde's dismay. But there wasn't anything he could do except agree, without sounding foolish. Let Annie pump Sophie for data. He didn't have anything to hide. Well, not much. Besides, Annie was right. He did have some urgent "computer things" to talk to Les about.

He returned Robert to Les and drew up two extra canvas director chairs for them. Try as he might, he couldn't resist a covert glance in the direction of the back porch, where Sophie and Annie were walking.

"Nice woman." Les reclaimed his attention. "'Bout time," Jake thought he muttered.

"What?"

"Nothing. How's the work going?"

He picked up his empty wineglass and idly turned it in his hands. "Something's not kosher. As far as I can tell, someone's moving funds between accounts, then between banks, and then out to a bank that's not in the group I'm working for."

Les's eyebrows slid up to his hairline. "How much?"

"A little here, a little there. It's adding up to thousands."

"Is it someone in one of the bank's data-processing departments?"

That was the most likely place to look, but he'd eliminated that possibility immediately. Jake shook his head. "No. I traced the source to an outside PC. He could be from the D.P. department, because he knows his way around the system, but he isn't cracking it from inside. Whoever he is, he's good. He knows the systems and he's covered most of his tracks."

Les frowned. "Think you'll get enough to call in the police?"

"Yeah. And that's what's bothering me." He set his glass down on the picnic table and leaned forward to say very quietly, "Les, that outside PC is in Sophie's video store."

"Sophie, what in heaven's name have you done to Jake?" Annie's voice rose almost to a squeal with poorly suppressed excitement. Puzzled, Sophie met the other woman's sparkling green eyes and shook her head.

"It's like he's a different man," Annie told her.

"How do you mean?" She pulled out a kitchen chair for Annie, then opened the freezer and rummaged for the coffee cake. She tried to speak casually, but inside, she was dying of curiosity. Her relief that Annie wasn't Jake's special woman was doubled by the possibility of learning more about the man she suspected she was already falling for.

"I mean, three weeks ago, he was allergic to babies and would never have dinner alone with a woman unless she was a hacker and they were eating Mexican or Chinese take-out. In fact, two weeks ago, he was wearing glasses so thick, you wouldn't have been able to see his expression. And he's wearing new jeans. Mount Vesuvius erupts more often than Jake buys new jeans!"

Mulling that over, Sophie measured coffee grounds into the filter, then poured in the water and flipped the switch on. She still had a clear image of Jake in rumpled sweats and shirts when he first moved in. It hadn't occurred to her that that was his usual wardrobe. But surely, she hadn't influenced him to buy new clothes. Certainly, not consciously. But if he *had* bought new clothes after meeting her...

No, she wouldn't indulge in pointless speculation. If Jake had bought new jeans, it was because of his job, not because he wanted to impress her. After all, it was just a pair of jeans.

After putting the cake into the microwave oven to defrost, she opened the refrigerator and found what she wanted.

"Annie, would you like a glass of wine?" She held up the open bottle of California white.

Annie beamed. "You bet. I've been waiting twelve years to have this conversation."

That stopped her in midreach for wineglasses. "Pardon me?"

Annie's laughter pealed infectiously. "No, no! It's not some airy-fairy other-life experience or anything. I've known Jake for twelve years, and I've been hoping that one day he'd meet a woman who would knock his socks off."

Sophie tried to squelch the little jolt of hope Annie's words sparked. "I've never seen him wear socks."

"See what I mean?" Annie giggled. "Seriously, I've seen Jake go out with women from time to time, but he always looked like he was lost in space. You know, that absorbed, vague expression?"

Sophie nodded. Annie sighed. "Les gets like that when he's working, but I can usually make contact. But sometimes, we'd be out in a foursome, having dinner or sitting around talking, and Jake would simply forget his date was there. He even went home a couple of times without them. Just left, with that distracted look on his face."

"Oh, Annie!" Sophie gasped.

A trill of laughter burst from the other woman. "I swear it! And these were perfectly nice, successful, attractive women. Bank managers. Consultants. Teachers. Lawyers."

Sophie had no doubt she wasn't the only woman who'd ever found Jake attractive. She just didn't want to have the others enumerated for her. Especially not when, at least in her imagination, they all looked like Kim Basinger and Michelle Pfeiffer. She, on the other hand, was strictly the girl-next-door type.

Annie tamed her amusement with obvious effort. "Jake would wring my neck if he knew I was telling you this. But honestly, he's the original absentminded professor. Hackers are like that. Les certainly is. And Jake in particular. Did he tell you about his childhood?"

Sophie sipped her wine, torn between curiosity and worry that Jake would feel Annie's confidences were a betrayal. "A little."

"His parents were rarefied geniuses who lived in their own little world. Literally. They shared raising Jake with twelve other geniuses, which was great for his brain but terrible for his soul. Les's parents knew the whole group, and said they always wished they could rescue Jake. There was no overt affection. No playing and goofing around, just being a kid. He didn't get pictures of Mickey Mouse to color. He got anatomically correct diagrams of the human circulatory and respiratory systems to color. You know, red for veins, blue for arteries."

Annie paused for a sip of wine. Sophie listened to the coffee dripping into the pot and thought about Jake's unorthodox childhood. What kind of man did a child like that become? A man who could love, who could build a solid, lifelong relationship? Or a man who was so wrapped up in his thoughts that he could forget whatever woman happened to be with him?

"Apparently," Annie went on more quietly, "Jake had a rough time when he was at university and grad school. He was so much younger than everyone else. Les was in a similar situation, but his parents were pretty normal. By the time I met the two of them, Jake was so shy, he hardly spoke except about computers. Or to order soup and sandwiches at the health food restaurant my parents own."

"Is that how you met Les?" Sophie guessed.

Annie smiled. "Mmm. He was a health-food fanatic. Whenever he came in, we'd talk about the relative merits of various vitamins, or hydroponic gardening, but he was flirting in his own way. Jake just came along for the ride. I'm sure he never noticed how many women tried to get his attention."

The microwave beeped twice to signal that it was almost finished defrosting the cake. Sophie glanced at the coffeepot. It was full. She took a last sip of her wine.

"I hope Jake won't quit swimming because of the accident." Annie's face reflected her suddenly serious tone.

"He said something before that made me think he might," Sophie confided.

"Swimming was something he loved. Twelve years ago, he was this curly-haired beanpole who always had a cold. Then he traded some computer consulting for a lifetime membership in a health club and started swimming." Annie offered a quick smile over the rim of her wineglass. "He stopped having colds and developed that gorgeous physique, but it was more than that. It was a way for him to do something physical and sensual and get outside of his brain. I'm afraid he won't go back to it if he stays out of the water too long. You know, like not getting back on a horse or a bike after you fall."

Sophie nodded. "I can't say I blame him. I think I'd feel the same way."

"Mmm. Well, maybe when he gets home, and he's on his own turf again, he'll get back to swimming. I imagine he's under a fair amount of pressure to finish this job. He's always got projects lined up."

Sophie felt her heart sink. How could she have forgotten even for a moment, that Jake was leaving soon? What a fool she could be, thinking with her feelings instead of her head. She got up and set dishes and forks on a tray with the thawed coffee cake.

"I guess we should join the men."

"If they're really talking about computers, they didn't notice we ever left." Annie gave her a wry smile and reached for the tray while Sophie carried the coffeepot and mugs on another tray.

Once again, she had to ask herself why, when she knew so many perfectly nice men, was she even *thinking* about a man who was leaving town in two months? A man who was prone to obsessions, had a habit of forgetting the women he was with and came from a background where love was probably considered an unnecessary option, possibly an undesirable nuisance?

Extra-virgin *olive oil!* Extra-*virgin? Isn't what you've got enough of a problem? How can something be* extra-*virgin?*

"Shut up, will you?" Jake muttered.

"Did you say something?" Sophie called from her kitchen.

"No," he called back from her living room and thinking ugly thoughts to Dean.

Les and Annie had finally left, but not before carrying all the dishes and things upstairs to Sophie's apartment, which put him where he wanted to be. Sophie had invited him to stay for a movie, then told him to choose one. He stood scanning the shelves beside the TV, not having a clue which one to select. The last thing he wanted was to pick something that would spoil the mood between them.

Good thinking.

"Thank you very much," Jake muttered. Patronizing wannabe, he added silently, running his forefinger absently along the video boxes. "You can butt out, now. I'll take it from here."

"Did you find something you want to see?" Sophie asked, appearing in the doorway.

Startled, he glanced down at the title under his fingertip. "What's this one about?"

"It's about a dead man who tries to get in touch with his lover," she told him with a smile. "I don't want to tell you any more, or it will spoil the fun."

It was too much of a coincidence. And he couldn't imagine what fun there was in having a persistent dead guy around.

Try being one, Wilde told him. He told Wilde to try doing something anatomically and spiritually impossible. This wasn't the time for interruptions.

Sophie came closer, close enough that he could smell the sweetness of her perfume and the delicate musk of her skin. With her face tipped up toward him, her neck arched, exposed, vulnerable. He could see the pulse surging at the hollow of her throat. Her dark hair fell like silk on the creamy skin of her shoulders.

"You might find it frivolous," she said softly. "I mean, it's about ghosts and romance. Are you sure you wouldn't prefer something like *The Hunt for Red October?* Or *Terminator 2?* The special effects were done by computer, and are really amazing."

He clenched his hands at his sides, trying to control the impulse to touch her. What was it about her that made him feel like this? She was beautiful, but he'd met other beautiful women who hadn't made a dent in his emotions. She was bright, but he knew other women whose IQs were astronomical—and who left him feeling empty. He'd never met a woman who made him follow the impulse to bare his soul, until he met Sophie.

He wasn't sure he liked what she did to him. Until now, he'd been safe from the fear that had lurked in his mind whenever he thought about getting involved with a woman. Now he found himself reluctantly confronting the fear that he might not have the capacity for emotions a relationship would require. Before, he'd shrugged off the possibility that his unorthodox childhood had crippled his ability to feel. He'd rationalized that his brain was far more important than his heart.

For the first time, he wanted to care, and he didn't know if he could.

Sophie gazed up at him, sweetly trusting, sweetly giving, not suspecting the doubts that raged in his head. Because he couldn't resist touching her any longer, he reached up and traced the curve of her cheek. Her skin felt like porcelain under his fingertip. Her eyes darkened and her lips parted. This time, he knew for sure that the urge to kiss Sophie was his own, not Wilde's.

He cupped her chin in his hand and lowered his head. Her lips felt warm and incredibly soft under his. Yielding. The delicate scent of her skin intoxicated him far more than the wine they'd shared. He wanted to take his time, to savor the sweetness of every particle of her. And he wanted to rush to possess her, to be consumed by the fire that was roaring inside him.

Ye-e-e-s! Closer, man. Closer and deeper! Forget the movie.

Jake broke the kiss abruptly. Damn! He'd forgotten about Wilde. Sophie blinked up at him.

"We should watch that movie before it gets too late," he told her, his voice coming out strangled, which was exactly what he'd love to do to Wilde.

By the time Sophie felt her pulse return to normal, the male lead had taken outrageous chances and female lead had given him hell for not thinking about anyone else beside himself. On the couch beside her, Jake watched the screen with an intensity she could feel. He had kissed her with that same intensity, she thought. Despite all her reservations, those kisses could have seduced her. Had he broken away because he didn't want to rush her? Or because he didn't want her to have any claims on him?

Jake chuckled at a minor character's antics. Sophie stole a glance at him and marveled at how appealing he looked when he smiled.

Of course, he was pretty darn appealing even when he was serious. And when he was kissing her...

Trailing smoke and flames, the hero's plane went down just as Sophie's phone rang. She gave a startled yelp, then clapped her hand over her mouth in embarrassment. Jake pressed the Pause button on the remote control while she reached for the receiver.

"Ms. Quinn? Patrolman Martino, West Hartford Police. We apprehended an individual attempting to break into your store."

A chill ran up her spine. "Yes?"

"We'd like you to come to the station, if you could."

"Now?"

"Yes, ma'am."

"I... I'll be right there." She set the receiver down and looked at Jake to find him watching her.

"I have to go to the police station. They caught someone trying to break in."

"I'll drive you. Come on."

He took her hands in his and drew her up from the couch. As she stood, she wished she knew him well enough to lean on him, just for a moment. And, as if he could read her mind, he wrapped his strong arms around her back and held her close to his chest for a brief, fortifying hug.

"Thanks," she whispered, easing away before she embarrassed herself by snuggling closer and seeking a replay of his sweet kisses. "I have to get my purse."

The phone's ring shattered the silence in the apartment. Sophie jumped, her hand going to her heart.

"Hello?"

"Sophie? It's me. Rick. I'm in trouble."

"Rick? What's wrong?" The police could wait, she thought, while she heard what Rick needed from her.

"I got busted at the store. I hate to ask, but the cops won't believe I was working. Can you come down here? And can you find me a lawyer?"

Chapter Seven

"I'm going to walk Sophie upstairs," Jake told Rick when they reached the second-floor landing. He kept his voice low to avoid waking Mrs. Mandel in the middle of the night. "You go inside and wait for me in the kitchen."

Rick nodded and faded into the darkness of the apartment. *What a loser,* Wilde muttered. Jake gritted his teeth and willed Wilde back into the recesses of his mind. He didn't know if it would work, but it was worth a try.

The silence behind his own thoughts told him either he had some power over Wilde after all, or his resident ghost was sulking. At the moment, he didn't care which. He didn't even have the patience to deal with the possibility that he'd actually *accepted* having a ghost—or whatever—in his head. The only important thing was to find out what was happening to Sophie's store, and to eradicate it.

He glanced down to find Sophie looking up into his face. Even in the dim porch light, he could see faint shadows under her eyes. Her smile quivered. Deep inside him, he felt something unknown expand. He reached down to take her small hand in his. The way she clutched his hand sent a special, unfamiliar warmth through him.

He recognized the instinct to protect her, and marveled that it was so strong in him. He'd never felt protective—or possessive—about a woman before. A computer, often. A particularly elegant software program, certainly. But never had he felt this sense of connection with a woman.

He also felt his anger growing over the way someone was using Sophie. And determination to find out who. If it really were Rick—and at the moment, he was inclined to agree with the cops that Rick was involved somehow—after the way Sophie had trusted him and defended him... Never before had he considered doing anything violent to another human being.

Then again, the stakes had never been this high before.

"Come on, Sophie," he said, drawing her closer to his side. "You need some sleep. We'll get this solved. Don't worry." Easy to say. He hoped he could make it true.

Beside him, she climbed the stairs like an exhausted child, letting him pull her up, her feet barely moving on their own. He was torn between relishing her dependence on him and his respect for her independence. With other women, the idea of being clung to had been as appealing as being tied to a hill of red ants.

He'd noticed the difference the other night. Normally, he shied away from being needed, except on a computer-related project. Probably because of the way his parents and their colleagues avoided emotional attachments like they avoided static around their computers. He'd learned at an early age that they resented being needed, being depended on. Need was an imposition.

But he didn't resent Sophie depending on him. Far from it. What was even more astounding was that he wanted her to ask for more. He wanted to be her hero. In the morning, she would probably be back on her own feet again, but for now he would let himself savor the way she leaned on him. He'd just hope and pray he could give her whatever she needed. He didn't want to face the possibility that he just didn't have what she needed. And that in itself was pretty unsettling, without any complications from Dean Wilde and the parasite who was getting fat from Sophie's computer.

He unlocked her back door and tugged her inside the kitchen. A soft light glowed from one of the outlets. The trace odors of flowers and baking perfumed the room. But the deep breath he drew filled his head with the sweet scent of the woman beside him.

"Jake, thank you for taking Rick's word," she said softly.

To his surprise, he felt a stab of jealousy at her concern over the other man. He wanted her to be thinking of him, not Rick. But that was petty.

Well, so what? Where was it written that he had to be perfect? It was time he let himself be human.

Right. But first you gotta figure out what human is. All you know is computers. The only interfacing you do is between systems.

He stopped short, unable to determine whether the words in his head were Wilde's, or his own. What did it matter whose thought it was? It was true. He knew as much about emotions, about relationships, as a cat knew about computers; he knew they existed, but he sure didn't know how to make them work.

"Go to bed, Sophie," he muttered, unwilling to confess that he didn't, in fact, believe Rick's story. Sophie didn't need any more grief tonight.

She nodded, but she didn't move. "Will you be all right alone?" he asked, wondering in the next second what he could possibly do to help her if she wasn't going to be all right.

"I'll be fine. Thanks." Her voice come out even softer, as if she were fading.

"Sure," he said, not believing her.

Following some primitive impulse that surprised the hell out of him, he scooped her up in his arms. She squeaked, then wrapped her arms around his neck and held on to him tightly. Sensations rioted through him. The warmth of her body. The intoxicating scent of her. The softness of her breasts against his chest. The whisper of her breath on his neck.

She couldn't know what she was doing to him. He shouldn't be thinking about his own needs when she was so upset. But he suspected he needed to touch her, comfort her, at least as much as she needed him to.

Slowly, wanting to prolong the moments that he could hold her like this, he made his way to her bedroom. With his foot, he nudged the door open, then paused at the threshold of the dimly lit room. In the center of the room stood a wide antique four-poster bed covered with lacy stuff. He carried Sophie to the edge of the bed and set her down, fighting the desire that surged in his blood.

The way she looked up at him shook his resolve. He didn't need Wilde's prompting to know that if he kissed her now, she would return his kisses. And if he took her into his arms and slipped her dress off and stroked the satin skin revealed, she would let him take her.

But he couldn't. Not now. Not when Sophie was so vulnerable because of events that had nothing to do with whatever there was between them. Not when Rick was downstairs in his apartment, waiting, probably concocting some lame excuses. Not when Wilde lurked somewhere in his psyche, both rival and voyeur.

But more important, not when he didn't know which feelings were his and which were Wilde's. Or even if he was capable of having feelings, beyond intellectual curiosity and physical desire. Sophie deserved honesty.

"I'll see you in the morning," he somehow managed to choke out. Then, before she could do or say anything to sabotage his flimsy willpower, he hustled out of her apartment and downstairs to his own, where Rick waited for him. If Wilde was planning to mess with his head anymore, he was going to have to get in line.

Rick sat at the kitchen table in the dark, his head cradled on his arms. When Jake stepped inside and flipped on the lights, Rick slowly straightened in the chair and looked at him. Deliberately dragging out the moment, hoping to force Rick to lower his guard, Jake pulled out a kitchen chair for himself. He turned it around and straddled it, facing Rick.

"Okay, man. Let's have it straight. What's going on?"

"Nothing. I told the cops the truth. I wasn't breaking in. Hell, I owe my life to Sophie. She gave me a chance when no one wanted to hire me except to pick shade tobacco. The last thing I'm going to do is rip her off."

Jake's brain warned him to be wary, but his gut heard the ring of sincerity in Rick's voice. He found himself wanting Sophie to be right about trusting Rick. But not quite ready to be as trusting as she was.

"Then what were you doing there an hour after closing?"

"I went back to check the alarm. Whoever tried to bust in before knew how to disarm it, right?" Jake nodded, anticipating where Rick was going but wanting to hear him say it. "So, I wanted to make sure it was okay. Something's been nagging at me about that night, and I finally figured it out. I wanted to see if I was right."

"About what?" Did Rick know something about the bank connection, Jake wondered, or was there something else going on?

"Well, I never was convinced we should keep the system running twenty-four hours. I don't think turning it on once and off once a day is going to do significant damage to the hard drive. So, I got to thinking about the B and E try. It was the only night in two months—"

"That the computer was shut down for the night."

Rick's eyes narrowed. "What do you know about this, Warren? If you're doing something that puts Sophie in—"

"Relax. I was about to say the same thing to you."

Jake pondered the situation, then decided to give Rick enough rope to hang himself. If he wasn't involved in the scam using Sophie's computer, he'd be the best man to help. And if he was involved, Jake would take him apart bit by bit.

"Want a beer?"

The tension melted out of Rick's pose. "Yeah. Thanks."

After they'd both taken long swallows of the cold, bitter drink, Rick met his eyes. Jake saw concern, a little defensiveness, but no guilt. He decided either Rick was a psychopath, or he was being straight with him. Whatever Rick's past—and the arresting officer had been happy to detail it for him and Sophie—he wanted to believe Rick had put it behind him. In a way, he supposed that Sophie's success with Rick compensated in her mind for what she probably saw as her failure with Dean Wilde.

Rick lowered his beer. "So, what's the skinny on the computer?" He kept his eyes on Jake while taking another drink. "Why would anyone want to break in just because it wasn't on?"

Jake tugged at the hair falling over his forehead. "I'm not sure." He still wasn't ready to reveal his hand. "I want to take a look inside that CPU. What kind of modem is in there?"

Rick stopped in midgulp. "Modem?"

Jake nodded.

Rick shook his head. "There isn't any modem in that computer. Dennis offered her a sweet deal on one that handled faxes, too, but Sophie didn't see any need to have one. She didn't want to tie up her phone lines. She doesn't do her banking by computer, and she doesn't have any branch stores to connect with this one. She already had a fax machine in the office that she's happy with. She says that's enough high technology for her for this lifetime."

Jake got up and paced across the kitchen. The floor in the corner near the refrigerator creaked. He stopped in his tracks and looked at Rick. Rick dug at the label on his beer bottle. What kind of game was he playing?

"I'm telling you, there's a modem in that computer."

"And I'm telling you there isn't."

"Have you opened it up?"

Rick looked up from the pile of shredded paper, looking both surprised and suspicious. "No," he said slowly. Jake waited, knowing exactly what path the other man's thoughts should be taking, if he weren't covering his own tracks. "If there is . . . ?"

"If there is, Sophie may be in trouble."

Rick took a long moment to digest that. "You're the expert, here, Warren. Is there anything you can do?"

"Yeah. But I'll need your help."

"You got it. Anything for Sophie."

"You need something to take your mind off all these hassles, Sophie," Lynne said over coffee in the office. "And I need a friendly face that isn't in banking and investments to get me through this barbecue Craig is doing Friday night. Please?"

Sophie paced her office, weighing the invitation carefully. The impulse to ask Lynne if she could invite Jake fought with her common sense. After the way he'd taken care of her last night, she was more afraid than ever that her feelings were growing too deep, too fast. It would be so easy to fall for Jake, too hard to watch him walk out of her life in six weeks.

Common sense won, but it was a hollow victory.

"Okay. You've twisted my arm. What time and what should I wear?"

Lynne grinned. "Seven, and wear that violet halter dress with the long, floaty skirt. There are a couple of unattached men on the guest list."

Sophie groaned. "You're incorrigible."

Lynne shook her head, her smile replaced by a frown. "I plan to get your mind off Jake Warren. The man's too sexy to be a nerd."

Sophie turned her back, pretending to straighten an already neat stack of papers so Lynne couldn't see her face. She didn't want her friend to suspect the effect Jake's kisses—drunk or not—had on her.

"What if I don't want my mind off Jake?" she asked, playing devil's advocate. In fact, she'd welcome any good reasons not to be attracted to Jake.

"Come on, Sophie. The man's leaving in less than two months. Maybe it's none of my business, but you've never been the kind of woman who got herself into dead-end affairs just because a guy was irresistible. I don't want you to get hurt."

Sophie smiled. "That's why it's your business. You're the voice of my conscience. And you're right. Jake is attractive, but he's leaving and I'm not into disposable relationships." She stifled a yawn, still exhausted from being awake most of the night. "Anyway, Jake isn't interested in me."

"That's okay, then." Lynne stood and tossed her napkin into the garbage. "Besides, who knows who he's going back to? Maybe he's got a wife and kiddies stashed away in Silicon Valley. Or a modest harem of adoring nerdettes keeping his computers warm for him while he toys with your affections."

Sophie forced a laugh, stinging from Lynne's easy agreement that Jake really wasn't interested in her. "*Nerdettes?* That sounds like an all-girl rock band. Go away so I can do some work."

Lynne strolled toward the door. "Okay, okay. Just promise you'll come Friday."

"Promise."

Lynne paused in the doorway. "Alone," she said sternly.

"Alone," Sophie echoed, still smiling. But the moment Lynne passed through the doorway, Sophie felt her smile fade. Their joking about "nerdettes" made her wonder about the life Jake had left behind for two months. No one, not even a computer wizard, could live in a complete vacuum. And Jake was one very attractive computer wizard.

Her imagination perversely conjured up a picture of Jake and a woman seated before a computer screen, their heads together, their hands touching over the keyboard. And, of course, the other woman—the nerdette—would take off her black-framed glasses and unpin her long honey-blond hair from its severe bun. "Ms. Smith, you're beautiful!" Jake would say, then take her in his arms and—

"Sophie, you idiot!" she muttered. "You've seen too many movies! Stop torturing yourself and get back to work."

You can't keep doing this to me, Wilde growled while Jake unlocked his bike from Mrs. Mandel's back porch.

The sun was already hot at 10:00 a.m., the air heavy and humid, but he needed to work off the energy that vibrated inside him. He needed the mindless motion of riding the bike to help him think. He *didn't* need a figment of his imagination nagging at him about his choice of transportation.

"Go back where you came from, Wilde," Jake muttered back. He wrapped the chain around his waist and snapped the lock shut. "I don't care what you want—"

Look, I'll settle for any motorcycle.

Jake wrenched his bike off the porch and set it on the ground with an angry bounce. "You'll settle for a mountain bike or find someone else to haunt. Isn't there a chapter of Hell's Angels around here?"

I'm no angel, Warren.

"Don't I know it."

"Good morning, Jake!" Mrs. Mandel stepped out onto the porch and glanced around. "I heard voices. Are you and Sophie going for a bicycle ride?"

He felt his face tingle. Foo! Now he looked like he had bats in his belfry to go with the ghost—or whatever—in his head.

"Uh, no. I was just talking to myself. Thinking out loud. Sophie went to work early."

Mrs. Mandel nodded, but the way she narrowed her eyes told him he wasn't quite off the hook. He dusted off the seat of the bike and waited.

"Was there a problem last night, Jake? I heard voices very late."

He nodded. "Sorry. I was hoping we wouldn't wake you."

"We? Does that mean you finally took my advice about asking Sophie out?"

Her self-satisfied smile brought the heat back to his face. "Not exactly. The police thought there was another break-in, so I took Sophie to check it out."

The way Mrs. Mandel's smile faded made him feel guilty that nothing had happened between him and Sophie.

Wouldn't his landlady be surprised to learn that she had an ally in the not-so-dear departed Dean, although they didn't exactly share motives. Mrs. Mandel had permanent matchmaking on her mind, but his alter ego wasn't thinking past seduction. Vicarious, at that. And there he was, caught in the middle, not knowing what the hell he wanted. All he knew was that he still wanted . . . something.

"I see," Mrs. Mandel said, her tone conveying that she saw more than the obvious. She shrugged. "Well, maybe you aren't the right man for my Sophie."

Jake froze, gaping at his sweet-faced landlady as his earlier words to that effect came back to him. At that moment, he knew exactly how a hard disk would feel as it crashed. Useless. Helpless to retrieve the data stored in good faith. Hollow. The way he'd felt when he'd realized he was drowning, just before his first vision of Sophie beckoning him back to life.

He shook his head. "I don't know if I'm the right man for Sophie, Mrs. Mandel," he said quietly, "but I have to do what I think is right." Like not taking when he had nothing to offer in return . . .

I hear violins, Wilde muttered.

Jake clenched his teeth to keep from telling Wilde to shut up. Then he saw the smile that lit Mrs. Mandel's face.

"Do you like pot roast, Jake?" she asked.

Bemused, he nodded. Apparently, he'd said something right, because his landlady went back into her apartment nodding to herself, but inside he wasn't so sure. Like a computer, a man couldn't do more than he was programmed to do, and he'd never been programmed for the kinds of emotions rioting through him.

Screw emotions. Stop thinking so much and just do *something. We're supposed to be a team, man, but so far, I've been doing all the work. You could have had Sophie last night. If you don't want her, that's your hang-up, not mine.*

Jake ignored Wilde's nagging. He wheeled the bicycle out to the curb and started pedaling east, toward downtown Hartford. The sun burned through his thin black cycling pants. Within minutes, his T-shirt was stuck to his back, and he couldn't pick up enough speed to create a breeze.

Cars and trucks sped past, choking him with exhaust and spitting small stones up into his spokes. The door of a parked car opened without warning just as he passed, nearly hitting him. A minivan turned right without signaling, forcing him to half bail out onto the sidewalk. His attempt to make a left turn set up a cacophony of horns as impatient drivers swirled past him, trapping him in the intersection through an extra light change.

Two hours later, he walked out of the Harley-Davidson dealership fastening his new helmet, a spare hanging on his arm. The black motorcycle in front of him gleamed in the sunlight. Tiny waves of heat shimmered above the blacktop of the parking lot. He swung his right leg over the bike and settled into the saddle, bracing his feet, in new leather boots, firmly on the ground.

His new pants and jacket creaked softly and released the warm scent of new leather. Through the slightly stiff black leather gloves, he felt the ridges of the handlebar grips. The sun baked into his back and shoulders. The roads stretched in all directions, waiting for him.

Jake turned the key in the electronic ignition. The bike rumbled to life. He grinned and eased into first gear. He'd owned a motorcycle years ago, a battered 250 c.c. toy that had a whine like a crazed sewing machine and virtually no padding on the seat. The Harley purring between his knees was a sweetly tuned example of precision bordering on perfection.

Told ya.

"Don't be so smug," he muttered as he rolled toward the exit. "I only got this because I wanted it. You just made the suggestion."

Yeah, yeah. Have I steered you wrong yet?

"There's always a first time."

Yeah, well, this is only one of the firsts you gotta get through.

Bad enough his imaginary playmate always had to get the last word, Jake thought as he guided the big bike into noontime traffic. He didn't always have to be so damn *right*.

Don't stop loving me, babe, Dean whispered. *Don't forget me, Soph. Don't leave me alone.* His breath stirred the wisps of hair at her neck. Blinded by the sun and the engulfing waves of heat, Sophie struggled to see him, to reach out and touch him.

She heard the rumble of his motorcycle and smiled. Dean was back. His boots crunched on gravel as he walked closer. The grass muted his steps, but she knew he was beside her when she smelled leather and sunshine and heard the rasping of his jacket zipper.

Dean had come back to her. That was why she'd never been able to love anyone else. It all made sense now. She'd been waiting for him all these years. She had to tell him....

"Dean?"

"Sophie, wake up."

But that wasn't Dean's voice. It was Jake's voice, but Dean was so close. She could feel him. Why couldn't she see him? Was she only dreaming again?

"You set me up, damn you," she heard him say. His voice—no, Jake's voice—vibrated with anger. That didn't make sense. "The hell you didn't," he added, still angry. Who was he talking to? Then he said her name again, gently, but with an edge of urgency. "Sophie, come on. Wake up before you get sunburned."

She struggled to open her eyes, yet she was afraid to lose him if she succeeded. "Dean?"

"Jake," he said sharply, and she knew she'd only been dreaming, lying on a blanket in the late-afternoon sun behind Mrs. Mandel's house. The dream dissolved, and Sophie took a firm grip on reality. Dean was a bittersweet part of her past she couldn't forget, but Jake was a disturbing part of her present.

For a moment, she felt as if the two men were pulling at her from different directions.

Sophie opened her eyes and blinked up at the dark figure silhouetted by the sun. All thoughts of Dean dissolved in the memory of the way Jake's arms had felt when he'd carried her to her bed last night. It had been Jake in her dreams, not Dean.

"Hi. Jake." Her voice felt heavy with sleep. She cleared her throat. "I must have been dreaming. I thought I heard a motorcycle in the yard."

He crouched beside her and she could see he was scowling as he met her eyes. "You did."

She propped herself up on one elbow and felt her eyes widen as she looked Jake over. In black leathers, with a black helmet dangling from one gloved hand, he looked like a modern knight ready to do battle. The supple pants hugged his powerful legs and lean hips. Over a plain white T-shirt, that clung to his flat belly, his leather jacket hung casually unzipped. The way he'd tied his dark hair back emphasized that fierce expression in his brilliant eyes. Behind him, in the driveway, stood a huge black motorcycle gleaming in the sun.

It was a Harley, like Dean's.

A brief replay of her dream flashed through her mind, bringing with it memories of Dean. Feeling vaguely disloyal, but not sure to which man, she shook the images away.

"You bought a bike!"

He shrugged and his cheeks reddened endearingly, diminishing only slightly his warrior demeanor. "Yeah. It went with the new jacket and pants."

Sophie laughed. "It sure does."

He flashed her a crooked grin. "Shouldn't you be at the store?"

"Rick sent me home. I didn't get much sleep last night so I kept falling asleep at my desk."

He nodded but said nothing, a distant expression on his face. Had her mention of last night reminded him of the disgustingly wimpy way she'd clung to him? She'd practically hauled him down onto her bed with her, but he'd escaped with that awful look of pity in his eyes. It hurt, but she was grateful that he hadn't taken advantage of her neediness.

"Feel like a ride?" he said gruffly, breaking the silence between them just as it was getting truly awkward.

"I'd love it. I haven't ridden on a motorcycle in years." Twelve years, to be exact. Not since just before Dean had died. But something told her she would be wise not to mention that to Jake.

He stood and held his hand out toward her. She reached up and placed her hand in his, hoping he couldn't feel how she trembled at his simple, friendly touch. Oh, Sophie, what a fool you are, she scolded herself. Between her memories of Dean and her infatuation for Jake, she was behaving like a besotted seventeen-year-old, not a mature, independent woman.

Jake pulled her to her feet, his hand warm and strong around hers. For a moment, she stood barely a few inches from him, the scent of leather and sunshine mingling with the scent of his skin. Looking up into his brilliant blue eyes, she felt the rest of the world fade away.

"You better put some real clothes on," he said curtly as he released her hand.

Her neck and cheeks stung with heat. Part of her felt like a fool standing there, practically naked in a tube top and running shorts. Part of her couldn't help wondering what it would feel like to step into his arms and wrap her bare arms and legs around his leather-covered body. Shivering in the heat, she turned and hurried to her apartment to get dressed.

Jake watched Sophie walk toward the porch. It wasn't just the sun baking him through the black leather that stoked the heat in his veins. He could still feel the soft pressure of her hand on his. And he swore he could feel the weight of her slender body against his, as if he'd really given in to the urge to pull her close and wrap her bare limbs around him. Talk about "virtual reality"!

Virtual reality, like hell! It's my reality, Warren. That's my *body you can feel her climbing on.* My *memories. And just because you think you have to do the right thing, don't expect me to help. Being noble got me diddly. I want Sophie now, even if you don't.*

Jake strode to the bike and released the spare helmet. "Back off, Wilde. I'm not going to seduce Sophie to satisfy your curiosity."

What about your *curiosity? You may live like a monk, man, but you're no saint. You want her, too.*

He couldn't argue with that. Or at least, he didn't think he could. Was it his own hunger for Sophie? Or Wilde's? Was this presence in his head—assuming it existed and he wasn't simply ready for a rubber room—capable of manipulating him? And if so, how far? What would Wilde be willing to do to get what he wanted?

You know what they say, bro'. That's for me to know, and you to find out.

Jake cursed. Wilde laughed.

Sophie reappeared at her back door, dressed in jeans and a blue-gray leather jacket. She'd tied her hair back, exposing the place behind her ear where he fantasized about tasting her skin. But was it his fantasy, or Wilde's memory? He wanted the truth, but he didn't. When she reached him, he silently held out the spare helmet.

Her lips looked so soft, so inviting, when she smiled. "Thanks." He recalled how soft they felt, how sweet she tasted. And he knew that no matter how much influence Wilde had on his thoughts and actions, Sophie's kisses, her sweetness on his tongue, were *his* memories. And the desire to taste her again, to peel away the layers of her clothes and lose himself in the sweetness of all of her, was *his* desire.

She slipped the helmet on and disappeared behind the tinted visor. He replaced his own helmet and straddled the bike. When the engine was idling smoothly, he turned and nodded to Sophie. The light pressure of her hand on his shoulder branded his flesh. When she settled herself behind him, hands at his waist, thighs resting around his hips, electricity charged every point of contact between their bodies.

Just don't forget, Warren. She's mine. I gave her up once. I won't do it again.

Damn Wilde! Jake swallowed hard. He eased the bike into first gear and steered toward the street. Although he'd never carried a passenger on his decrepit old bike, he had no trouble getting used to Sophie's presence behind him. Her hands barely rested at his sides, and she followed his shifting balance around corners as if they were one person with two bodies.

He aimed the bike west, following the sun along Route 44 toward the northwest corner of Connecticut. The dense green of the forests seemed to close in on them as they left the main road and flew along small, winding, climbing secondary roads. Used to the wide, rolling, bright expanses around Los Altos, he couldn't decide whether he liked the smaller, darker scale of the New England landscape. He felt something oppressive, almost foreboding, about the scenery.

The narrow road they sped along wound up a steeper hill than the others they'd traveled. Jake had to lean farther into the turns than before. Without thinking, he reached back and placed his hand on the small of Sophie's back, urging her closer. She wound her arms around his waist and pressed against his back, her thighs hugging his hips intimately.

It was bliss and it was torture.

Suddenly, as they crested the hill and leaned into the curve that began their descent, a vision flashed through his mind. A car—a small, beige car—stood stalled in the intersection at the bottom of the hill, hidden by the twists of the road. A small truck sped east toward the intersection from the next hill. They were going to run straight into that car. The truck was going to crash into them moments later.

He saw it happen even as he drove the bike toward the intersection. Like commands flashing across the monitor while a computer performed them, he saw the bike skid as he braked hard on gravel and sand. He saw the bike swerve and slide into the side of the car. He heard the dull thud, the breaking glass. And the screams. Then the second crash.

And then he saw Sophie. Lying beside the road, her slender, broken body covered by a gray blanket. And standing possessively, triumphantly, over Sophie, he saw a shadowy male figure he knew was Dean Wilde.

Chapter Eight

The scenery streaked by in a blur of greens and browns. The big bike wobbled when he applied the brakes. Jake geared down for another turn, so tight, it was almost a switchback.

Where the hell was that intersection? Was it even real? It sure had looked real, but how could he be sure? The road seemed to continue forever. His heart pounded so hard, he couldn't breathe. He fought gravity and momentum to slow the bike, certain he was losing the battle.

There! Through the trees, he saw a flash of beige. He guided the bike toward the narrow shoulder of the road. Still running too fast, the powerful machine fishtailed on the pebbles and sand. He braked hard as branches slapped at their legs. The bike stopped in the heart of a thick bush, away from the path of the speeding truck.

"Stay here!" he yelled at Sophie as he shoved himself off the bike.

"What—?"

"Just do it!"

He pulled his helmet off and rushed to the stalled car. Two young women sat inside. Jake yanked the driver's door open and pulled the woman out roughly. She screamed and slapped at him but he ignored her. When he reached inside to shift the car into neutral, the other woman screamed and pounded his hand.

"Get out!" she yelled at him. "Get out!"

"You get out!" he hollered back. He stood and braced his hands against the frame of the little car. "Help me push this thing out of the intersection. *Now!*"

Both women froze. Jake strained to push, his feet slipping on the sandy road. The car barely moved after the first shove. He sucked in a deep breath and pushed again. Suddenly the car gave. It rolled out of the intersection and slid gently down the small slope. The passenger inside screamed as the dense bushes engulfed the front fender. The driver ran after Jake, hitting him on the back and arm. He ducked her blows, looking for a chance to explain rationally what had happened.

"Are you crazy? Look what you did to my car!" she yelled.

"Jake?"

It was Sophie, much too close. She should be across the intersection and safely hidden at the side of the road. Jake pivoted toward the sound of her voice.

Sophie stood in the road, where the little car had been stalled a moment before. He realized that she'd come across to help him push the car when the driver hadn't. Now she was looking at him, her brow furrowed. He couldn't blame her.

He heard the clank of metal on metal and the squeal of tires. The truck. His heart stopped.

Time stopped.

The driver of the car grabbed at his arm again, shrieking in anger, but all he saw was Sophie standing in the path of the oncoming truck. With a growl, Jake shook off the other woman and charged toward Sophie. He caught her hand and dragged her roughly into his arms, staggering backward until they hit the side of the beige car. He leaned against the car and held Sophie hard, his heart pounding.

The red pickup sped through the empty intersection, spitting sand and stones in all directions. The open tailgate bounced, rattling heavy support chains. Seconds later, the truck was out of sight around the bend in the road, the rhythmic clanking fading into the distance. The driver didn't turn his head.

Jake heard the two women from the beige car babbling, but he didn't bother to listen. All he cared about was the trembling woman in his arms. He held her until his heart no longer hammered and her body no longer shook against his chest.

A million thoughts raced through his head. But when he finally eased his hold on her, and she looked up into his face with those wonderful, soft gray eyes, he couldn't think of anything to say.

He wanted to bend his head and kiss her, to prove she was real, and she was safe. He craved the taste of her, the feel of her yielding in his arms. The gentle pressure of her body against him sent heat rushing to his loins. Images of Sophie's sweet kisses, her soft body tangling naked and trembling with his, collided with the image of her broken, blanket-covered body. If they had been alone at the side of the road, he would have been tempted to draw her into the dark shelter of the thick trees.

But they weren't alone. He turned to face the now-silent driver. She gaped at him.

"What's wrong with your car?" he asked gruffly.

"I . . . I don't know."

"Open the hood. I've got some tools on the bike."

He left the three women to retrieve the tool kit from the Harley. When he reached the bike, he searched for Wilde's presence.

"Thanks," he said softly.

Hey, no sweat. You did the hard stuff.

"I wouldn't have known—"

I did it for Sophie. I couldn't. . .

He read Wilde's pause. "Yeah, I know."

You move pretty fast for a nerd.

Jake clenched his hands into fists, wishing Wilde's neck was available for wringing. But, as usual, his ghost had the last word on that, too.

Jake stopped the bike at a red light. "Want to stop for a beer or head back?"

Sophie's helmet bumped his when she leaned closer. Her arms ached from holding him as tightly as she could, but she didn't ever want to stop touching him. "A beer sounds great."

"That steak house on the corner okay? We can grab some dinner."

"Sure."

Anything, she thought, anything to prolong the time with him. And maybe, to have a chance to talk about what had happened a half hour before. Jake had adjusted the cranky fuel pump of the little beige car, but he hadn't said a word to either of the other women or herself beyond "Hand me that wrench," and "Try it now." When the women, Donna and Terry, had thanked him profusely, he'd simply shrugged and said, "No big deal."

Well, it might not have been a big deal in the life of a computer wizard, but Sophie was still shaking at the memory of that red pickup truck barreling through the very spot she'd been standing in before Jake grabbed her.

She still trembled at the primitive urge to celebrate being alive by making love with Jake. The memory of his solid body supporting her, the comforting crush of his strong arms around her, felt branded on her flesh. If those women from the stalled car hadn't been standing there, she would have led Jake into the thick cover of the woods.

What a glorious mistake that would have been, she thought as they dismounted in the restaurant parking lot. Obviously, the incident had made more of an impression on her than it had on Jake. From the instant he'd released her to fix the car, Jake had behaved as if nothing out of the ordinary had happened.

Still, she wanted to savor the time with him. It was barely seven on a summer evening. The steak house was nearly empty. A hostess in a short black dress and fishnet stockings showed them to a secluded table beside a window and promised to bring the pitcher of draft light beer Jake ordered. He nodded absently and opened his menu.

Sophie studied his handsome face and felt a wave of emotion that scared her almost as much as her brush with death. With every hour they spent together, she was getting more deeply involved and he was getting closer to leaving. Not saying the words didn't erase the feelings in her heart.

Life could be so short, so fragile. Would it be a mistake if she followed her feelings about Jake and ignored her better judgment? If she took the responsibility for getting hurt when he left and didn't try to blame him or expect anything more from him?

"Jake?" Her voice came out too softly. He continued to pore over the menu. It took her two more tries to get his attention. Then she couldn't find the courage to say what she wanted to. "How did you know what to do?" she asked instead.

He shrugged. "I've worked on a lot of cars, tinkering for fun. The fuel pump on that make tends to—"

"That's not what I meant. How did you know to push the car out of the intersection?"

He slid his gaze away from hers and appeared to be very interested in a nick in the shiny wooden tabletop. "When a car stalls in an intersection, that's the logical thing to do."

"But how did you know it was there? I didn't see it until you'd parked the bike and charged down the road."

"What? Oh, I, uh, saw it through the bushes when we were coming down the hill. When you cycle on hills as much as I do, you get in the habit of looking ahead any way you can. Always try to minimize surprises. I wasn't sure the car was actually in the intersection until we were almost on top of it."

"But—"

"It was only a matter of time before someone came around that corner too fast. Hell, we almost did."

He looked up, but still didn't quite meet her eyes. It was as if he were embarrassed to have saved three people from injury, if not worse. Well, he had a right to his modesty, but she had a right to her gratitude. She wanted him to know how spectacular his actions were.

"And the truck? It came out of nowhere. But you seemed to know it was coming."

He shrugged and lowered his gaze to the menu again. "I heard it. You know, the chains and the tailgate. Didn't you?"

"No." She swallowed. "No, I didn't. I probably wouldn't have known what to do if I had heard it. Jake? You saved my life. I'm trying to get a grip on what almost happened, and say thank you."

He looked at her then, his eyes laser-bright, his brow furrowed. "Forget it, Sophie. It's a little too close to home to talk about it, okay?"

How could she have forgotten his own, much closer, brush with death? "Oh, Jake, I'm sorry. I didn't think—"

"Here we are, people!" a waitress announced, transferring an overflowing pitcher of beer from her tray to the center of their table. She placed napkins in front of each of them, then set glasses down and poured beer into each glass. Sophie wanted to scream in impatience over the prolonged interruption, but she knew the woman was just doing her job.

"Ready to order?" The waitress took her pen and pad from her apron pocket and looked at Jake with an obvious combination of interest in his order and interest in him. Sophie couldn't blame her. Jake looked dangerous and wild in his black leathers, with his long hair rebelling against the elastic holding it back. Dangerous until you looked into his face, Sophie mused. Then he looked intelligent and gentle... and, as Lynne kept saying, much too sexy for a nerd.

When the waitress finally finished grilling them about what they wanted to accompany their main courses—baked, mashed or rice, salad or coleslaw—Sophie knew it was too late to return to their previous conversation. And maybe, given the way her thoughts had begun to resemble her impulses, that wasn't such a bad thing. It was one thing to get hurt without being able to anticipate it, but quite something else to rush headlong into disappointment.

She lifted her glass and took a sip of the cold beer. Jake drank some of his beer, then set his glass down and began turning his napkin around on the table. The silence between them seemed louder than the country-rock music on the restaurant sound system. Sophie took another sip of beer, casting around in her mind for a suitably neutral topic of conversation.

Suddenly Jake made a strange sound, like a strangled cough. Sophie looked up in alarm. Jake smothered another cough.

"Are you all right? Should I get you some water?"

He shook his head. "I'm fine," he said, choking.

Sophie shrugged. He sure didn't look or sound fine. But the last time she'd fussed over him, when he'd had that awful headache, he'd practically tossed her out of his apartment. She took another sip of her beer, then blotted the foam on her lip with her bar napkin. Uncomfortable with the silence, she turned her napkin around until she could make sense of the design and the words.

With a gasp, she glanced across the table at Jake. No wonder he'd choked. The napkin had a drawing of a condom in its wrapper. The bold lettering around it said Please Let This Come Between Us. She'd forgotten all about the state's Department of Health campaign to promote safer sex.

Jake met her eyes and Sophie felt her neck and face flame.

"How are things—?" she rushed to say.

"Is the computer—?" he said at the same time.

She couldn't help it. Awkward as the moment was, it was also funny. She smiled, and then a little laugh escaped her. Jake looked startled, then grinned crookedly. A second later, Sophie was laughing so hard that tears down her cheeks.

Finally she caught her breath and looked across the table at Jake. His expression was surprisingly serious. Self-consciously, she realized he probably didn't appreciate the assumption that they were potential lovers. The reminder that the attraction was one-sided stole the last of her amusement. Thank goodness she hadn't followed her impulse to throw herself at him earlier. She crumpled her napkin and pushed it to the side of the table.

"Sorry," she said. "You were saying something about the computer?"

He nodded. "How is it working now? Any more problems with data recovery?"

"No. It's been fine. Whatever Dennis did when he finally made his service call seems to have fixed whatever wasn't working."

Jake stared at his beer glass. His expression was so distant, Sophie wondered if he'd heard her. Then he looked into her eyes. The intensity of his gaze sent a rush of heat through her. He looked at her the way he had before each time he'd kissed her. Hungry. Predatory. Had she read him wrong earlier? Or was she reading too much into his expression now?

"I'd be glad to look at the system, Sophie. Just to make sure there isn't something that Dennis is overlooking. Is he a computer engineer?"

"I don't think so, but he seems to know what he's talking about. At least, I figure he does because he's been servicing my bank's computer system." She offered an apologetic smile. "Not that I understood even half of what he ever says. But I have Rick to translate for me."

Jake frowned fiercely. Sophie wondered if he really did believe Rick wasn't trying to break into her store. He looked so disapproving whenever she mentioned Rick. She was tempted to ask him, but she hated confrontations.

"How are things going with your work for the banks?" she asked instead.

"Pretty good."

Now, that was enlightening. "I can't imagine they really have security problems. I mean, all those stories about tellers siphoning off a tenth of a cent from accounts and escaping to Mexico... And movies where hackers move huge fortunes into numbered accounts in the Cayman Islands or whatever... People can't really do things like that anymore, can they?"

"Depends."

"Jake, if you aren't supposed to be discussing the job, just tell me."

The waitress arrived with their salads.

"I probably shouldn't talk about the work while it's still in progress," he said as he dug his fork into his salad. "But, uh, I could tell you about some other jobs I've worked on. If you're interested. I mean, not everyone thinks cracking is all that fascinating."

"Cracking?"

He nodded. "Hacking is basically just fooling around with a computer, to see what it can do. Like fine-tuning a program to make it as elegant, as close to perfection as possible. That's pretty much how software is developed and customized. Cracking is using computers to break into other systems."

"I've always wondered about that. I mean, in the movies, someone just sits down at a terminal and starts typing, and the next thing you know, they're monkeying around in someone else's computer. How do you do that?"

Over salad, main courses, pecan pie and decaffeinated coffee, Sophie heard more about modems, passwords, data banks, lurking, viruses and worms than she'd ever want to have to take a test on. More compelling than Jake's information and his tales of crimes and attempted scams he'd uncovered was his sudden enthusiasm, his animation as he talked. She could have listened to him all night.

Unfortunately, their cheerful waitress brought their bill and Jake retreated to silence. Sophie insisted on splitting the check after he refused her offer to buy dinner. When they went back outside to the bike, brilliant streaks of fuchsia, purple and gold painted the sky. The air was still warm—a perfect summer night. She didn't want it to end.

At the edge of the parking lot exit, Sophie looked to the east, into the falling darkness, the direction of her home. Then she looked west, into the spectacle of the sunset, the direction of Jake's home.

He revved the engine, balancing the heavy machine with one foot on the pavement until traffic cleared. She bit back the impulse to tell him to follow the sun. Instead, she wound her arms a little tighter around his waist. Immediately, he stiffened. Stung by his silent rejection, she unwound her arms and rested her hands on his sides.

Too soon, yet not soon enough, they were rumbling down the driveway of Mrs. Mandel's house. Sophie hopped off the bike before Jake cut the engine. She wanted to escape before she made a fool of herself by touching him, offering something he obviously didn't want.

"Thanks for the ride," she said hastily. She thrust the spare helmet into his gloved hands. "It's a great bike. Good—"

"Sophie, wait." She hesitated, watching him remove his own helmet. "Are you...?" He cleared his throat. His beautiful eyes seemed to hold a question he struggled to ask. Had she misread him after all? Her heart gave a little leap.

"Are you sure you're okay?" he asked.

Her heart sank. Dumb, dumb Sophie! she scolded herself even as she smiled and nodded. Jake was just being nice, and you're plotting to throw yourself at him. Wake up, Soph! Mike is the kind of man you need, not this unattainable combination of genius and outlaw.

What the hell was that all about? You were going to ask her out. After what happened today, she's more than ready to jump your bones, man. Don't tell me you're scared.

"Okay, I won't tell you," Jake grumbled at the nagging voice in his head.

"Dean, my boy." The Adviser gave him that weak smile he used to hate. Now he could see the old man was just tired. He even felt a little guilty for all the trouble he'd caused. Maybe hanging around with Mr. Clean was having some kind of effect on him. Wouldn't that be a riot, if Jake helped him become an angel?

"How ya doing, Adviser? Spreading yourself kinda thin with all us apprentice spooks, huh?"

The Adviser's little snort of laughter made Dean feel good. The old boy was loosening up a little more all the time.

"One could say that, yes. But I'm pleased to see that you're doing so well without close supervision. Of course, you *did* bend the rules a little...."

Dean shrugged, secretly hoping he wasn't going to blow his chances in this afterlife game. "Hey, rules are for people who can't think creatively."

The Adviser's eyes pinned him. Dean was glad he wasn't guilty of something serious. "That's one way of looking at the situation."

He felt a wave of panic. "I didn't screw things up for Warren, did I? I mean, it was *Sophie*.... I couldn't let that happen to her." He shrugged. "I guess I finally figured out I have to let her go. What would you have done?"

He'd never seen the Adviser smile like that, as if he really meant it. "Exactly as you did, my boy. I'm very gratified by your progress, Dean. You've turned an important corner. And no, you haven't exerted any negative influence over Jake. He took control and acted on his own once you gave him that, um, *hint* of impending disaster."

Thinking about how Warren had chickened out of asking Sophie out, Dean snorted. "I don't exert any kind of influence over him, man."

"Ah, but you do, my boy. The trouble is, Jake isn't sure what kind of influence you have."

"So?"

"So, you'll have to choose your next step very carefully." He smiled and patted Dean's arm. "Good night, Dean."

"But—"

The Adviser was gone. Dean looked around at the vaguely cloudlike terrain of Jake's sleep. *Next* step? He was still having trouble with his last one. The one Warren had missed.

We're late.

"I got hung up," Jake muttered as he dismounted from the Harley. "It was work I had to do. If I starve to death, you'll have to find someone else to haunt."

Very funny. Third World countries couldn't starve on the money you make. Besides, that stuff wasn't that important. Loosen up, man. Have a few brews, shoot the breeze with the banker types. No sweat.

Jake hung his helmet from the handlebar and shrugged out of his jacket. Hooking it over his shoulder, he followed the sound of reggae music to the cedar-fenced backyard. He didn't really want to spend an evening making small talk, but Craig Gardiner's bank was paying his fee. Given a choice, he'd rather chew tinfoil than shmooze with a yard full of suits and their wives.

He'd wanted to ask Sophie. Craig had suggested several times that he was welcome to bring a date to the barbecue. But Sophie had been so careful not to get close.... So he'd chosen the coward's way out and not risked rejection.

If he could do it over again, he would take the risk. Hell, he would insist she go with him. If he knew how to read women a fraction as well as he could read a computer program—

"Warren! Glad you could make it!" Craig Gardiner's voice cut into his thoughts. "I've got a cold beer with your name on it and a yard full of people who want to meet a famous computer wizard."

Just his luck. He shook Craig's offered hand, then followed him through the back gate to the yard. The scent of grilling steaks reminded him that he hadn't eaten since breakfast. Craig introduced his wife, Lynne, who looked vaguely familiar, then fished a can of beer out of a pail of melting ice. Jake took a swallow of beer and looked around the yard, assessing the crowd. He had to grin. Even in jeans and polo shirts, the men looked like bankers.

From a small group of men and women in the far corner of the flagstone patio, Jake caught the full force of a hostile glare. Mike Riordan. No surprise there. And facing Riordan, a slender, black-haired woman in a pale purple dress that left her back naked from her shoulders to the tempting curve of her waist. *Sophie.* Surprise and confusion, even a little anger, rose at the sight of her. She must have known he'd be there, but she hadn't said anything. Was she there with Riordan?

"There's someone who wants to meet you," Gardiner said before he could act on the impulse to cross the yard and pull Sophie away from the other man.

He'd bide his time. Aware of Sophie's presence as if his nerve endings were scorching, he answered the probing questions of bank president Harold Eames. He'd never felt his attention split like this before. The time dragged, despite his genuine interest in Eames's conversation. Technical and logistical problems of system security couldn't compete with the knowledge that Sophie stood near Riordan.

Suddenly all his senses came awake. He turned and Sophie was beside him, smiling.

"Jake, this is Karen Swan, Donald Swan's wife."

He shook the limp, bony hand of a plastic-looking blond woman dressed in a white strapless top that made her look like a skeleton with chalky skin. She gave him a smile that made him feel like the blue-plate special and she continued to hold his hand.

"I've heard a lot about you, Jake." The way she said that made him wonder what she'd heard.

He nodded, but his attention stayed fixed on Sophie even while he met Karen Swan's heavily made-up eyes. Riordan strolled over and put his hand on Sophie's shoulder. Jake fought the urge to shove his fist in the guy's smug face.

"I've never met a computer wizard before, Jake," Karen said in a husky voice, "but I read somewhere that there are two types. The nerds, who know a hundred and one ways to make love to a woman but don't *know* any, and the hippies, who know the women."

Her smile widened, reminding him of a barracuda. "Tell me, Jake, are you a hippie or a nerd?"

Chapter Nine

Sophie gasped at Karen's audacity.

Granted, she'd love to know the answer, but she certainly wouldn't have asked the question like that. Someone in the group surrounding them snickered, then the others chuckled. Jake looked around, his expression clearly saying the comment had come out of left field. Mike's hand on her shoulder began to feel like a lead weight. She shrugged him off, then met Jake's eyes, expecting him to be red-faced with embarrassment.

To her astonishment, he grinned—a wicked, teasing grin that triggered images of Dean at his most devilish.

Still looking into her eyes, Jake said, "I'd say I'm a little of both."

The others laughed. Someone clapped Jake's shoulder in male appreciation of his retort.

"Sophie, you lucky girl," Karen muttered, her tone grudging.

Sophie felt her eyes widen at Karen's implication. Her cheeks stung with sudden heat. Jake's grin stayed steady. Sophie couldn't decide whether to laugh or hit him.

Lynne's voice rang out, calling everyone to dinner, breaking the tension. The people around them wandered toward the tables set up around the yard. Mike hovered over her, making her feel claustrophobic. He was clearly intent on not letting her have a moment alone with Jake. She knew she should be flattered at his attentions, but it was impossible to think romantically about another man when Jake filled her consciousness.

"Come on, Sophie. Craig and Lynne are holding a place for us at their table," Mike murmured. He cupped her elbow.

His presumptuousness irritated her, especially after she'd made it clear earlier, when he'd offered to drive her to the barbecue, that she wasn't his date. "I'm sure there's room at the table for Jake, too." She moved her elbow out of Mike's grasp. "After all, he's Craig's guest of honor."

Mike's lips thinned and his eyes narrowed, but he didn't say a word. Lynne came to lead Jake to their table, casting a puzzled glance back at Sophie. Sophie shrugged. Lynne shook her head. Well, Sophie thought as she took the seat Craig pulled out for her, it looks like everyone thinks Jake is wrong for me.

Over dinner, Jake only spoke in answer to direct questions, yet he seemed to be the center of everyone's attention. She stole glances at him as he talked earnestly, using technical terms that baffled her but had his listeners nodding. Mike, seated across from her, between managers of two other bank branches, glowered whenever he looked at Jake beside her.

Not that Mike had a right to be jealous, Sophie mused, but he had nothing to worry about. After teasingly giving the impression that they were lovers, Jake had barely glanced at her.

"Sophie, remember what happened at the shoe store near my boutique?" Lynne startled her out of her thoughts. She looked at her friend blankly and waited for Lynne to continue.

"Something awful happened to their computer. They lost all their records, and it took some consultant about two weeks and a fat fee to get them back. I thought once those electronic dots, or blips, or whatever they are, were gone, they were gone."

Jake grinned and shook his head. "Sometimes. But there are some pretty sophisticated utilities that can retrieve data if you know what you're doing. I've worked on cases that took six weeks, and even then, some data was lost. But that was industrial sabotage, so the lossage was deliberate."

"Is it true that all computers die eventually?" Lynne asked. "I'd hate to have the one in my store go belly-up just when I'm finally getting the hang of using it."

"Hard drives don't last forever," Jake said, "but if you back everything up every day, you shouldn't lose too much."

Lynne wrinkled her nose. "That's such a pain. When the day is over and I lock the door, I want to go home and soak in a hot tub, not feed disks into the computer."

"If you'd like, I can program your computer to automatically back up all new data after closing, then turn itself off. All you have to do is put in a floppy disk and run the program. You can also send the data to your printer, if you want a hard copy."

"Can you really do that?" Lynne leaned forward, her beautiful face animated. Mike made a disparaging noise.

"Sure. Or you can get a tape backup. They're not too expensive when you compare them to the fees consultants charge to retrieve data."

Then he turned his piercing gaze to Sophie. "You should have an automatic backup like that on your system. Maybe then you could figure out why some days the computer, uh, sulks?" His gentle teasing made her smile.

"Don't you have some sort of maintenance contract on your system?" Mike asked Sophie. She nodded, thinking of how unreliable Dennis had been. Mike smiled. "You know what they say about too many cooks. Besides, your system is small potatoes for a wizard like Warren here. Can you imagine what he'd charge you for customized software?"

Somehow, as innocent as Mike looked and sounded, Sophie didn't think he was referring to money. She decided to take some of the wind out of his sails.

"Actually, I'd be interested in doing something like that for my system," she told Jake. As she spoke, she recognized the wisdom of that decision, regardless of her motive for making it. "Whatever is bothering the poor thing is too complicated for Rick to figure out. I guess it needs either a hacker or a shrink."

The rest of the group crowded around their table laughed at her feeble joke. Then someone mentioned an article about animal psychiatrists and, to Sophie's relief, the conversation got very silly very quickly. Laughter from the other tables drifted toward them, as well. When Lynne served coffee and dessert, Craig switched the music from lively to romantic, altering the mood as the sun set and the party lights around the yard glowed like multicolored moons.

Without warning, Jake stood. He took her hand and drew her to her feet in front of him. Startled, she gazed up at him. His eyes looked as dark as the night sky. His expression was the same as it was the night he'd kissed her—before he apologized for it. His hand closed warmly around hers.

"Dance," he said simply, the way Dean used to do so many years ago. Not an invitation. Not a question. A statement of fact.

But Jake wasn't Dean. And right now, she was very, very aware of who he was and how she felt about him. If only Jake could feel the same way about her....

She nodded and let him lead her into the middle of the stone patio. The song that was playing was about a male wallflower who wonders what the beautiful girl dancing with him sees in him. The first verse was almost over. Jake slipped his arm around her waist, hesitated for a brief moment, then began move to the slow, steady backbeat. Sophie closed her eyes and followed as if they'd been dancing together for a lifetime.

His subtle scent filled her head like the sweetest drug. The warm pressure of his hand on her bare back invited her to arch into him. Did she dare to give in to that impulse? Where could it lead, except to a dead-end affair? Sex wasn't worth the heartbreak of watching Jake walk away from her in a couple of weeks, when his contract with the banks was fulfilled.

But love... What was love worth?

Jake bent over her and gathered her a little closer. Her breasts brushed his hard chest. His breath rushed warmly past her ear, stirring her hair, stirring her senses. She slid her left hand a little farther around the back of his neck, daring to touch the warm skin beneath the long, silky hair. Jake's warm fingers moved softly over her bare back. She caught her breath at the electricity his light touch generated.

The singer was wondering if what he felt was love, why did it scare him? She could tell him why, she thought. Love was scary because it left you vulnerable. It made you take chances you knew you shouldn't take. It made colors brighter and kisses sweeter...and pain sharper.

The song was almost over. Without warning, Jake gathered her close and whirled her around. As the last notes faded into the next song, he lowered her over his left arm in a deep, sweeping dip, the way Dean used to do. And, just the way Dean used to do, he held her there, gazing down into her eyes, for a few extra seconds.

When he swung her upright again, Sophie stared deeply into the brilliant intensity of his eyes. Before she could do more than return his sudden, infectious grin, Mike appeared at her side. He put his hand on her shoulder and turned her away from Jake, who continued to rest his hand at her waist.

"My turn, Warren," he said softly.

"That's Sophie's decision, Riordan," Jake said, even more softly.

He sounded rather dangerous, like a guard dog growling low in its throat. It was sweet of him to think he had to protect her from Mike, but even that was a patronizing gesture. The simplest solution, the one that might drive the point home to both of them, was to refuse to dance with either of them.

"She'll dance with me," Mike insisted before she could open her mouth to speak for herself. "She doesn't need some fly-by-night Romeo to take advantage of her good nature."

That did it! Who did Mike think he was, to make assumptions about her vulnerability and naiveté, let alone with whom she wanted—or needed—to dance? Just because there was a sliver of wisdom in what he was saying... But it wasn't his place to tell her what to think or do, and she wasn't going to stand here like some lawn ornament and let him—

She didn't hear what Mike said next, or what Jake replied. But suddenly she was being moved aside and Mike had his fist wrapped in Jake's shirtfront. She stepped toward them, intending to pull them apart, but the expression on Mike's face stopped her. His normally handsome face was frighteningly contorted in anger.

Her scolding words stuck in her throat and her heart began to race.

Jake! Oh, God, Jake was standing there and Mike had been on his university wrestling team and Jake was just a nice computer wizard, a nerd by his own admission, and Mike was going to hurt him!

"Go ahead," Jake said quietly.

Sophie gasped. He couldn't be so reckless! Dean, yes. He'd taken perverse pleasure in beating odds like this. But studious, absentminded Jake—

"Make it your best shot," he practically growled, "because you'll only get one."

Sophie held her breath, certain that Mike would call his bluff. Then she remembered the almost superhuman strength Jake had shown when he'd pushed the stalled car out of the path of the speeding truck. Was she worried over nothing?

She risked a glance around, hoping some of the other men would be able to intervene before Jake got hurt. No one else seemed aware of what was happening in the middle of the patio. Should she call for help, or might that distract Jake and give Mike an opportunity to slug him? Her heart pounded against her ribs. Oh, Lord, she was standing there practically wringing her hands, and—

Then Mike snarled something ugly and released Jake's shirt. "I'm warning you, Warren. Sophie's too good for you. I won't let you use her and dump her."

Jake didn't speak, didn't move. Mike glared at him for another long moment, then turned and stalked away. He went inside the house, taking exaggerated care not to let the screen door slam behind him. Sophie let her breath escape slowly.

Jake's broad shoulders relaxed slightly. She reached out to touch his arm and saw that her hand was shaking. Before she could draw it back, Jake turned his head. He caught her fingers in his and grinned.

"Whew! Dirty Harry, move over, huh?" he murmured. He looked very pleased with himself.

Sophie gaped at him. If she weren't such a pacifist, she'd take a swing at him herself!

Nice goin', Warren. Took the words right out of my mouth.

Jake registered Dean's approval, but at the moment, he didn't give a damn. His elation at having dealt successfully with Riordan on his own terms was fading at the fury crackling in Sophie's eyes. With an impatient little sound, she pulled her fingers out of his grasp.

What was she angry about? He'd defused an unpleasant situation before it erupted into something really ugly. Riordan was well and truly ticked off, but no one was bleeding. And he'd defended her right to choose her dance partners. So what was her problem?

Women! Go figure 'em, huh?

"Of all the stupid macho things to do!" Sophie hissed. He felt his jaw drop.

Uh-oh! you're on your own, pal. I'm outta here.

Somehow he wasn't surprised by Wilde's sudden retreat.

"If you'd given me a chance to tell Mike I was perfectly capable of deciding who I want to dance with, you wouldn't have risked getting your face broken. Mike has a room full of trophies and medals for varsity wrestling."

He couldn't believe she was taking Riordan's side! "But—"

"Do you have any idea," she interrupted, her voice quietly intense, her eyes flashing, "how embarrassing it is to have two supposedly intelligent, grown men practically brawling over who I can dance with? This is Connecticut, for pity's sake! Not the wild West!"

"But—"

"At least no one noticed! Now, if you'll excuse me. . . ."

She brushed past him, her scent wafting up to him as she moved. Her shoulders were squared, her chin up. In a daze, he watched the way her skirt floated around her slender, very rapidly moving legs. Her dark hair swung with each step. It had felt like silk against his arm when they were dancing. Her bare back had felt like warm satin under his hand. Holding her in his arms, dancing with her, had felt like heaven.

He'd give her a few minutes to simmer down, then apologize. Having her angry with him felt like hell.

He felt even worse when he discovered that she had left the party immediately, after telling Lynne she had a headache. He wanted to leave, to follow her, but someone stopped him with a question about time bombs in computer systems. One question led to another, thwarting his escape.

Finally he managed to get away. Disappointment stabbed at him when he saw from the street that Sophie's apartment was dark. He wanted to talk to her now, to apologize for whatever she thought he'd done wrong, and explain why. By tomorrow, it would just sound lame. But if he woke her, she might be even more angry.

Coasting the bike up the driveway, he caught a glimpse of flickering blue light reflected in her living room window. She was awake. He'd take his chances, although he couldn't say why it was so important. It just was.

You still don't get it, do you?

Damn Wilde! "Get what?" He didn't get a lot of things. Being a genius wasn't always all it was cracked up to be. He and the rest of the world were seldom on the same wavelength.

The reason Sophie was so ticked off at you, man. She wasn't taking Riordan's side. She was scared to death you'd get killed or maimed. She cares, *pal. She* cares.

Sophie cared? About him? Jake parked the bike and locked it, frowning. That was good news, and bad news. He wanted her to care. He just wasn't sure what he was going to do about it.

As tears slid down the actress's cheeks, Sophie sniffed and reached for another tissue. Why was she watching this stupid, soppy movie? She should be watching something energizing, not something that was guaranteed to push every emotional button repeatedly. Maybe it was just safer to feel for someone else, to cry for someone else, than to face her own emotions.

A sip of Baileys Irish Cream on ice cooled her throat, but it did nothing to soothe her thoughts. Damn Mike! Damn Jake! And damn Dean, for that matter! What was she supposed to think about them? Mike's willingness to fight over her made her feel guilty for not being in love with him. But if she'd learned anything in thirty years, it was that love had its own rhyme and reasons.

And the scene between Mike and Jake tonight had crystallized her realization that she did, indeed, love Jake. Not the way she'd loved Dean, with stars in her eyes, too immature to know what love really meant. But with a quiet, deep resonance that said this was real, this could last.

And why not? Jake was a very lovable man. Her heart couldn't stop loving him just because he didn't love her, and was going to disappear from her life.

Absorbed in her thoughts, Sophie gave a startled yelp at the knock on her front door. Heart pounding, she pressed the pause button on the remote control and sidled toward the door. Through the peephole, she saw the back of Jake's tousled head. He turned and scowled at the door, looking determined and sexy despite the distortion of the lens in the door.

She clutched the lapels of her thin robe together at her throat and unlocked the dead bolt. Opening the door a few inches, she gazed up at him. The wistful expression in his beautiful eyes melted her heart.

"I saw your light," he said softly. "I wanted to apologize."

She shook her head. "No. I was wrong." She kept her voice low, too, unwilling to waken Mrs. Mandel. "I overreacted. I guess I was scared."

He offered her a crooked grin. "For me, or for Riordan?"

That made her smile. "In retrospect, for Mike, I think."

His grin faded. "Oh. Well..." He shrugged and half turned away.

He'd misunderstood.

"I mean, any man who can push cars around can probably do serious bodily damage to a mere mortal, even a champion varsity wrestler."

Jake's grin lit his eyes and melted her heart. She opened the door wider. "Would you like to come in? I'm watching a silly, sentimental movie."

He stepped forward, filling the doorway, then looked her over. "Are you sure?"

She followed his glance down the front of her silky lilac kimono with a wedge of gray lace from her teddy peeking from the V of the robe. She looked more ready for bed than for company. Heat rushed to her face. "I...I should change into something more decent."

"You look pretty decent to me."

Her face grew even warmer. Before she could think of a reply, the television blared. The pause control on the VCR had run out of time. Tightening the slippery belt of her robe, she hurried to the couch and turned down the volume.

"Would you like some Baileys?"

He nodded. "Thanks."

"I'll get you a glass. Ice?"

He nodded again. She hurried into the dining room to take another crystal wineglass from the built-in china closet. When she came back into the living room, glass in one hand, dish of ice in the other, Jake sat in the middle of the couch, dominating the space, leaving her very little room on either side. After setting the glass and bowl down in front of him, she gestured for him to help himself. Feeling nervous and restless, she turned away briefly to tighten the belt of her robe again. When she turned back, she discovered that he'd topped up her glass.

"I haven't seen this one yet. How far into it are you?"

"Not far. I can rewind it."

"If you don't mind."

She squeezed herself against the corner of the couch and drew her knees up beside her. Jake held her glass out to her and smiled. She smiled over the rim, nervous about what might happen between them that night—and petrified that it might not. Then she recalled the incredibly sensuous love scene with the clay and the potter's wheel. . . . Would Jake think she rewound the tape for that scene? Would he think she was hinting? *Was* she hinting?

When that scene unfolded, Jake reached over and captured her hand. His thumb stroked softly over her palm, creating a pool of electricity in the center of her hand. It felt natural, when the male lead was murdered, for Jake to slide his arm comfortingly around her shoulders. When the ghost tried to convince the disbelieving, phony medium that he had to contact his girlfriend to warn her about the danger she was in, Jake's laughter vibrated through her where her side pressed against his.

Sitting close to Jake, snuggled in his light embrace, felt so right, almost familiar in its rightness. It could only be a matter of time, she thought, until he forgot about the movie and bent to kiss her. But when the ghost tried desperately to move objects, exhausting his strength, Jake stiffened. And when the dead hero, using the medium's body, danced slowly one last time with his lover, Jake swore under his breath. At the end of the film, he pulled away enough to gaze into her eyes, a strange light in his.

"That's it?" he demanded as she pressed the rewind button. "After all that, the ghost just goes *pfft?*"

His indignation puzzled her. "Well, I think we're meant to believe he goes to heaven. He accomplished what he set out to do, so he doesn't have to be a ghost anymore." An unreadable series of expressions crossed Jake's face. "I mean, that's what the theory is, about why ghosts haunt people or places. That they have unfinished business that won't let them rest."

He snorted, making her feel a little foolish. "I'm a scientist, Sophie. Ghost theories are way out of my realm of understanding." He sounded apologetic, as if she expected him to believe in ghosts.

She smiled and took a last sip of her drink. "I think ghosts are a way people can make sense of things they otherwise can't explain. And I think it reassures people to think they can take care of something important even when they're no longer alive. I think that's why movies like this are so popular. People need hope."

He frowned in thought. "Maybe." He took the remote control from her hand, turning off the raucous television program while the VCR continued to rewind. "What if there really are ghosts, spirits who come back to finish something? Or spirits who won't let go of someone they knew when they were alive?"

His intensity surprised her. "Hey, you're the scientist, remember?"

She loved that crooked grin. Without thinking about consequences, she reached up and touched his lips with her forefinger. His eyes seemed to darken. He caught her wrist in gentle fingers and she couldn't look away.

Her name came out on a sigh, whispering warmly over her fingers. He pressed soft kisses into her palm, then drew her hand to rest against his smooth cheek. Her lids grew heavy, shuttering her from the intensity of his direct gaze. She felt him touch her hair, felt him stroke her cheek with one gentle fingertip. He drew patterns on her neck, sensitizing her skin, making her eager for more of his tantalizing touch.

His first kiss came softly, tentatively. She held her breath, held herself perfectly still, afraid to discover she was imagining this. But no, Jake was real. His kisses were real. He gathered her close to his chest and kissed her with increasing passion, like the building of a storm.

Sophie clung to him and parted her lips at the first touch of his tongue. He tasted sweet from the drink, sweet yet dark, male, exciting. He probed slowly, lingering, giving her time to savor the taste of him, and the hot, silky slide of his tongue on hers. Each gentle thrust sent sparks of desire flaring through her, threatening to consume her, promising to renew her.

Jake eased back against the couch, drawing Sophie down over him. Her robe parted when she twined her legs with his. There was something deliciously erotic about the feel of his jeans against her bare legs. One muscular thigh pressed upward between hers. She let herself sink down onto his torso, her breasts pushing against his chest. Against her middle, she felt him hard and powerfully aroused through his jeans.

She arched into him, telling him without words that she wanted him. Their kisses smothered his low moan. His hands swept down her sides, pushing aside the flimsy robe to rest on her bottom, holding, caressing, as his hips shifted upward to meet hers. His fingers slid under the edge of her teddy, seeking yet teasing. Her body responded, warm, pulsing, melting.

A few more inches and he would find the heart of her desire. A simple movement and he could undo the snaps of her teddy and free her. One touch and he would know how ready she was for him. Oh, how she ached for his touch!

Impatiently, boldly, she tugged at his shirt. She uncovered a patch of warm, smooth muscle at his side and struggled to reach farther inside. His sharp intake of breath fueled her need.

"Oh, Sophie! That feels so good!" he whispered hoarsely as she stroked his side with her fingertips.

His strong hand cupped her bottom, so close...so close....

"Jake!" she breathed. "Oh, Jake! Make love to me!"

Chapter Ten

Jake's low moan vibrated through her. With one restless hand, she caressed the warm, bare skin under his shirt. With the other, she sought his thigh and kneaded the hard muscle under the heavy denim. His fingers dug into the flesh of her hips and bottom, pressing her harder against his erection.

She wanted to be free of the barriers of clothing, free to feel him sink deeply into her waiting body, the way he had already entered her heart. As she returned for more of his sensuous kisses, she eased her hips away and slid her wandering hand between their bodies. Even through his jeans, he felt hot and heavy under her palm. She traced his shape with bold fingers, smiling into his kiss when he arched into her touch.

"Jake, touch me, too," she murmured, feeling drunk on his kisses, losing her normal inhibitions in the heat of her desire. "Make love to me."

She gave herself up to the sweet intoxication of his kisses but the hunger inside her burned for more. She needed the physical consummation of the emotions overflowing her heart.

"Sophie, no!" he gasped when she found the snap of his jeans. She felt as if she'd been burned and jerked her hand away.

"Sophie, I'm sorry. I . . . I can't make love to you." With gentle strength, he eased her away from him and sat up, his head in his hands.

She bit back the impulse to argue that he sure felt like he could. Instead, she waited for him to explain, trying to ignore the negative voice in her head that posed a dozen horrible reasons why Jake had stopped their lovemaking when he was still so obviously aroused. When she was so obviously ready and willing.

He was silent for several agonizingly long minutes.

Finally she couldn't stand waiting. "Jake? Can't you tell me why? I think you owe me that. Are you married? Or living with someone in California?" She twisted her fingers together, needing the truth yet afraid of what he might answer.

He snorted, but didn't look at her. "Hardly."

"Then . . . are you . . . ?" Her face grew hot. "Are you . . . ill?"

That got his attention. He looked at her, his eyes still dark as midnight, anger flashing like lightning. "Hell, no!"

He shook his head, then caught her hand in his. Gently he drew her hand up to his face and touched his lips to her knuckles. She gazed into his eyes, blinking away the tears in her own.

"Sophie, Riordan was right. You deserve better than me. I got greedy, but it isn't right. *I'm* not right. Let's . . ." He swallowed. "Let's just be friends. I'm almost finished with my work here, so I'll be out of your life soon enough."

The bottom dropped out of her world.

What the hell are you doing here?

"I live here."

Jake grabbed the towel from the hook and stepped out of the shower. His skin felt like ice, but underneath, he still simmered with arousal.

Yeah, but why are you taking a cold shower when you should be upstairs taking a warm woman?

Determined to ignore Wilde's taunting, he knotted the towel around his waist and started down the hall. Then he stopped short and scowled with suspicion. "Don't you know?"

If I knew, I wouldn't be asking, would I?

Jake yanked open the drawer where he'd stuffed his clean underwear. "You mean, you weren't there, spying on me?"

Hey, the man's a genius.

"Great. Sarcasm from a ghost—or whatever the hell you are."

Call me your guardian angel. Sounds better. But the question is what you *are... still. When I left, Sophie was begging you to make love to her. How could you screw that up? Pardon the pun.* Wilde had the bad taste to snicker.

He pulled a T-shirt over his head. "I can't make *love* to her. I wouldn't know what love is if it bit me. And Sophie deserves to be loved, not used."

Sit down, Warren. We have to talk.

"Forget it. I've got work to do. Go haunt at somebody else."

"Adviser? Got a minute?"

The Adviser appeared out of the fog of Jake's sleep, frowning at the black notebook he was forever writing notes in. Dean caught him just before they collided. The old guy was getting more and more absentminded these days.

"Oh! Dean, my boy. I thought I heard you calling. Do you have a problem?"

Suddenly he didn't know what to do with the nervous energy that pulsated through him. He started to pace. Jake turned over and muttered in his sleep.

"Well, sort of a problem. Sort of a question." He felt his face burn. Jeez, you'd think an angel—even an apprentice one—would be beyond blushing like a girl at her first dance! "I need to ask you about something."

"About what?"

His face got even hotter. "About love," he managed to choke out.

The Adviser's smile made him grit his teeth. He needed the answer more than he needed to get off some smart-ass comment.

"Hi, Sophie. Got a minute to spare for a contrite macho jerk?" Mike's voice broke into her thoughts, startling her badly. "Sorry. I guess I'm batting zero."

With one hand on her chest, as if to calm her heart, she looked up from the bill of lading she'd been studying without seeing for some time. Even knowing it was Mike, not Jake, she felt a stab of disappointment at the sight of his handsome face smiling ruefully from the doorway to her office.

She forced an answering smile. "Hi, Mike. Come on in."

He shut the door behind him. "Sophie, I want to apologize for being such an overbearing jerk Friday night. I still care for you, Soph. I guess I'm a sore loser."

Why couldn't she care for this man? Why was she sitting in her office on Sunday night hoping—*praying*—that Jake would come by or call?

"You're forgiven, Mike, but please don't think of me as a prize you can win or lose."

He spread his hands in a gesture of surrender. "I know, I know. Even us banker types have cave memories. I saw Warren acting like you belonged to him, and I lost it. Honestly, Soph, I understand you're the one who makes the final decision. I just wish it had been me. I don't want to see you get hurt."

"Mike, you're very sweet. But I don't belong to Jake, either. And I won't be getting hurt."

And her siblings said she couldn't lie with a straight face? She belonged to Jake, heart and soul, and because of that, she knew darn well she was going to get hurt.

"Does that mean you and Warren aren't...?"

"We're friends, the way you and I are friends." She shrugged, trying to appear casual, hoping Mike would believe this latest lie. "That's all."

He grinned and his shoulders relaxed slightly. "Well, friend to friend, how about packing up and going for a pizza or a burger before they roll the streets up?"

She wanted to be alone, here in her office, or at her apartment, in case Jake called or... "Well, I..."

"Come on, Soph. It's five minutes before closing, and there's no one out there. I promise to have you home in time to get a good night's sleep, so you can spend the morning logging in the hundreds of tapes rented over the weekend. Okay?"

His teasing made her smile. "Okay. Just let me tell Larry I'm leaving, so he'll have to lock up."

Mike waited outside, pacing in the empty parking lot while she made sure Larry knew all the steps to follow for locking up. It was the first time she'd left the young part-timer to close the store on his own. But as Mike had pointed out, the store was quiet and there wasn't much to do except turn off the lights and the computer and switch on the security lights and the alarm. Larry assured her he could do it all without help.

After spending the afternoon and evening in the air-conditioned store, Sophie welcomed the warm, muggy night that wrapped around her. Of course, she would have preferred to be leaving with Jake, having his arms around her in the sultry night air, but after last night's fiasco, she didn't expect Jake to get within embracing distance. His rejection had hurt so much. She still felt like a zombie.

She started her car and watched Mike climb into his BMW. He followed her home so she could leave her car, instead of having to pick it up later. His thoughtfulness touched her. In spite of her rejection of him as a lover, he was still so attentive and sweet. Why couldn't she feel more for Mike than friendly fondness?

Jake's Harley wasn't in the parking area behind the house. His apartment was dark, except for the porch light over the back door. Gnawing her lower lip, she wondered where he could have gone for the weekend. Anywhere, she supposed, to get away from her after she'd embarrassed them both by throwing herself at him.

True to his word, Mike brought her home before eleven, which probably had something to do with her constant yawning. He walked her to her door, his hands in his pockets, and gave her the briefest of friendly kisses on her cheek when she said good-night. Sophie went into her apartment still wondering where Jake was. Somehow, despite the thoughts colliding inside her head, she fell asleep almost instantly after she lay down.

The trilling of the phone by her bed woke her. Blinking, she reached for the receiver and peered at the clock radio. It was ten o'clock on Monday morning. She hadn't turned on her alarm last night. Or else she'd slept through fifty-nine minutes of rock music. Either way, she'd missed opening the store. She'd never done that before.

Her head felt thick and woolly, and she had trouble getting her voice to work well enough to answer the phone.

"Ms. Quinn? Sergeant Benoit, West Hartford Police."

She had expected to hear Rick's voice, teasing her for being late. A chill of dread ran through her, clearing her head. She sat up and hugged herself. "Yes?"

"I'm afraid there was another break-in at your store last night, ma'am. Does a Mr. Larry Doan work for you?"

"Larry?" She fought down a wave of panic and nausea. "Yes, of course. He closed the store last night. Did anything happen to him?"

"He was struck on the head, then tied up behind the front counter. He was hurt pretty badly. It seems he managed to crawl toward the door during the night. A customer discovered him this morning. He's on his way to Hartford Hospital. You'll be able to get a report on his condition in a few hours."

"Oh my God! Poor Larry! It's my fault. I left him alone to lock up. I shouldn't have gone. I should have stayed there."

"Hard to say, ma'am. You might be the one in the hospital, then."

She understood he was trying to calm her down, but that wasn't the important point. "It's my store, Sergeant. Larry shouldn't have been in the position of having to defend it. What about the alarm system? Why didn't that go off?"

"The alarm was never set but the closed-circuit videotape may tell us something. It's possible that Mr. Doan let his attacker in just before closing, or that the perpetrator was hiding somewhere in the store, waiting. We need you to come to the store and report any losses or damage. A Mr. Rick Zarillo is here. He says he works for you, but, ah, Mr. Zarillo is under suspicion of—"

"No, he isn't, Sergeant," she snapped. "Not in my book. I'll be there in twenty minutes."

* * *

"Mr. Warren?" The soft voice seemed to come from far away. "Mr. Warren, there's a phone call for you." He glanced away from the monitor just long enough to see the young trainee receptionist smile shyly. "I knew you were in here," she added, "so I figured you probably didn't hear the intercom buzzer."

"Thanks, uh, Noreen, right?"

Her smile widened. "Yes. Line twelve."

He nodded and reached for the phone. Noreen hesitated by his desk, then picked up his empty coffee cup and the wrappers from his sandwiches. Her face turned pink when he looked at her, and she scurried out of the small office he'd been assigned by the bank.

"Warren."

"It's me—Rick. What do you think about what happened at the store last night?"

He scowled. "What happened?"

"Didn't you talk to Sophie today?"

He beat a slow rhythm on his thigh with his fist. "I, uh, haven't seen Sophie for a couple of days. What happened?"

As Rick described the break-in and the attack on Larry, Jake's fist clenched tighter. If anything had happened to Sophie because he was playing cat and mouse...

"Larry's still unconscious," Rick told him. "The cops are hoping to get a positive ID when he comes to. *If* he really saw the guy *and* can remember. Getting bonked like that can scramble your coconut pretty bad."

Tell him something he didn't know. "But Sophie's okay?"

"She's spitting mad. If she ever gets her hands on the perp, he's a chew toy."

Jake bit back a grin. The memory of Noreen standing by his desk prompted him to be cautious. "Meet me in fifteen minutes at the ice-cream shop in the Center. I don't want to talk about this over the phone."

He saved his work, told a startled Noreen he was going out for an hour and went to retrieve the Harley from the employee parking lot. A few minutes later, he halted in a parking space on South Main Street, across from the remnants of the old village green. The ice-cream parlor was almost empty. Rick was already at a booth toward the back, idly toying with a long-handled sundae spoon.

Jake ordered a root beer float. A little sugar surge might come in handy. "Okay. What was missing?" he asked as soon as the waitress left the table.

"Some tapes, a little petty cash. I couldn't tell about the computer. The cops wouldn't let me breathe on anything that might be a clue. Don't want me to smudge usable prints, especially if they're mine."

Jake frowned. "Anything on the closed-circuit video?"

Rick shook his head. "You think the cops are going to tell me about that? They're checking my alibi about being with my girl, but they're hoping I'm going to confess. It'll save them a lot of work."

"I can save them a lot of work. It had to be this Dennis, the guy who set up the system. He has to figure that by now I'm breathing down his neck pretty hard through the banks' computers."

"Right. You and I know that. And you've got evidence from the banks and the store. But are the cops going to swallow that theory when the modem isn't even there anymore? Because I'll bet dollars to doughnuts that it isn't."

Jake grunted. "I know. There's more than enough proof of *what* was going on, but no way to connect it with *who* was doing it."

"See that you keep your proof in a safe place, Warren. If Mike Riordan hadn't shown up just before closing to take Sophie to dinner, she'd be the one in the hospital. Or worse.

Whoever hit Larry didn't give him a love tap. He meant to take him out.''

Jake didn't think he'd ever be grateful for anything Riordan did that involved Sophie. The concept of bittersweet was taking on a whole new meaning.

At that moment, the waitress arrived with Rick's marshmallow sundae and Jake's float. For a few minutes, they ate in silence. Jake wrestled with the urge to ask Rick how Sophie really was, aside from being upset over the break-in. Had she'd mentioned him at all? But he didn't want to look like a fool.

''Rick, stay close to Sophie. I, uh, I can't be with her as much as I'd like. I've got this bank job to finish, and something else came along. Until they catch this guy, I don't think she should be alone.''

Rick regarded him with narrowed eyes. ''Exactly what I was thinking. But if I do a flypaper act with Sophie, she'll know something's up.'' He pointed the sticky spoon. ''You can get away with it better than I can. I've seen her look at you, Warren. She doesn't look at me that way. I'm just a friend.''

He wouldn't let himself believe what Rick was implying. Sophie had agreed to keeping their relationship strictly friendly so fast, he'd wondered if he'd imagined her asking him to make love to her.

''That's all she needs. A friend.''

Rick's expression altered. Now he looked smugly amused. ''Aren't you supposed to be a genius?''

Damn, he hated when people said that! It made him think he was missing something.

By a mile.

Sophie left Larry's parents huddled together in the waiting room of the intensive-care unit. After wiping away a stray tear, she slid a quarter into a pay phone and called the store. Rick answered.

"It's me. Busy?"

"Nah. It's always quiet in the middle of the day. How's Larry?"

"Still unconscious. The doctors don't seem to know what to say. I guess it's hard to predict when or if he'll come to. They did warn Sergeant Benoit that Larry might not remember anything about what happened. At least we still have the security-camera tape. Did the police say anything to you about what they saw on the tape?"

Rick swore mildly, under his breath. "The camera wasn't working, Sophie. The cops already gave me the third degree about it. It wasn't recording that night. Maybe the guy who broke in disabled it. They aren't sure yet, and they aren't taking Jennifer's word that I was with her, 'cause we were alone together. So unless Larry wakes up and remembers or the cops find proof the modem was there, I'm the prime suspect."

She swore more emphatically than Rick had. "And I'm the Queen of Sheba."

Rick's snort of laughter almost made her smile. "Hey, I almost forgot. You've got a message. The lady said it was urgent. Annie something. Want her number?"

The only Annie she could think of was Jake's friend. Her heart did a clumsy flip. Had something happened to Jake while she was running around worrying about Larry and her store?

She barely said goodbye to Rick after writing Annie's phone number on the palm of her hand. Fumbling, she fed another quarter into the pay phone and pushed the numbers. Her heart pounded. Annie's phone rang four, five, six times. Sophie's arm seemed to weigh a ton as she moved slowly to hang up the receiver. A faint click made her pause.

"Hello? Hello?"

In relief at getting an answer, Sophie leaned on the wall beside the phone. "Annie? Hi. It's Sophie Quinn."

"Oh, Sophie! I'm so glad you called. It's about Jake. I'm really worried about him. I think he's going to do something really foolish."

"Annie, Jake is the least likely man I know to do something foolish. Take a deep breath and tell me what's going on."

"I'm sorry, Sophie. I guess I sound a little hysterical. I feel like it's my fault, but I can't do anything to stop him because Robert is sick and Les is away at a conference."

Her heart plummeted. "Stop him doing what, Annie?"

"Swimming. Alone. I just have this feeling he's going to try to swim alone."

Annie's shrill tone struck a responsive chord in Sophie. She straightened abruptly, yanking on the short phone cord, almost pulling the receiver from her hand. "*What?* Where?"

"At some bank president's house. I think that's what Jake said. Jake stayed at our place Saturday, and we were talking about his accident, and I reminded him that he should think about trying to swim again. I didn't even remember saying it until he called from this guy's house to tell me there was an indoor pool. The guy and his family went off somewhere and told Jake he could have the use of the house for a couple of days in exchange for some computer work."

"Did Jake give you a name?" As if she knew all the Connecticut bank presidents by name!

"James? Robert was crying and I couldn't hear Jake clearly."

"What about an address."

"I don't have one. Jake wouldn't even leave the phone number. He said it was unlisted, so it wasn't right to give it out. I'm sorry, Sophie. You must think I'm totally ditsy, but with Robert sick, I'm scraping by on almost no sleep."

"I understand, Annie. Just think for a minute if there's anything else you remember."

Annie sighed into the phone. After a long silence, she said, "I think he said this Mr. James or Aimes or whatever lives in Simsbury."

Eames! She'd met the bank president and his wife at Craig and Lynne's barbecue. He'd spent a lot of time talking with Jake.

"Annie, I know who it is. I think I can find out where he lives, or at least get a phone number."

And then what? Jake wouldn't want her nosing around. Her feminine instincts told her that his line about being friends was just that: a line. She'd offered herself to him, freely, with no strings, and for whatever reasons he wouldn't explain, he'd rejected her. The fact that Jake had disappeared early Saturday morning, so he wouldn't have to see her around Mrs. Mandel's house, spoke volumes.

Still, Annie was worried. Sophie honestly believed Jake was totally sensible and practical, but on the other hand, hadn't he told her himself that he could get obsessed beyond reasonable limits? What if he decided to swim until he was exhausted, just to prove he could? If Annie, who knew Jake so well, was concerned, maybe there was reason for Sophie to be, also.

"If I can locate him, do you want me to call you back so you can check on him?"

"I can't go anywhere, Sophie. Robert's running a fever, and I'm beat. I understand you and Jake had some sort of...whatever. He wouldn't admit it, but I figured that's why he was hiding out at our place. But if you care for him at all... Please, Sophie? I'm worried sick that he'll jump in that pool and there won't be anyone there this time, if he..."

Sophie heard the tears—of panic or exhaustion, she didn't know—in Annie's voice. Her own heart was thumping uncomfortably. The cold weight of fear settled in her stomach. She cared for Jake more than she knew was wise, but that didn't mean she wanted to risk making fools of both of them if Annie was overreacting.

But what if Annie were right?

Annie was right. He had to get back to swimming, the sooner, the better.

Easier said than done, huh?

"Who asked you?"

Hey! We're in this together.

He turned on his heel and paced in the opposite direction, away from the glass wall between the sunken family room and the indoor pool. He didn't have to look to see the way the sunlight sparkled on the tiny ripples made by the circulating pump. He didn't need to stick his toes in to know that the water temperature was exactly what he liked. The monitoring software he'd been customizing, for Eames's state-of-the-art amusements, reported and adjusted the condition of the pool hourly.

Two days alone in the sprawling house, all too aware of the pool, was worse than being haunted.

Well, thanks for that.

"Take a number, Wilde. I've got more important things to worry about than hurting your feelings."

Yeah? Like hurting Sophie's feelings?

Feeling as if he'd taken a punch to the gut, he sat on the carpeted stair into the family room. "Yeah. Like hurting Sophie's feelings. Now or later, I'm going to hurt her if I let her think I can love her." He rested his elbows on his knees and buried his face in his hands.

You're chicken.

His head jerked up. "Chicken! Where do you get off calling *me* a chicken? You died because you were afraid to make a commitment to Sophie."

What? Man, you don't know anything—

"Yeah? Tell me you didn't push your luck to scare Sophie away. You were afraid she'd tie you down. Afraid she'd expect more from you than you thought you could give."

The anger pumping inside him astounded him. "You were afraid everyone else was right about you being a useless excuse for a human being, and that Sophie was wrong about you having any redeeming qualities. Or are you too chicken to face the truth?"

Where the hell do you get off saying—

"Hey, you've been lurking in my head, Wilde, but you left a data trail of your own. I know your thoughts and feelings the same as you know mine."

Well, well, well. Welcome to the monkey house.

He let out a snort of pure exasperation. "That's another thing you do. You hide behind smart-ass comments because you're afraid people will take you seriously until you fail. Then they'll be on your case."

You wanna play hardball, Warren? Okay. We'll play hardball. You do the same damn chicken things you're laying on me. You're afraid to let Sophie get close because you're afraid you can't love anyone. Great excuse, Einstein! If you didn't love her, you wouldn't be on the spin cycle about hurting her. You'd just get your jollies and split for sunny California.

He couldn't take this sitting down. He started pacing again. "That's not quite the same as getting yourself killed taking a totally no-brain dare. I'm *supposed* to leave."

He stood at the glass wall and stared at the rippling water. "Besides, Sophie lives here. This is her home. She has her business here. What if I ask her to give up her life here and she's miserable in California?"

He turned on his heel and marched back toward the steps from the family room to the chrome-and-red-tile kitchen. But there was no escaping Dean's voice inside his head, putting words to the thoughts that had him tied up in knots.

What if you fail her? What if you let her down? What if you really are *the miserable excuse for a human being you're afraid you are? What if you really can't love anyone, and Sophie finds out you're hollow inside? Like some science-fiction android, all wires and no feelings. Like your brilliant parents and their intellectual friends.*

Jake slammed his fist on the counter. The impact sent a jolt up to his shoulder and rattled the ceramic containers.

"You tell me!" he practically roared at the voice in his head. "You've been skulking around my thoughts long enough. Is there anything that could pass for love in there?"

In your thoughts, no. Love isn't something you think. *It's something you* feel. *But I've been letting myself into some unused places, when I had some time on my hands. Not everyone is interested in algorithms, whatever the hell they are. At first, I gotta admit you were pretty light in the feelings department. Then you met Sophie.*

"Maybe you're just seeing your own feelings for Sophie. How am I supposed to know if what I feel is real?"

Ask yourself this, man. Do you want to live the rest of your life, and maybe even after, without her?

Jake realized he'd been asking himself that question in a million different ways, almost every time he breathed. And he knew damn well that the rest of his life without Sophie was a pretty grim prospect. She was like a sweet river, making his desert of a soul bloom, turning him into a human being. Without her, he'd return to being a spiritual desert. He'd never known one person could give so much to another.

Yeah, so ask yourself what you'd do for Sophie? How far are you willing to go for her? When you get your answer to that, you'll have your answer about love.

Jake leaned on the counter and growled in frustration. The worst of it all was, he was beginning to wonder if it was Wilde talking to him, or if he was really talking to himself.

By the time she found the hidden, narrow private road, on her third pass along the winding, heavily wooded back road, Sophie felt close to panic. It had taken her almost an hour to track down Craig Gardiner, at a meeting at another bank branch. Then she'd had to convince him, without spelling out the reason why, that she could be trusted with his bank president's unlisted phone number and address.

After one last call to the hospital to hear the distressing news that Larry was still unconscious, she left Rick in charge of the store. As she pulled out of the parking lot, the gas gauge light went on, forcing her to stop to refuel. Even the knowledge that she'd prevented herself from running out of gas somewhere in rural Connecticut didn't keep her from gnawing on her lower lip in impatience.

Every second that ticked by was another second that Jake could be closer to drowning.

"Don't be so melodramatic," she muttered as she maneuvered down the narrow, winding road toward the Eames house. "Have some faith. Why should Jake drown just because he jumps in the pool?"

Panic. That was why. Panic could paralyze a person. Even a strong-willed, sensible person. If he let himself remember the accident . . . Lord, how could he *not* remember?

The house that appeared at the end of the road would have impressed her at any other time. It was huge, sprawling, constructed of naturally aged cedar and tinted glass, set harmoniously into the wooded landscape, overlooking the edge of the hill it crested. The only signs of life were the birds that darted and trilled overhead, and the squirrels that scurried away from her car and scolded from the safety of mature trees. Her heart gave a thump at the sight of Jake's Harley parked under the overhang beside the three-car garage.

Sophie halted her car in front of the garage and shoved open the door. Not bothering to take her keys or shut the door behind her, she ran to the front of the house. The door was locked. She rang the bell, pressing repeatedly, her ragged breathing sounding louder in her ears than the chimes inside the house. No response.

Frantic, she ran around the circumference of the house, hoping belatedly that Eames didn't have guard dogs patrolling the grounds. The ground was dry, but she slipped several times as she followed the flagstone path down the ridge to the back of the house. It seemed to take forever. Finally she turned the corner and found herself gaping at a totally glass-enclosed room—glass she couldn't see through.

But there were stairs up from the first of several decks on the landscaped hillside. And the stairs led to wide sliding glass doors. Stumbling in her haste, she ran to the stairs and tried the door. With a gasp and a whisper, the door slid open, revealing a blindingly bright, tiled room. In the center of the room, a pool sparkled with blue and silver ripples.

And at the far end of the pool, leaning over the edge, staring into the seductive ripples, stood Jake. Oh, God, he was going to jump in, fully clothed. Sophie's heart stopped.

"Jake, no!" she cried.

His head jerked up. "Sophie?" he said, and stepped forward.

As water splashed up and Jake's head went under the surface, her scream echoed off the glass walls, mocking her.

Chapter Eleven

A kaleidoscope of thoughts and images exploded in his brain as the water closed over his head. Dragged down by the weight of his jeans, he struggled to reach the surface. His shocked gasp came too late to fill his lungs with air. Instead, chlorinated water seared his nose and throat, forcing him to hold what little breath he had. The sensation was distressingly familiar.

At least this time, he was fully conscious. If he let himself sink to the bottom, eight feet deep, he could push off and get to the surface. Momentum and a few hard strokes would carry him to the edge of the pool.

And Sophie.

Sophie! Was she real, or a hallucination conjured up from his misery without her? Or a figment of Wilde's imagination? If a figment of his imagination could have one of his own....

He stopped thrashing his arms and let his body slip farther into the water. The bottom, less than two feet over his head, met his searching toes. His lungs burned. He bent his knees, making himself heavier, getting a solid stance on the pool floor. Then he sprang hard, breaking the surface. With a shout, he cleared his lungs and sucked in fresh air. He shook the water and his hair out of his eyes and saw that he was only a stroke or two from the edge. He reached out.

Suddenly, Sophie *was* there, clinging to him, dragging him back down. He took a quick breath before the water closed over their heads. With one arm around her slender body, he pushed off again from the bottom, angling them toward the pool edge. With his free arm, he caught the curved concrete lip and anchored them, his heart pounding.

Sophie clung to his neck, her legs wrapped around his hips, her dress drifting around them. She made soft sounds, of fear or relief he couldn't tell. He almost didn't care. All he was aware of, now that he could take stock of the situation, was the warm, wet woman in his arms.

Like the vision he'd had when he was dying, she wore white and her dark hair floated around her shoulders. But this time, she was real, and she was *his* vision, not Wilde's. In time, he would ask why she was here, but for now, all he wanted to do was peel off the wet layers of their clothes and make slow, sweet love to her.

I'm outta here, Warren. You're on your own. You don't need me anymore. Sophie's... Sophie's yours, man. Be good to her.

He grinned, then shook the wet hair out of his face so he could see her more clearly. *His!* There were black streaks under her eyes where her makeup had liquified, and her face looked deathly white. Her smoky gray eyes gazed wildly back at him. Her teeth caught at her full lower lip. He ached inside at her beauty.

Suddenly he remembered that empty yearning feeling that had assaulted him the night he'd moved into the apartment below Sophie's. Now he knew exactly what his soul had craved. He held all he needed in his arms.

She freed one hand to touch his face, her fingertips cool and hot and shaking. "Oh, Jake! Jake! Why did you do it?" she sobbed at him.

Confused, he stared at her. "Do what?"

"Throw yourself into the pool."

He snorted. "I didn't."

He tightened his grip, lifting her shoulders farther out of the water. Her dress clung to her breasts, leaving no question that she was braless. Swallowing hard, he forced himself to lift his gaze.

"I saw you come in, and I was so surprised, I forgot about the water. I just sort of walked in."

She gasped. "You walked into the pool because I startled you?"

He nodded, torn between the rush of heat stirring in his loins and the urge to laugh at the absurdity of the situation.

"Oh my God!" she wailed. "I was trying to save you but I could have killed you!" Her beautiful eyes turned silver with tears. "Oh, Jake! I'm so sorry!"

His laughter died at the first frantic touch of her mouth on his. Her lips parted at the first touch of his tongue. The sweetness of her kiss erased the burn of chlorine. His guilt at her dismay evaporated. The hunger that he'd tried to deny twisted inside him, aching, demanding fulfillment.

But not here, not like this, dragged down by their soaked clothes, clumsy, desperate, uncomfortable.

"Sophie, shh! It's okay. I'm okay. Just wet." She shook in his arms. He kissed away the tears streaking down her cheeks. "Don't cry. You didn't do anything to me, except prove I can still swim. Everything's fine. No one's in any danger."

The tenderness, the protectiveness welled up inside him, and with them, the words to hint at his feelings—even without Wilde's coaching. Despite the embarrassing fact that he'd just absentmindedly walked into a swimming pool, he felt strong, in control. He'd gladly make an ass of himself any day—*every* day—if that would bring Sophie into his arms.

For the first time in his life, he was getting a handle on being human. It was a condition fraught with pitfalls. And occasional pratfalls. But it was worth it, if Sophie could be part of his life.

He kissed Sophie's temple and hugged her, hoping to reassure her. "Let's get out of the water. Come on. The ladder is just a few feet away. Help me a little, Sophie. Hold on so I can use both hands. Okay?"

She sniffled, then nodded, her trembling barely perceptible now. With her arms and legs wrapped around him, he eased them along the side of the pool to the metal ladder in the corner. He grasped the handrails and stood on the first step, letting the water pour off them as he straightened. Gravity and the water pulled down at him. Common sense told him it would be easier and safer to let Sophie climb out of the pool by herself. But he didn't want to release her.

Even when he stood firmly on the tiled pool deck, with no more excuse or need to hold her, he couldn't let her go just yet. So he held her and started walking slowly, every nerve in his body firing like crazy at every point of contact between them. Their bodies began warming their soaked clothes, and the heat branded his flesh. He wanted to simply wrench off his jeans and slip deep into her before reality caught up with them.

"Jake?" Her breath warmed his ear, giving him chills. "Where are we going?"

"To get out of these clothes and shower," he told her, when he wanted to tell her he was carrying her to bed. "I've got clothes here, but I'll see if there's something you can borrow from Mrs. Eames until your dress dries."

It was the honorable thing to do. Riordan's warning still nagged at him. He didn't want to take advantage of Sophie's fear, of her being soaked and vulnerable. Hell, he couldn't assume she still wanted to make love, after the way he'd shut her down the other night.

He ached to make love to her, but everything had to be right. The first time was too important to let circumstances dictate when and where. He didn't want Sophie to believe he'd been carried away by the moment, by the opportunity. He needed her to understand that what he felt might be expressed by sex, but could never be limited to physical desire.

"Oh." Her voice sounded curiously flat. "A robe will do, if you don't think she'd mind."

Was it his imagination, or had she loosened her hold around his neck? He had the sinking feeling he'd done something wrong, made some tactical misstep, but he couldn't think what it could be. This man-woman stuff wasn't like writing software, for damn sure! If he'd made a mistake, he couldn't just look at a printout until he could pinpoint the error.

Where was Wilde when he needed him?

He reached the doorway to one of the Eames's guest rooms. Reluctantly, he let Sophie slide from his embrace, instantly chilled by the loss of her body heat. She hardly looked at him when she regained her balance and stepped into the room.

Whatever was wrong, he'd have to correct it somehow. He had to figure out some way to get them back to where they were Friday night, when she wanted him, too. Sophie was a loss he couldn't afford. It had been a colossal mistake to think he could settle for simple friendship with this woman.

He started to back out of the room. Sophie turned and looked steadily at him. He didn't need Wilde's tutoring to read the invitation in Sophie's soft eyes. Her sweet half smile kick-started his heart and made it hammer against his ribs until he could hardly breathe.

"Jake?"

"Sophie, we have to talk."

"We can talk," she murmured, "later."

She held her hands out toward him, exactly the way she had in his vision. Time slowed. Reality faded. Her smile widened a fraction, encouraging him. Moving as if trapped in thick fog, he stepped toward her. It was all exactly the way he'd seen her—in his vision or in a dream. Her long, dark hair, her soft, wise eyes, her smile, the white dress that outlined the enticing curves he longed to lose himself in.

But first, he had a confession to make, and he prayed that what he had to tell her wouldn't be the beginning of the end.

She'd made her decision. Nothing short of a flat rejection could dissuade her. The future didn't matter. Only the present, and loving Jake. He was the first man she'd been able to love since Dean's death. Her love shimmered inside her, as magical and pure as a rainbow after a storm. All that mattered to her now was the need to share that love in the most intimate, basic, profound way possible.

"There's something I have to tell you, Sophie," he murmured, stopping just out of her reach.

She knew what he wanted to tell her, that he was making no commitments, no promises. She understood they lived in different worlds, both figuratively and literally, and had little except this simmering attraction to hold them together. But her pride demanded that she be the one to assure him there were no strings. She couldn't bear to hear words of rejection from him. It would hurt too much.

"Jake, I—"

He shook his head. She bit off her words. The look in his beautiful eyes told her he needed to speak first. What did her pride matter? She would do anything for Jake.

"I want to make love to you," he said with an intensity that stole her breath. "I wanted to make love to you from the first time I saw you. Maybe even before that. The last thing I wanted to do Friday night was walk out of your apartment alone."

The heat of his declaration sent spirals of desire pulsing through her. Unable to think of a reply to his bold statement, she gazed helplessly at him. He gave her a crooked little smile.

"Remember when Karen Swan asked me if I was a nerd or a hippie, and I said I was a little of both?" Surprised at his unexpected change of topic, she nodded. "It's true. I probably do know a hundred and one ways to make love to a woman."

Endearingly, he blushed. Her own cheeks burned at the suggestiveness of his comment.

Then he cleared his throat. "And I do know a lot of women—sort of."

Her heart sank. She didn't want to know about Jake's many conquests. "Jake, I don't care how many women—"

"None."

It took a moment to realize what he was saying. Then her eyes widened and she barely caught her jaw before it dropped open. His cheeks were crimson now, but he held her gaze.

"None?" she echoed.

He shook his head, his brilliant eyes wary. His posture was rigid, on guard, waiting for her reaction. Did he expect laughter or derision? Not from her. Not after the hell Dean had put her through, alternately teasing her that a virgin was too much trouble for him to bother with, then pressuring her to let him be the first. And Dean hadn't been the only man sending mixed signals.

"Oh, Jake, that's so special," she whispered, her heart melting at the relief in his beautiful eyes.

His shoulders relaxed and a sweet smile lit his face. "I didn't think so, until now." His voice lowered to a husky growl that only hinted at the hunger now lurking in his eyes. "With you, it will be very special."

Suddenly, the enormity of his confession, and the responsibility he was giving her, dawned on her. Her brave resolve—to make love with Jake regardless of what the future might hold—wilted. Never mind the future. The present was about to shake what little confidence she had in herself. Given her few and dismal sexual experiences, how was she going to teach this sweet and beautiful man how to make love?

"Do you . . . ? Do you want to talk . . . about . . . ?"

He shook his head, his long, tangled curls dripping onto his already soaked blue shirt. "Later. It's a long story. *Too* long. There are other things I'd rather do than talk about close encounters of the failed kind."

She barely managed to summon a smile at his self-denigrating wit. He strode to her and cupped her face in his big, warm hands. There was fire in his eyes as he lowered his face toward hers. Overwhelmed by the intensity of his gaze, she let her eyelids flutter shut. His lips brushed hers, softly, almost hesitantly, but she felt the banked flames behind that kiss.

She rested her hands on his shoulders for balance a second before he deepened the kiss, giving her a further taste of the desire burning inside him. Her small sound of welcome caught in her throat as his tongue pushed past her teeth. The dark sweetness of his kiss sizzled on her tongue as she tipped her head back to give him free access to her mouth.

He took what she offered. Heat rushed through her. Her knees buckled. He slipped one arm around her, supporting her, bringing their bodies together. Through their sodden clothes, she felt his arousal. He pressed against her, hard, insistent. Her hips shifted, teasing, inviting, drawing a moan from deep inside him.

Her own desire caught fire at the sound. Jake's hand slid down her bare back to cup her bottom and hold her, the heat of his hand burning through her wet, cold dress. His tongue echoed the slow, suggestive thrusts of his hips, driving her higher. Then, with his free hand, he gently cupped her breast. His touch sent a jolt of sensation straight to the heart of her desire.

All her worries about teaching Jake anything about making love dissolved. He was already way ahead of her.

"We've got to get out of these clothes," he murmured, his lips brushing her cheek.

Inspiration flashed at his words. She nodded slowly, an excuse to rub her face against the smooth planes of his. "And into a shower, I think you said?"

He eased his hold, an odd expression on his face. "Sure. There's one in here. I'll meet you—"

He'd misunderstood. "Where do you usually shower?" she murmured close to his ear, letting her lips brush his warm skin. Then she tipped her head back and smiled. "Is there room for two?"

His eyes reflected confusion. "For two?"

"Unless you'd rather shower alone?" She hardly recognized herself in the seductive boldness. It was as if that dunk in the pool had washed away years of repression. She felt new, trembling with possibilities.

Understanding dawned in Jake's eyes, and with it, that hungry look returned. Before she could anticipate his intentions, he'd scooped her up into his arms and was striding down the long hallway toward another bedroom.

Smiling, Sophie clung to his shoulders and teased the warm skin of his neck with soft kisses.

He set her on her feet in a spacious, white-tiled bathroom with a whirlpool tub and a large glass-enclosed shower. "People keep telling me that being a genius doesn't make me so smart." He grinned, a little sheepishly, she thought. "I hate to admit it, but sometimes they're right. Especially about things between men and women." His grin turned wickedly suggestive. "All the interfacing I do is between computers."

A delighted laugh escaped her. She stepped back into his arms. "I think we can change your programming."

"You already have, Sophie."

His words touched her soul with the sweetness of an angel's kiss.

She heard him sigh; then he released her. When he turned away to run the water in the shower, she understood that he was sorting through his feelings, seeking equilibrium on shaky, unfamiliar ground. When he turned back to her, the stark hunger in his eyes made her shiver in anticipation. Her worry was no longer whether she could teach him to make love. Now she was petrified that she wouldn't be able to keep up with him.

"Sophie, are you sure?" he asked softly.

She couldn't find her voice. All she could do was stare into his compelling eyes and nod. He pulled his wet polo shirt over his head so roughly, she heard stitches tear. She let her gaze drift over his smooth-muscled body.

"You don't look like a nerd," she told him, her voice barely above a whisper. She smiled. "Or a hippie."

His eyebrows lifted. "What do I look like?"

Boldly, she placed her hands flat on the hard swells of his chest. "Like a man. A very beautiful man," she whispered dreamily, feeling as if she were falling under a spell.

His sharp intake of breath told her he liked her answer, liked the way her hands drifted over his broad shoulders. She didn't have to look to know he was blushing. Jake truly didn't have a clue how attractive he was.

She feathered the silky dark curls that spread across his chest, then stopped to tease his nipples with her fingertips. Sudden shyness halted her impulse to place her lips on his warm skin and use her tongue to continue what her fingers started.

Then Jake reached out and unbuttoned the back of her halter dress. With agonizing slowness, he drew the bodice down to her waist, leaving her bare to his hungry gaze. Even before his fingers found her nipples, they were hard and tingling. His first gentle touch elicited a gasp from her. But he didn't linger to tease. Instead, he traced tantalizing patterns over all her exposed skin, turning every inch he touched into a highly charged erogenous zone, and making her tremble.

Her hands shook as she fumbled with the snap of his jeans, the heavy cloth stubbornly resisting her efforts. Finally he took her hands in his and drew them up to kiss her knuckles.

"I think I'd better do that," he told her. "But not just yet."

Instead, he circled her waist with his hands, then slid the zipper at the back of the dress down from her waist. When he stepped back, the wet fabric fell to her bare feet, leaving her only in pink French-cut panties. Jake's slow study of her body brought a flush of heat to her neck and cheeks, but her initial shyness flared into desire when she saw his eyes darken with arousal.

He took her hand and she stepped over her wet dress to follow him into the rushing warm water of the big stall shower. She moved into his arms. Her breasts pressed against his chest, his heartbeat vibrating through her, as she lifted her face for his kiss. His mouth came down hot and hungry on hers. She let her lips part and his tongue delved deeply into her mouth, stirring the flames within her.

The texture of his jeans contrasted erotically with the wet smoothness of her bare skin. Her thin panties were plastered to her, no serious barrier to the obvious arousal straining at his jeans. Impatient to feel his flesh on her, within her, she tugged at the sodden denim at his hips.

He tore his lips from hers, his breathing ragged. "Sophie, wait." Gently he eased her away until they were no longer pressed together. "I've been celibate for thirty-four years," he said, sounding as if he were in pain. "I don't want this over before it starts."

Between desire and fear, he was paralyzed. He'd never imagined anything as breathtakingly beautiful as Sophie standing all but naked in front of him. She was a mermaid. A nymph. An angel. *His* angel. Did he dare touch her? What if he couldn't satisfy her? It would break his heart to let her down in any way.

Gazing down into her upturned face, he ran his tongue over his bottom lip, savoring the intoxicating taste of her lingering there. He wanted to drag her down to the shower floor, with the warm water pouring down over them, and bury himself inside her. But that was out of the question. She deserved better than that. She deserved to be pleasured in as many of the hundred and one ways he knew that wouldn't cause him to explode.

With his hands on her shoulders, he drew her closer. The brush of her bare breasts on his chest sent a shard of awareness through him. So soft, yet firm, round. Her breasts were beautiful. Her rosy pink nipples puckered against him, reminding him of the way she'd responded that day in her office, when his hands had accidentally closed on her.

Was she trembling, too, or was it only him, shaking like an earthquake? He ran one hand down the sleek, wet skin of her arm, then slid his palm up her ribs to cup her breast. His thumb brushed over her nipple, making it swell and harden even more. A tiny sound escaped her lips.

Did her skin taste as sweet as her mouth? Only one way to find out. He bent and sampled the tender side of her neck. Her head tipped back, giving him free access to her throat. With the tip of his tongue, he traced the delicate lines of her throat and collarbones. She clung to his shoulders and leaned into the support of his arm around her back. He bent and touched the erect nipple with his tongue. Soft whimpers rewarded him.

Success made him bolder. He opened his mouth around her nipple and began to suckle. She tasted so sweet, and the sound of her tiny cries increased his arousal. Nature amazed him with her wisdom, giving him pleasure while he gave pleasure to Sophie.

But it wasn't enough. Before he laid her on the bed and buried himself in her body, he intended to have her limp with satisfaction.

Somehow he managed to support her while easing himself down on one knee. Nuzzling at the undersides of her breasts, he hooked his fingers into the elastic of her panties and drew them past her hips and down her legs. He knelt and pressed her close, listening to the erratic beating of her heart. Her firm, round bottom fit against his open palms. Her fingers tangled in his hair. The shower pouring down her back sent warm spray at him when she shifted her balance, reminding him of the less practical aspects of their location.

With a last kiss between her breasts, he got to his feet, silently cursing the painful state of arousal and his heavy, soaking jeans. Taking the bar of strawberry glycerine soap in his hands, he worked up a lather, then placed his hands on her shoulders. Her eyes met his, letting him see the effect his touch was having on her. He cupped her breasts, then slid his hands down her narrow ribs to her waist to stroke her flat belly with soapy thumbs. Her eyes were wide, smoky, unfocused, her breathing softly shallow.

Obviously, he was doing something right.

He slid one hand lower, his fingers just brushing the soft curls between her legs. Then she gasped and her eyes fluttered shut. He touched her again, more boldly, cupping her, finding her heat with his shaking hand. Sophie gave a small cry and clutched at his shoulders.

Had he done something wrong?

"Jake! Hold me!" she whispered, reassuring him.

He circled her waist with one arm and she leaned against him. Gently, reverently, he touched her, exploring the secrets of her body. She was so soft, so mysterious, so small. He didn't want to hurt her.

"Sophie, tell me what you like," he whispered. "Tell me what to do."

A tiny shock ran through her body. "I thought you knew," she whispered back after a long silence.

So much for bragging. "In theory, sure." He frowned, then kissed her forehead. "But you aren't theoretical. You're very, very real." Carefully, he deepened his exploring touch. Her knees buckled, sending her leaning even more against him. It was rather gratifying, considering his crisis of confidence.

"Help me please you, Sophie. Tell me how to satisfy you."

She buried her head in his neck. "I can't! I don't know! No one ever..." Her words came out in a smothered little wail. She took a breath. "I'm not a virgin, Jake, but I might as well be. I've been told I'm as responsive as mud."

Disbelief flashed through his head, replaced instantly by anger, sorrow and awe. Anger at the men who hadn't loved

Sophie enough. Sorrow for this beautiful, sweet woman who deserved to be loved. And awe that he—unworthy as he was—was the one she had just entrusted with her innocence.

He hugged her to him and kissed the top of her head, which was all he could reach. "It's okay, Sophie. I like solving problems no one else can figure out."

She went very still against him. He held his breath. *Now* what had he done wrong?

"I'm trying to take that in the spirit I believe it was meant," Sophie muttered into his chest hair. Leave it to Jake to put making love in the shower into the context of a problem of logic! Embarrassed as she was by her confession, she felt the need to reassure him that he hadn't made matters worse.

She heard him sigh, then felt him gather her closer. "Tell me how you like to be touched," he murmured as his strong, gentle fingers continued to explore her intimately. The sensations he created made her tremble with increasing pleasure and stoked the hungry fire that had never before burned so high. She felt as if she were melting.

"Like this?" he whispered, his touch sending lightning streaking through her. "Or like this?" And his touch stirred tiny sparks. She shuddered with pleasure, almost afraid of sensations brighter and deeper than any she'd ever known.

"Yes!" she managed to gasp.

"Hook your leg around me," he ordered hoarsely. "I won't let you fall."

In a sensual trance, she did as he told her. He continued to stroke her, bringing her higher with every caress. He took her mouth in a long, deep kiss that left her breathless, then pressed his lips to her throat. With his strong arm around her, she let herself lean back, offering him her aching breasts. The first tug of his hot mouth ignited a flash fire deep inside her.

It was too much, and it wasn't enough. The sensations he sparked began to swirl and tighten in a spiral until she was caught. Helplessly, she cried out, then sagged against him, trembling. He held her close and the warm water poured over them. She lost track of time, nestled in his arms.

Jake stroked her hair back from her face and kissed her so softly, so reverently that tears came into her eyes. She wove her fingers into his wet, silky hair and held him to prolong the kiss. This time, she stroked his lips, seeking entrance. This time, she led him in a slow, sweet mating of tongues and lips until they were both gasping for breath.

"Make love to me, Jake," she whispered.

His low growl echoed off the tiled walls. Still kissing her, he reached between them to struggle with his jeans. She heard the scrape of his zipper, felt his knuckles brush her belly and realized he was taking her request literally.

If he couldn't get out of his damn jeans, he was going to go from Romeo to the Nutty Professor in a nanosecond. The trouble was, he couldn't seem to keep his hands off Sophie, or stop kissing her, long enough to concentrate on the zipper. It also didn't help that his hands were shaking so badly, he could hardly grasp the zipper tab.

He still couldn't believe the way Sophie had responded. Shy. Sweet. Abandoned. And so, so trusting.

In an agony of impatience and arousal, he finally worked the zipper down. Sophie's fingers trailed fire over his chest while he kissed her and struggled to shove his jeans down. Her mouth was so hot, so sweet. Her wet breasts pressed against him, tempting him to cover them with his hands and caress them. But the hunger inside him blinded him to everything except one goal: to bury himself deep in Sophie and make love to her. Make her his.

He kicked his jeans and shorts into a corner of the shower, then grasped her waist and pulled her to him. He was so hard, so painfully aroused, that the first touch of her resilient belly almost undid him. Tearing his mouth from hers, he bit his lip hard. As if she understood, she held herself motionless against him. But his self-control was hanging by the thinnest filament.

"Sophie? I can't protect you here," he managed to choke out. "I don't want to get you pregnant." Not now, not yet.

He felt a tremor run through her. "I'm on the Pill," she murmured. For reasons he couldn't fathom, had no patience to examine at that moment, her assurance made him feel something almost like regret.

The rational part of his brain shut down. Instincts took over, coursing through his blood with the heat of desire. He wanted this woman, wanted to possess her, to brand her and bond with her. Without conscious thought, he captured her mouth in a probing kiss and lifted her high against him.

Sophie clutched his neck and wrapped her legs around his hips. His manhood moved against the slick, honeyed folds of her, striking sparks. It was the most exquisite torture to stroke against her like that, but he knew he wouldn't last more than a few seconds. Desperate, he broke the kiss.

"Help me, Sophie!"

The first touch of her hand nearly sent him over the edge. He clenched his teeth and smothered the roar that tried to burst from his lungs when she guided him to the molten center of her body. Pain and pleasure exploded into fireworks as he thrust into her. She was so hot, so tight, so soft and yielding.

The universe contracted, imploded, focusing on the joining of their bodies. Nothing else existed except the soft, wet woman clinging to him, surrounding him. Her tiny cries and whimpers echoed his groans. Her hips moved in perfect counterpoint to his.

Make it last, make it last, he ordered himself. But he felt Sophie tighten around him, heard her stifled cry and knew they'd both gone past the point of no return. He clutched her to him, determined to keep her safe no matter how carried away he became. Lightning and darkness, all the colors of the universe, exploded inside his head as he thrust wildly into her, unable to inhibit the primitive power that overwhelmed him.

Then all conscious thought burst into glowing fragments as he shattered.

He didn't know whether to laugh or cry. Feeling exhausted and weak, yet strong, invincible, he leaned against the cold tile wall and cradled Sophie's limp body. Vaguely, he was aware of the water pouring over them. But physical sensations had given way to a tidal wave of emotions, love above all.

Oh, how he loved Sophie!

Was this really happening? Sophie clung to Jake, barely conscious of the sound and feel of the water pouring over them. At his plea, she guided him to her and felt the shock of her touch rip through him. She held her breath as he entered her, slowly at first, tension pulsing through his body. Then, with a smothered groan, he drove himself deep into her, igniting sparks.

With each powerful thrust, Jake took her higher. She'd never responded like this before. The intensity frightened her even as it excited her. Pleasure spiraled within her, drawing tighter and tighter. Beyond the pleasure—deeper, sweeter than sensation—Sophie felt as if their souls were joining together.

Her climax washed over her, wave after powerful wave. With a cry of surprise and completion, she clutched at Jake for safety. A moment later, he clasped her even more tightly and his groan echoed in the enclosure as he gave himself up to his own wild release.

He sagged against the wall, his arms still strong around her. His chest heaved with his breathing, rhythmically pressing her sensitized breasts, and his heart thundered through her. The taste of his mouth lingered on her lips. It was as if he had become a part of her. She couldn't tell where she ended and he began.

And finally she understood why she'd never responded to any other man in this profound, elemental way. Guilt and unrealistic expectations had kept her trapped in the past. She hadn't been able to fall in love because she hadn't really come to terms with Dean's death, no matter how much she'd wanted to. But something had freed her to love Jake, and that made all the difference.

Suddenly she realized Jake was shaking. Leaning back a little, she looked into his face. He was laughing.

"Make that a hundred and two ways," he murmured.

She smiled, too mellow to speak. With gentle hands and many kisses, he lifted her down, then held her close. "I think we're about to run out of hot water," he said.

Sophie felt as if she were still in a trance. Somehow they managed to disentangle themselves enough to get out of the shower. With exquisite tenderness, Jake wrapped her in a thick white bath sheet, and gently toweled her wet, tangled hair.

When she turned around to face him, Jake looked into her eyes as if seeking assurance that she was all right. Instead of answering with words, she boldly leaned forward and licked at the droplets of water glistening on his collarbone and throat. His sharp intake of breath made her smile.

"There's a bed in the other room," he told her hoarsely. "I think we still have some unfinished business."

"We do?" She couldn't imagine what they had left to do!

He nodded solemnly, then pulled her into his arms. The towels between them couldn't hide the fact that he was once again powerfully aroused.

"Oh!" She felt her cheeks flame at the thought that she'd had such an effect on him. This might take some getting used to!

Jake chuckled softly, sounding very self-satisfied. "I'm usually a very methodical guy, Sophie, and it seems to me we've left out a number of critical steps."

Chapter Twelve

Sophie awoke slowly, dreamily aware of the warm weight of Jake's arm over her side, and his chest and legs cradling her. His slow, rhythmic breathing stirred her hair gently, and when she took a breath, the scent of his skin filled her head.

Being in a strange bed gave her a feeling of timelessness, as well as physical disorientation. Blinking, she tried to focus on the clock radio on the sleek black-lacquer bedside table. Only half past eight in the evening. It felt later, but the sun was still lighting the summer sky.

It was an odd feeling to wake up before dark, after sleeping away part of the afternoon. And after making love for part of the afternoon.

Just thinking about the way she'd abandoned herself to Jake brought heat rushing to her cheeks. She could still hear the echoes of Jake's low groans and smothered shouts, her own cries and the muted creaking of the bed. Love had certainly banished most of her inhibitions, and awakened a sensuality she'd thought had died with Dean.

Jake stirred then, and all other thoughts fled at the first touch of his hand on her ribs. Like a contented cat, she stretched and leaned closer into him. She couldn't imagine another place she'd rather be, another man she'd rather be with.

"I want to make love to you again," he murmured, "but we have to talk, too." He must have sensed her disappointment, because he kissed her shoulder lightly and added, "In that order."

The pealing of the phone made her start and wrung a grunt from Jake. "It's probably not for me," he said, stroking her breast. "I think I left the machine on," he added when the phone kept ringing. After the sixth ring, he swore softly and rolled away to grab the receiver.

Sophie snuggled up behind him, stroking his flat belly, still a little too shy to reach lower. This was all so new, so fragile.... Should she say anything to Jake about her feelings? Or wait for him to say something to her? Or—her hand stilled on his chest—what if he didn't feel the same way? Just because she was the first woman he'd made love to didn't necessarily mean he loved her. Maybe that was what he wanted to talk about. Maybe he had no place in his life for love.

The direction of her thoughts disturbed her so badly that she hardly heard Jake speaking on the phone. She felt him reach out to hang up. Then he turned and looked into her eyes. There was an odd light in his.

"We really have to talk now, Sophie. Maybe we should get dressed. I don't think you're going to like what I have to tell you."

A chill raced up her spine. She fumbled for the white terry-cloth robe they'd found earlier in the guest room closet. Her dress was in the dryer in the laundry room off the kitchen. She didn't want to wait that long to hear what Jake had to say.

She knotted the belt around her waist as if fastening emotional armor around her heart. Then she sat on the black leather director's chair near the bed.

"Okay. What do you have to tell me that I won't like?" To her relief, her voice came out without a hint of the tremors that were coursing through her. She'd been prepared to let him go when he had to, but this was too soon. A lifetime too soon.

She gripped the armrest of the chair and waited. With his back to her, he zipped his clean jeans. Still bare-chested, he turned and started pacing, only looking at her occasionally. Then, abruptly, he faced her, his expression unreadable. A rush of fear rippled through her.

"I won't throw a lot of jargon at you, but someone rigged your store computer to crack one of the banks I'm working for, through the remote banking system."

Her jaw dropped, relief vying with astonishment. He wasn't giving her the brush-off. At least not yet. He was only telling her that someone was using her computer system to commit grand theft, just like in the movies!

"*My* computer? That's impossible. Jake, I don't have a whatchamacallit. You know." She shrugged helplessly at her unfamiliarity with computers. "A thing."

He paused in his pacing and flashed her a grin. "A modem."

That grin did more than she could have predicted to make her feel better, despite the situation Jake was describing. It was his normal grin, and it told her that things between them were still good. She simply wouldn't let herself think beyond the moment.

"Right. A modem thing. I don't trust myself to do my banking that way without hitting the wrong keys, and I didn't plan to break into any federal-agency computers, so

I didn't have a modem thing installed when I got the new system."

Her attempt at levity fell flat when she considered the reality. What if whoever was using her computer was doing something even worse than moving funds from bank to bank? What if he—or she—was playing with national or even international security? The thought made her feel ill.

Jake sat heavily on the edge of the bed, his beautiful eyes troubled. "Sophie, you did have a modem. I checked it out myself. It was installed internally, and tapped into your third phone line. The wires were hidden under the counter in your office. You'd have to know it was there to find it."

She tried to make sense of what he'd said. "I *did* have one? Does that mean I don't anymore?" He nodded. "But . . . ?"

"I figure whoever knocked Larry out the other night was there to remove it before I blew the whistle."

She let that sink in. "*Before* you blew the whistle? So you haven't yet?"

He looked indignant. "Are you kidding? I went to the FBI as soon as I saw what was happening. Someone is robbing *banks*."

"Oh." She only felt a little stupid. "Sorry."

"Remember I told you at Lynne and Craig's barbecue that I could program the computer to record all activity and tally it after hours? I'd already done it. There's plenty of evidence of nocturnal activity on disk, in your safe. But the Feds won't do anything until the West Hartford police or the state cops find the guy who beaned Larry. That's a state crime, not federal. They won't even take the back-up disks until they think there's an investigation to pursue."

Something clicked. "Nocturnal? Is that why Dennis told me to keep the system running all the time?" The expression on his face confirmed her suspicion. "Dennis?" She shook her head. "No. He's a little irresponsible, but I can't believe he'd be so vicious. I also can't believe he's a computerized bank robber. Anyway, you told me people can't do things like that anymore."

He sighed and shoved his hair away from his face. "It isn't as easy as it used to be, but crackers don't give up easy. The challenge is the kick. Whoever is doing this figured a way to get in the back door, so to speak. He tapped into your computer from a remote location, so that all the activity was traced back to your store. Probably used a laptop computer with a modem, calling from a different pay phone every time, so he couldn't be pinned down or anticipated."

She hugged herself, feeling violated. But she still couldn't believe that brash, flirtatious, somewhat lazy Dennis was the culprit. She couldn't imagine him hitting Larry so hard that his life was in danger. She didn't want to imagine it.

"That was Rick on the phone," Jake told her, his voice sober.

"Rick?" That alarmed her. "What's he got to do with this? He's not in any trouble, is he?"

"No. I thought for a while that Rick was behind the scam, because he knows computers and you give him free rein. And he has the right background. But he's straight. We had a little talk after he got busted, and I threatened to rearrange his face if he was involved."

Sophie gaped at Jake. This was twice he'd been willing to fight over her. It was a thoroughly unsettling notion.

Jake shook his head. "After the way you gave him a second chance, he'd do anything for you. Rick's the reason I was able to get into your CPU to find the modem. He was as convinced as I was that it had to be this Dennis character who's the cracker, but it turns out we were wrong. Larry finally woke up this afternoon. He saw the guy who hit him."

She leaned forward, unable to breathe until Jake told her what Rick had reported. "Who was it? Jake, tell me!"

He shrugged. "We don't know. Larry said the guy was average height, average build, average looks, with medium dark hair. That lets Dennis out, since Rick says he's got red hair."

Sophie nodded. Dennis did, indeed, have red hair. Brick red, not flaming carrot-top red, but no one could mistake it for brown. Oddly, she felt disappointed that Larry wasn't better able to identify the person who hit him, even though it meant Dennis couldn't have done it. She hated to be wrong about where she placed her trust, but she wanted this solved, wanted whoever hurt Larry and exploited her store to be caught and to pay.

She thought carefully. "But you said you've got evidence . . ."

"Yeah." His mouth twisted in a look of disgust. "A few disks full of suspicious activities stored in your safe, and my printouts from the banks. But there are no fingerprints inside the CPU besides Dennis's, from when he installed the system. It would be a lot more suspicious if his prints weren't there. Without a likely suspect, all we've really got is a mystery."

She shivered. In a heartbeat, Jake was kneeling at her feet, his strong hands grasping her shoulders, his brilliant eyes focused on hers. Instinctively, she held on to his muscular arms for support.

"You'll be safe, Sophie. I promise. Whoever the cracker was, he took his modem and went underground. There's nothing happening at the bank now. Not through your system, anyway."

He leaned forward and kissed her sweetly. Immediately, she felt calmer, safer.

"The cops are watching the store, and the FBI is on alert, but your computer isn't any use to him now. That's why he ripped out the modem. There's a good possibility he's done this before, or will do it again. Sooner or later, he'll get sloppy or too ambitious, and they'll get him."

Still, she wasn't perfectly satisfied. She'd read plenty of mysteries, seen dozens of suspense and mystery movies. "But what if he knows Larry saw him? Do the cops think he might try..." She couldn't say the words. "You know."

He smiled gently. "I know." Another sweet kiss went a long way toward soothing her fears. "Sophie, the cops and the Feds expect me to tell them everything I know, but they don't see it as a two-way street. And hell, I'm not Rambo." He shrugged. "I'm betting he's long gone, though. I'm just glad Riordan got you out of there just before closing. The guy could have been lurking behind the shelves. When I think that it could have been you..."

He swore softly, then kissed her hard, until she was shaking and gasping for breath.

"Oh, God, I shouldn't have done that," he muttered. "Rick said Larry was asking for you. He thought we should drop in."

She stroked his tangled hair back from his temple and smiled into his eyes. "Isn't it too late to visit him tonight?"

He smiled back. "Yeah. Why don't you call him and tell him you'll be by tomorrow?"

"And then?"

He shrugged, but she saw the devilish light in his eyes. "Don't know. I'm so hungry, my stomach's wrapped around my backbone, but I don't know anyplace that's open late."

She loved this side of him, teasing, unguarded. "Hmm. I've probably got something edible in the freezer at my apartment."

A slow grin curved his lips. "Give me ten minutes to pack up my stuff and straighten this place enough so Eames's maid doesn't pitch a fit tomorrow."

* * *

Just his luck, Mrs. Mandel was rocking on her front porch when he followed Sophie's car to their driveway. She waved, so he knew they'd have to stop and say hello. He really liked their landlady, but he had making love with Sophie on his mind. It was all so new to him. He was still having trouble believing it was real

He was also wondering, since he had a healthy respect for Murphy's Law, when Dean Wilde would make another appearance. Not, he hoped, when Sophie was in his arms, letting him make love to her. There was no way he would share her with Wilde.

He propped the Harley on its stand and waited for Sophie to lock her car door. Sudden doubts hit him. This was all so new. It was like being given software without any instructions. Should he take her hand? Put his arm around her? Or would she think he was being presumptuous? She might not want their landlady to know they were . . . close.

Sophie solved his dilemma by smiling sweetly and taking his hand. "She'll be hurt if we don't say hello. Just don't mention food, or we'll never escape."

"Hello, children," Mrs. Mandel called. "Come have some cookies."

He glanced down at Sophie, who snickered and refused to look at him. Mrs. Mandel, on the other hand, eyed him sharply. "Sophie, darling, that nice Mike Riordan was here looking for you earlier. He said he'll drop by the store tomorrow."

Jake frowned, but there wasn't anything he could say. This thing with Sophie was too new, too fragile, for him to go primitive. But he'd love to find an excuse to make sure Riordan stopped sniffing around Sophie—permanently.

* * *

"Well, Dean?" The Adviser gave him that raised-eyebrow look, but couldn't fool him. There was a definite twinkle in those eyes.

He grinned. "As far as I know, all pistons are firing."

"As far as you know?"

"Well, hell!" The Adviser winced at the reference. "I'm not a Peeping Tom! Last I checked, Sophie had that dreamy look in her eyes and Warren couldn't stop grinning." He'd expected to be jealous, but all he'd felt—all he *still* felt—was glad. Deep-down, bottom-of-his-black-little-heart glad.

"Ah." The Adviser gave him a smile—a real one. "Mission accomplished."

Dean pondered that. "No, I don't think so."

"But they're in love, are they not?"

"Oh, yeah. They're nuts about each other. But something's still not right. I can't pinpoint it, but I can feel it. Like when an engine isn't running as sweetly as she could. You know?"

The Adviser nodded slowly. "Yes, Dean. I believe your instincts are correct."

It was like that old joke about the good news and the bad news. Nice to know he was right about something, but he didn't want to be right about something being wrong. He wanted everything to be right for Sophie—and Jake.

"So what should I do?"

The Adviser smiled. "What is the saying? Ah, yes. Deal with it."

"*Deal* with it? I don't even know what *it* is!" he sputtered, but he was already talking to himself. Maybe he should ask Warren. Hell, the guy was a genius.

Much as she loved Mrs. Mandel, Sophie was relieved when their landlady finally dismissed them. She was still tingling from Jake's last kiss, less than an hour ago. The last thing she wanted was Mrs. Mandel's well-meant hints about marriage to scare Jake off. His expression of dismay—guilt, perhaps?—had been like a neon sign warning that his thoughts had not been traveling down the same road at their landlady's—or her own.

But instinct told her that the surest way to lose whatever precious little time she had left with Jake was to try to hold on, to try for more. She'd have to learn to treasure the moment, live in the present and let him go when he was ready.

Perhaps, if she'd understood that about Dean, he'd be alive today.

Jake stopped at his own back porch. When she looked up at him, he didn't meet her eyes. Her heart sank.

"Well, um..." He stared at their hands, clasped together.

Hastily she tugged her hand from his. She wouldn't have him thinking she was hanging on to him, even if her soul cried out for her to hold on with every ounce of her strength.

"Oh," he said, as if she'd answered some unspoken question. "Well..." He turned toward his door. She bit her lip to keep from asking him to stay, to take her with him, to go upstairs with her—anything, but this awkward parting.

Suddenly he faced her, his eyes glittering in the porch light. For a fraction of a second, she saw a predatory gleam that unnerved her, and at the same time, gave her hope. He still wanted her.

"Sophie, what the hell is the protocol here?"

"Pardon me?"

"The protocol. The communication parameters." He shook his head. "Do I follow you upstairs, or ask you in, or say good-night here?"

Her heart melted. Smiling, she took his hand in hers again. "You *don't* say good-night here. Come upstairs for dinner."

He drew her hand up to his lips and kissed her knuckles. Her heart pounded at the intent so clear in his beautiful eyes. In a dreamy daze, she let him lead her up the stairs to her own apartment. Once inside, she felt as if she were on automatic pilot, hardly aware of anything except Jake. A quick check of the freezer yielded a vegetable lasagna she could defrost and heat in the microwave. Jake found a bottle of white wine in the refrigerator and poured two glasses while she took care of the lasagna.

"Do you mind if I change into something that doesn't smell like chlorine?" she asked. "I won't be long. You can put on some music, if you'd like. Dinner won't be ready for at least twenty minutes, but there are some potato chips in the—"

He chuckled. "Sophie, relax. I won't starve. I must have scarfed down at least a dozen of Mrs. Mandel's cookies."

She flashed him a quick smile, then hurried to her room to grab another lightweight summer dress from the closet. After tiptoeing to the bathroom, she took a quick shower, blessing the inventor of shampoos with conditioners for saving her a few minutes. Once her hair was almost dry, she slipped into the sunset-pink sundress, sprayed cologne on her throat and wrists and walked barefoot to the living room.

The sound of a David Foster CD floated down the hall, making her smile. It was her favorite. Jake sat on the couch, watching her walk into the room. Smoothing the skirt of her dress with suddenly damp palms, she sank down beside him and picked up her wineglass. The music swirled softly around the dimly lit room, setting a very romantic mood that surprised and pleased her.

Jake captured her free hand in his. She looked into his beautiful eyes. "This afternoon was...very special, Sophie." His intimate tone gave her chills. Nice, warm chills.

Wide-eyed, she nodded. "It was for me, too," she admitted in a voice that was barely over a whisper.

He gave her a crooked little grin. "I was afraid I wouldn't be able to make it good for you. Theoretical knowledge has a way of dissolving in a crisis."

"It's never been like that before for me, Jake. If you hadn't said anything, I never would have known..." She felt her cheeks burn. "You know." He squeezed her fingers gently.

"Yeah. It's not something I liked to admit. But I wanted you to know. I'm glad you were the first."

She smiled shyly, wishing she had the courage to tell him she wanted to be the last, too. But if she said too much, too soon, she might ruin this sweet moment. Memories of Dean weighed heavily on her heart. If he'd lived, he would be Jake's age. He'd be the best motorcycle mechanic in New England, at least. If she hadn't chased him to his death by trying to tie him down. Well, she wouldn't make the same mistake with Jake. She'd follow his lead and keep things as light and unencumbered emotionally as he obviously intended.

So she smiled and said, "I just can't imagine how all the women in California missed you."

He snorted. "They didn't." Her brows rose at that. Was he playing on her gullibility, which everyone always claimed was of legendary proportions? "I told you, it's a long story."

"I'm not going anywhere." She smiled. "It's my apartment."

"Hey, I'm not that absentminded. I could tell by the fact that there's actual food here."

"You're stalling." She took a sip of her wine, then set her glass down. When she sat back again, Jake's arm slid around her shoulders. As if it were the most natural thing in the world, she settled against him, but inside, she was trembling. His scent and his warmth, the sultry night, the whimsical, soft music, the low rumble of his voice, made her think of how easy it would be for them to make love right then, right there.

Jake took a deep breath. "Yeah, I'm stalling. Okay, picture the scrawny, nerdy kid I told you about, starting university classes part-time at eleven. I was like the class mascot. The freshman girls used to offer to baby-sit for me in exchange for help with their math and science assignments. By the time I was in graduate school, at sixteen, I was in another world from kids my own age, and I was still a geeky kid to the women in the grad program."

She pictured that awkward little boy and her heart ached for him. "That must have been very lonely for you."

"I pretended not to care, but getting laughed at is tough on even the strongest male ego."

He finished his wine, then leaned forward to set the glass on the coffee table. When he sat back, he angled slightly away. Sophie wanted to touch him again, to reassure him. His rejection hurt.

"When I finally got brave enough to try to seduce a woman, one I'd heard was easy, I got so drunk that I passed out before anything happened. The next thing I knew, it seemed as if every undergraduate female on campus was trying to drag me into bed." He snorted. "It turns out there was a bet on. I felt like a piece of meat."

Tears stung her eyes. "But there must have been other women who were genuinely interested in you."

He shrugged. "It was easier to pretend to be above all that. After a while, I convinced myself I didn't need anyone. Hell, I was raised by a committee. My parents weren't married. When I thought about it later, I was always amazed that they'd managed to produce me. I never knew what a real family was. So I told myself I wasn't missing what I didn't know. I buried myself in work and burned off excess energy swimming and cycling like a maniac."

She put her hand on his hard thigh. "Jake—"

"For God's sake, don't feel sorry for me, Sophie." He covered her hand with his own and pressed her palm flat over the corded muscles. His smile didn't quite light his eyes.

"It's not like I ended up a street person or a lunatic. I've got a great career and more money than I know what to do with, and I'm no more neurotic than anyone else. Maybe less neurotic, since I'm not running in circles like everyone else seems to be, looking for whatever love is."

That hurt. Reflexively, she tried to pull her hand away from his. He held tighter. Caught, miserable, fearing what he would say next, she looked down at their joined hands framed by the faded denim of his jeans.

"Hell, does anyone know what love is?" he added, the quiet intimacy of his voice torturing her.

Sophie risked meeting his eyes. He gazed back, his expression unreadable. "I guess love is what makes us want someone to be safe and happy, even if it means we have to give something up to make it happen," she ventured, praying he'd understand what she was trying to say.

His eyes glittered in the dim light. "I think you're a very wise woman," he said softly.

His arm around her shoulder tightened, drawing her closer. His other hand released hers and gently cupped her head. Breathlessly, she closed her eyes and received his soft, sweet kiss. Then he drew back.

His meaning was clear, she thought. She had the wisdom to love him and let him go. God help her, she did, but she knew it was going to break her heart. Silently, she lifted her free hand to stroke the smooth, warm plane of his cheek and touch her fingertips to his full lips.

"Be patient with me, Sophie. This is all new to me." He gave her that crooked grin that always made her heart melt.

His fingers tangled in her hair. "We'll take it one step at a time, okay? And you'll stop me if you feel like I'm rushing you. Promise?"

"Promise," she echoed, but she wanted to plead with him to rush her.

He took her mouth in a kiss that started softly, sweetly. But the instant she parted her lips for him, he deepened the kiss until she was breathless. The banked fires within her flared up, fueled by the taste, the scent, the feel of him. Her last conscious act was to glance at her windows to be sure her curtains were closed. Then she gave herself up to the pleasures of loving Jake.

With unsteady hands, he eased the straps of her dress down off her arms. His fingertips trailed fire over her sensitive skin. She worked her hands up under his shirt, causing him to break the kiss to catch his breath when she found his nipples and teased them. She smiled at the power of that simple caress, then lost all strength when he bent to kiss her breasts. Every touch of his lips, tongue and teeth set off ripples of sensation through her.

The need to share this shimmering pleasure sent her hands to his waist. He sucked in his lean stomach when she fumbled with the snap of his jeans. He was powerfully aroused behind the soft denim. Sophie felt his big body vibrate with tension as she drew the zipper down. At the first touch of her hand, he went rigid and groaned.

Abruptly, Jake moved away, shoving his jeans and briefs off, then turned to her with a fiercely hungry look in his eyes. Her skirt had twisted around her hips. Without unfastening it at the waist, he roughly tore the skirt and her panties down her legs. The sound of fabric tearing, the unexpected intensity of his impatience, fueled her own desire.

His hands returned, so gentle now, caressing her thighs, seeking and finding the curls hiding her feminine secrets.

Once again, his mouth found her breasts. With a soft cry, she arched into his caresses.

Somewhere, a chime rang five times.

"What the hell is that?" he muttered, tickling her breast with his lips.

"The microwave," she managed. "Dinner's ready."

He lifted his head to look into her eyes. Slowly he explored her with gentle fingers. Her eyes went wide, then shut, letting her focus on the exquisite pleasure he was creating.

"So are we," he murmured. "Can dinner wait?" Unable to speak, she nodded. "Good." He eased her down onto her back and held himself over her. "Because I can't."

She couldn't wait, either. Clutching his hips, she urged him down to her. With a shuddering breath, he thrust into her and she absorbed his wildness. The spiral of sensations tightened almost painfully, then splintered into a rainbow kaleidoscope. Before she could catch her breath, Jake gave an inarticulate shout and climaxed, his ecstasy sending her over the edge once more.

Time and place dissolved. All she knew was Jake. He surrounded her, he possessed her. Their bodies were so warm, so slick with sweat it was as if they had melted into each other. She felt fused to him, body and soul. Sooner or later, reality would intrude. But for the present, the sweet, dreamy present, loving Jake was reality enough.

Jake tucked his helmet under his arm and smiled down at Sophie walking by his side. The smells, the sounds and sights of the hospital surrounded them, but he was so pumped up on adrenaline, on pure joy, that he couldn't care less where he was, as long as he was with Sophie.

He'd thought about what Sophie had said, about love and sacrifices. That certainly was the way he felt about her. He'd do anything, give up anything, to keep her safe and happy.

Not that a computer guy like him had much opportunity for grand gestures, but he'd be willing to die—or kill—to protect her.

Dean Wilde had finally understood that, Jake realized. He'd let her go, let her love again, because he'd finally learned what love was. Jake almost chuckled out loud at his next thought. Dean had thought he'd come back to teach sex education to a socially backward computer jockey, and ended up teaching himself about love.

It was ironic, but he missed Wilde. He wanted his guardian angel to know it was working out between him and Sophie. Of course, he reasoned, all that haunted stuff could have been a product of his imagination set off by a hell of a smack on the skull. But he kind of hoped not. Wilde could be a pain in the butt, but he had a good heart. Once he got a handle on the idea that he couldn't actually have Sophie, he'd been pretty decent. Hell, without Wilde's coaching, he—Jake—would probably still be standing, totally tongue-tied, on Sophie's porch. He never would have—

"This is Larry's room," Sophie said, breaking into his thoughts.

"Want me to wait out here? I don't exactly know him."

She smiled, that sweet smile that always sent warm little waves through him. "Don't be silly. He'll probably be very uncomfortable if his female boss shows up alone. He's barely nineteen, and pretty shy."

Well, he knew what that was like. He followed Sophie inside the four-bed room. Three of the beds were occupied, two by middle-aged men. The third bed held a gangly kid with a huge white bandage on his head and a pile of comics on his lap. Jake couldn't help wondering how Larry's vision was—or if he'd been hearing strange voices since getting knocked out.

Sophie greeted the guy and made introductions. The kid had a crush on his boss, Jake saw immediately. Not that he could blame anyone for having a crush on Sophie. But she was *his*.

"I'm supposed to be walking around a little," Larry said after some stilted conversation about how he was feeling, and how revolting the hospital food was. "You guys wanna come? That way I don't have to call for an orderly. I hate feeling like I need a baby-sitter."

Sophie glanced up, then smiled at Larry. "Sure."

The kid started to whip off the sheet over his legs, then turned beet red. "Uh, can one of you hand me my robe? It's hanging in the closet."

Sympathizing with Larry about the draftiness of those hospital gowns, Jake went to the narrow closet. There were three robes hanging there. "Which one?"

"The brown one," Larry told him.

He looked at the robes. One plaid, one striped and one red. No brown robe.

"There's a red one here," he said.

"Oh, is it red?" Larry looked surprised. "I wouldn't know. I'm color-blind. A lot of stuff looks muddy brown to me."

The gears meshed. The tumblers dropped into place. The bell rang. He looked at Sophie and knew without a word that she was thinking the same thing.

"You're color-blind?" he asked, to be sure.

"*Red* color-blind?" Sophie added.

"Yeah."

"Sophie, did Larry ever meet Dennis?" She shook her head. He turned back to the kid now sitting on the edge of the bed, his knobby knees showing below the edge of the blue hospital gown. "Sorry, man, but you'll have to get an orderly after all."

He tossed the red robe onto Larry's lap. The kid was gaping at him as if he'd sprouted horns. He grabbed Sophie's hand and tugged her toward the door. She stopped short and turned back to Larry. Despite his sense of urgency, he had to wait for her. He knew what was on her mind, and he loved her for it. Sophie would always think of others first.

"Larry, please don't tell anyone about being color-blind, except the police. Not anyone else. Please? It's very important."

Without waiting for Larry to answer, Jake hustled Sophie out of the hospital. Too much time had already been wasted.

Chapter Thirteen

Sophie hung up the front desk phone after taking a reserve request and smiled. Good for Bob Manetti, she thought. He'd finally found a special woman who shared his fondness for horror movies and homemade pizzas. More importantly, a woman who thought he was special, too.

"You look happy," Mike Riordan said, startling her.

"Oh! I didn't see you come in. Hi."

"Hi, yourself." He smiled. "I heard the kid who got himself knocked out woke up and the cops have a positive ID. They plan to bust the guy any minute."

She nodded. "How did you hear?"

"From Warren, when he finally showed up at eleven-thirty. I guess it doesn't matter when he wanders in, since he's a consultant, not an employee. And he's almost done, anyway. But it's bad for morale when a hotshot shows up late all the time."

Sophie straightened the pens on the desk, unwilling to let Mike see her expression when he announced that Jake was almost finished, several weeks early. She hadn't known that. Was he planning to wait until the last minute to tell her?

Mike's brows drew together. "Have you figured out what was taken, besides the videos?"

A quick glance showed her that the closest customers were out of hearing range, but she still leaned forward and kept her voice low. "We think that someone put a modem into my computer, then removed it after breaking into at least one bank."

He snorted. "So Warren claims. But he hasn't got any hard proof. I think he's just trying to cover his . . . act. The banks are secure, but he's got to say something to justify his fee, especially since it's taking him less time to do the job than he estimated."

His obvious scorn for Jake stung. She understood that Mike thought of Jake as a rival, and it bothered her to think that she'd been instrumental in hurting Mike. But her loyalty—and her love—belonged to Jake. She wouldn't stand there and let Mike criticize Jake for being brilliant at his work.

"Jake is the best in his field, Mike," she reminded him gently. "If he says he traced illegal activity to my computer, then I believe him. Anyway, I've seen the proof."

Mike's expression softened. "You're really hung up on him, huh?" He gave her a rueful smile before she could do more than blink in surprise at his sudden change of tone and subject. "Hey, he's not my type, but I guess I can understand."

She smiled, relieved. "Thanks, Mike."

He shrugged. "So Warren really has proof that someone was cracking through your system? I guess he is pretty good. How did he do it?"

"You know how hopeless I am about computer jargon. All I know is that he installed something to record everything the computer did."

Mike whistled softly. "Just like in the movies. Did you see a printout? It must be miles long. I hate those things after I've been staring at them for a few hours. I don't envy the Feds." He shook his head. "They must be going blind sorting out your video rentals from the illegal stuff."

"Well, the printout looked pretty long, but Jake has it all on disk, too. He said the FBI was waiting for the local police to catch the guy who broke in, before they go to the trouble of combing through the records." Mike frowned slightly, then nodded. "Anyway, I think Jake inserted some sort of code to sort the cracker's trail from my store data." She laughed. "Good grief, I'm starting to use computer jargon!"

Mike grinned. "It's contagious." Then he peered at her, all traces of humor gone. "I hope Warren put his proof in a safe place, then. I'd like to see that sleaze-bucket who did this put away for a long time," he added fiercely.

His concern touched her. "The disks are in my safe, until the FBI wants them."

Mike's brows lifted. "Do you know who broke in and hit the kid Sunday night? Warren was playing his cards kinda close to his chest. That made me wonder if he already knew."

She couldn't bring herself to accuse Dennis. That was for the police to do. As far as she was concerned, he was a likely suspect, but it wasn't fair for her to point a finger at him. She shook her head.

"I don't know."

Mike took her hands in his. He looked straight into her eyes, his expression troubled. "When I think that it was just a lucky break that I took you out of here Sunday night and left the kid to lock up.... It made me crazy to think it could have been you getting hurt."

She tried to ease her hands from his. "Mike, I—"

He gave her a rueful half smile. "I know. You and Warren have got a thing going. I told you, Sophie, I understand." His voice dropped even lower. "But that doesn't mean I have to stop caring about you. When Warren leaves, I'll still be here. I hope you'll remember that, Sophie. I still care about you."

She swallowed past the lump in her throat. "Thank you, Mike," she murmured, touched but uncomfortable with his declaration. She loathed the thought of Jake leaving her behind and she didn't want the guilt of Mike waiting for her to fall in love with him instead.

"Don't thank me. I'm just being honest." He grinned and straightened, releasing her hands. "And if I don't get out of here, I'm also going to be late from lunch. Gotta set a good example."

He gave her a wink, then sauntered out of the store. She watched him get into his black BMW and sighed, relieved that he hadn't hassled her about Jake after all. Still, Mike had made her wonder about Jake, and that made her uneasy. She loved Jake. She wanted to trust him. She didn't like having even the tiniest doubts about him.

So, it looks like you don't need me, huh? Now that you're swimming again and everything's copacetic between you and Sophie.

Jake nearly missed the next stair on his way to Sophie's porch. "Just because you're a ghost, doesn't mean you have to sneak up on me," he grumbled, stopping in his tracks.

Touchy, touchy. Wilde snickered. *Now what?*

Jake leaned against the stair rail, enjoying the familiar give and take. "Now, as in this minute? Or now, as in the future?"

Well, I don't have to be a genius to figure out what you're going to do now, like this minute. I meant after tonight. I'm looking to tie up somr loose ends and get on to something more interesting.

"Hey, you're lurking in my head. You know damn well what I plan to do."

Yeah, well, just do it right. Down on one knee. Flowers. Not roses. She always said they die too soon. Wilde snorted a short, ironic laugh. *Those big pom-pom things are good. She likes them. And a ring—*

"You're worse than Mrs. Mandel. I know what I'm doing, Wilde."

Well, hell. I'm just trying to help. Guess you're on your own now. Stay out of hot water, huh? I won't be around to bail you out.

A strange sense of loss stole over him. He'd had a few close friends, like Les and Annie, over the years, but never a friend like Dean. It would be like losing a part of himself when the irreverent, sarcastic ghost left to torment someone else in the name of assistance.

Torment, huh? Thanks a whole bunch. Without me—

"Yeah. I know." He couldn't believe this. He was getting choked up about saying goodbye to a figment of his imagination.

Take care of her, Warren. Love her for both of us.

He had to clear his throat twice before he could say, "I will."

He felt a brief wave of dizziness, then his head cleared and he knew Dean was gone. He expected the world to suddenly go out of focus, but his vision stayed sharp. A lasting souvenir of this strange alliance between them. Would his eyes return to their normal pale blue, or would they, too, remain as vivid as they'd been since Dean had saved his life? Or maybe both would fade with time.

But why was he wasting time standing around on the porch stairs when he could be upstairs holding Sophie, kissing her and hearing those little sounds she made that sent his pulse into overdrive? He'd worked late at the bank, impatient to finish the job, but aching to be with Sophie. And she was up there now, waiting for him.

He took the stairs two at a time. Sophie answered his knock, her smile sweet, a little shy. She was wearing a pale pink silky shirt that ended at the middle of her bare thighs. When he looked her over, her toes curled. Something deep inside him swelled and warmed at the sight of her, at the thought that she was his.

"Hi. Did you have dinner?"

He pulled her into his arms and held her close, breathing in the clean scent of her skin, her hair. She curved against him, so pliant, so giving. Blood rushed to his loins and desire made him shake.

"I don't need dinner. I need to make love to you," he muttered, feeling like a caveman and not caring.

She tipped her head back to look up into his eyes. "The air conditioner is on in the bedroom."

Knowing she'd been anticipating making love made his heart skip a beat. With a nod, he released her enough to walk down the hall with her clasped to his side. Her hand roamed over his back, sending electrifying messages to his brain to get his feet moving faster. The cold air from her closed bedroom wrapped around them when Sophie opened the door, but he knew that, soon enough, the room would be sizzling from the heat between them.

She turned and faced him, a sweet smile of invitation curving her lips. With trembling hands, he unfastened the six pearly buttons of her shirt, then left it hanging open. The shirt allowed him tantalizing glimpses of her satiny white flesh and pale pink panties when he stood back to rip his own shirt off. Several buttons pinged across the room, testifying to his impatience.

His shoes were already off, downstairs, the first thing he always did when he got into his own apartment. He could barely work the tab on his jeans, barely slide the zipper down. She reached out to help. He caught her wrists and stopped her just in time. If she touched him, even through his briefs, he would explode.

Tonight was too special to rush.

Gently he set her hands by her sides and stepped back to get out of his trousers and briefs. Then he moved closer until he could run his fingers down the open front of her silky shirt. He barely touched the inner curves of her breasts. She caught her breath. Through the shiny cloth, he saw her nipples harden. He brushed his fingertips over them, letting the silk add to his caress.

Kneeling, he pushed the shirt open, freeing her breasts for his hands. Her heart fluttered into his touch, like the beating of a bird's wings. He pressed his lips to the heated place between her soft breasts, then touched his tongue to her skin. A tiny cry escaped her, and she slid her fingers into his hair, making his scalp tingle.

Her scent filled his senses. He settled his open mouth over one nipple. The sweet taste of her, the sound of her rapid breathing, the heat of her skin and the cool slide of the silk shirt on his cheek swirled through his consciousness like a drug. He cupped her firm, satin-covered bottom in his hands and drew her closer. Her soft moan echoed the groan rising from deep inside him. Her hips shifted subtly, echoing the rhythm of his mouth on her breast.

The satin panties slid easily down her thighs to pool at her feet. He released her breast to bend and help her step out of the bit of cloth. Her slender legs trembled. He held her hips to steady her and pressed his mouth against her flat belly.

Someday, he prayed, their child would grow there, close to her heart.

With shaking fingers, he feathered the dark curls that hid her feminine mysteries. Until now, she'd shied away from total possession, as if she'd felt she had to hold something back. Until tonight, he'd felt a vague uncertainty about his own ability to love her the way she deserved to be loved.

But tonight would be the turning point. He wanted to possess all of her, to imprint himself on her psyche, leaving her no question that they belonged together.

She moaned his name as he pressed a kiss into the heat of her secret flesh. The sound ripped through him like lightning tearing apart the midnight sky. With an answering growl, so primitive, so primal he didn't recognize his own voice, he stood and lifted her into his arms. The silky shirt flowed around her pale body and trailed over his heated flesh as he carried her to the bed. She lay back and gazed up at him with stormy gray eyes full of trust . . . and more, he hoped.

He slid kisses down her quivering body until the soft curls brushed his cheek. Reverently, he touched his lips to her and felt her softening, surrendering. With his heart thundering against his ribs, he caressed her, growing drunk on the sweet spice of her. Her soft whimpers, her responsiveness, drove him higher.

Her climax rippled through her, wringing a cry from her. Close to the edge himself, Jake surged into her. She wrapped her legs around his hips, welcoming him, following him, leading him. He felt her body tighten, then felt release wash over her, the waves carrying him away, too, like a tidal wave. Possessing her, he was possessed by her. With a strangled shout, he poured himself into her, dying and being reborn in her arms.

Exhausted, satisfied, secure in his love for Sophie and hers for him, he held her close and drifted.

An explosion of thunder shook him out of a sound, dreamless sleep. The clock beside the bed said four in the morning. Lightning split the sky—multiple flashes. Another crack of thunder rattled the windows. Beside him, curled under the light summer blanket, Sophie started and whimpered softly. With a smile, he put his hand on her hip, massaging gently, offering comfort.

"Dean!" she cried out.

His smile faded and his hand on her hip stilled. Suddenly Sophie fought against the covers, thrashing until she'd knocked aside his hand and struggled to sit up. She reached out her arms as if calling back a lover.

"Dean! I love you!"

Every soft word sliced through him until he was sure he was bleeding.

"Sophie!" he hissed, unable to hear more. "Wake up!"

"Oh!" She lowered her arms and turned her head to look into his face in the shadowed room. Lightning flashed again, showing her face pale in the dark, her eyes enormous. "Dean?"

How many times had she called him Dean? Right from the first moment they met. Wilde had let her go, but Sophie would always love him.

"No, damn it! *Jake.*"

He stood and fumbled for his clothes in the dark. Inside, he felt shattered. He'd always laughed at the notion of heartbreak, but that was exactly what he was feeling. Nothing had ever hurt so much as hearing Sophie call out to Dean—*not* to him—that she loved him.

"Dean's *dead,* Sophie. *Dead.* You and I are alive. Let Dean go." She stared up at him, her confusion making him feel cruel, but he had to make her understand. "I won't compete with a dead man, Sophie. We can't have anything together until you *let Dean go.*"

"Dean?" she whispered, still looking straight at him.

With his heart in a million pieces, he walked away from the only woman he'd ever love.

"Sophie, go home." Rick's voice cut into her stupor. "You look like you're coming down with the flu. I can stay tonight and close up."

She met his eyes across her office but couldn't quite summon an answering smile. "Thanks, Rick. But really, I'm..." Her throat closed and tears sprang into her eyes. Helplessly, she shook her head.

Rick shut the office door and crossed the small room to her side. "Sophie, what is it? For God's sake, Soph, tell me. Let me help you, whatever it is." He perched on the edge of her desk, his eyes reflecting concern.

"There's...nothing you can...do," she choked out. "It's Jake..."

"What about Jake?"

"He's...gone. He left this morning before I woke up. Mrs. Mandel said he packed his clothes and computers and sent them somewhere by taxi. And he left her a n-note and extra money for inconvenience. All—all the note said was that his work was fi-finished so he was leaving."

Rick swore. "Did you guys have a fight?"

Utterly miserable, she wiped at the tears sliding down her cheeks. "No. Well, yes. Sort of. This morning. Early. The storm woke me. I must have been dreaming...about someone I knew a long time ago. Someone who used to be very special. I was dreaming that I was saying goodbye and I guess I said something...something like his name...."

"Oh, Soph!" Rick sighed. "That would do it."

"Obviously. Unless he was just looking for an excuse to go away without strings."

Rick appeared to ponder that. Then he shook his head slowly. "Some guys do that, yeah. But I didn't think Jake was like that."

"Neither did I. But I tend to give people the benefit of the doubt. Look how I trusted Dennis." She sniffed, trying to be brave when she felt as if she were dying inside. "Anyway, being here will keep my mind off Jake." At Rick's skeptical expression, she shrugged. "It's better than being home, knowing he's not there anymore."

"If you say so. Want anything from the convenience store before I take off?" She shook her head. "Okay. It's pretty quiet out there, with the rain."

She managed a smile for Rick as he waved from the doorway, but as soon as she was alone, she sank back into her thoughts.

The evening seemed to stretch on endlessly. The rain poured down as it had all day, a perfect reflection of her mood. Only a few people straggled into the store, dripping, commenting on the storm, eager to get home with the tapes they'd rented.

Then, finally, yet strangely too soon, it was closing time. She locked the front door and switched off the lights with a sense of relief mingled with dread. She didn't want to go back to her apartment, back to the bed she'd shared with Jake, knowing he wasn't there. Knowing he'd left without a word, left without saying where she could contact him... or if he wanted her to contact him. She could phone Annie and Les, but her pride wouldn't let her. If Jake wanted her, he would let her know. *If.*

In the semidarkness of the office, she sank down on the sofa and gave in to her tears. Head and throat aching, heart breaking, she let sleep wash over her. In her dreams, Dean and Jake stood shoulder to shoulder, mocking her with cruel smiles.

Suddenly a noise wrenched her out of sleep. Confused by waking in a strange place, she tried to orient herself in the darkness. Her office? Had she fallen asleep at work? What time was it?

The noise grated again. In the shadows, she saw something move. A shape. Tall. Moving slowly, stealthily. Bending low now, next to the file cabinets. The *safe!* She was being robbed!

A tiny gasp escaped her. She clamped her mouth shut but it was too late. The thief froze. Then, as she watched with eyes wide, trying to see as much as possible in the dark, the form straightened and turned toward her.

Her heart leapt and began to race painfully. She heard a click. Bright light blinded her. Instinctively, she sat up and shaded her eyes with her forearm, but could see nothing.

She heard him, though, walking slowly across the floor. He loomed over her, his breathing shallow. And she smelled him, a familiar men's cologne mixed with ozone from the rain.

"Oh, Sophie, you aren't supposed to be here now." He spoke softly, regretfully.

Adrenaline surged through her at the sound of that well-known voice, followed swiftly by a sense of betrayal as heavy as mud.

"Wha—What are you doing here?" Her voice came out in a hoarse whisper.

"Can't you figure that out yourself?" She still couldn't see his face, but she imagined him smiling. "No, of course not. You're too trusting."

The blinding light suddenly clicked off, leaving her even more sightless in the total dark.

"I'm stealing the disks and printouts from your safe. I'm getting rid of the evidence that I've been cracking into bank accounts through your computer and moving the funds into other accounts."

"*You!* What about Dennis?"

A snort came out of the dark. "Dennis is an idiot. He couldn't do anything without me, except screw up. Look what happened with Larry."

"But won't he tell the police? And the FBI?"

"Not if I get to him first." The quiet resolution of that statement sent chills shuddering through her. "And that's why I need to get rid of this stuff first."

In the silence that followed, Sophie understood what had to come next. Her heart pounded and the coppery taste of fear filled her suddenly dry mouth.

"I'm sorry, Soph. I tried to protect you. I even drugged your drink Sunday night so you wouldn't come back to check on the kid who was supposed to lock up. I didn't want you to get caught in the middle of that scene. I really do love you. I wasn't just using you to get into your computer." He paused, as if he were wrestling with what he had to say. "I don't want to hurt you, but you'll tell the cops about me. I can't let you."

She swallowed the bile that rose in her throat. "I know you wouldn't hurt me. You're a good person. Everyone can make mistakes. But you don't need to make it worse. Go now, and—"

"And what? You'll lie to the cops? To the FBI?" He swore sharply.

Desperate, shaking, she tried to think quickly, logically. There was no sign that the police were responding to her silent alarm. Had she set it before falling asleep? She didn't think so. She couldn't remember locking the back door. She was on her own, and she had to do something, anything.

"Take the disks," she suggested earnestly. "I can stall them for you. Give you time to get away. And I won't tell them anything they don't ask about. They'll only know what Dennis tells them, if they catch him."

"I've got a better idea. Come with me, Sophie. You can be my insurance policy. I've got plenty of money. I know people who can get us new passports, social security numbers, driver's licenses—the works. There are places we can go where no one will find us. We can make a life together."

He knelt beside the couch and took her hands in his. Her stomach twisted but she didn't dare give in to the urge to recoil. His bizarre offer was giving her the only hope she might have of escaping.

After a pause that vibrated painfully, she spoke again. "What about my store?" she asked in a choked whisper, hoping to make him think she was considering his offer. Hoping to stall for time, just in case the West Hartford police were patrolling, just in case they noticed something wasn't right.

"What about it? You can open another store. I've got enough money stashed away to set you up. I'll take care of you." He leaned closer and touched his lips to her forehead. Her skin crawled but she forced herself to sit as still as she could. "Sophie, please? Don't make me hurt you."

Logic told her that if she went with him, she would have far more opportunities to escape than if she didn't. It was a gamble either way, and she hated taking risks, but the odds were completely against her if she refused. He was desperate and she was defenseless.

"Okay," she whispered. "I'll go with you."

He sighed and pulled her up to embrace her. Shaking and repulsed, she numbly registered that the object digging into her was the handle of a gun tucked into the waistband of his jeans. She swallowed hard and fought against her tears.

"That's my girl," he murmured. "I knew I could count on you. Now," he went on briskly, "open the safe and clean it out. Take the disks and whatever cash you've got. Then we're out of here." He loosened his hold and turned her toward the safe.

"I don't think so, Riordan."

Jake's voice, low and vibrating with menace, came quietly out of the dark behind them. Sophie started to break away from Mike. He grabbed her arm and wrenched it up behind her, then pulled her against him. Pain shot up to her shoulder but she bit back her cry. She felt him use his free hand to remove the gun from his waistband, felt its hard, cold muzzle press under her chin. Fear twisted in her stomach.

"You lose, Warren. I've got the money, the disks and the girl. Sophie's coming with me."

"No."

"Yes. She just said so. She knows I'll take care of her."

"With a gun?"

"That's up to you. Get out of my way, and Sophie is safe." The pressure of the gun suddenly ceased. Instead, Mike held it aimed at Jake.

Oh, God, Mike would shoot Jake! She had to do something. "Jake, it's all right," she said, trying to sound calm, convincing. "I'll be fine. I know Mike doesn't want to hurt me."

"But he will, Sophie. He's in too much trouble already. He's got to get away, and he can go faster without you. Besides, you know too much. He'll use you to escape now, after he shoots me. Then you'll be a witness to murder. Right, Riordan?"

Mike's grip on her arm tightened painfully. Sophie bit her lip to keep from crying out. Tears spilled down her cheeks—tears of love, of fear, of helplessness. In the dim light, Jake filled her sight, his quiet determination giving her hope in spite of her despair.

Mike let his frightening silence drag on. Finally Jake spoke again, his tone quietly persuasive. To Sophie, it was the sound of life itself.

"What will you do then, after she watches you shoot me? Do you really think she'll run away with you, protect you, after you kill me? Sophie always believed you were a decent guy. Do you know what that will do to her, Riordan? How will she feel about you then?"

Mike's grip loosened as if the doubts Jake were planting had sapped his physical strength. Some primitive sense of survival told Sophie this was her only chance. Crying Jake's name, she threw herself into Mike's side. He staggered and clutched for her, but she wrenched her aching arm out of his fingers and dropped to the floor. With a growl, he turned the gun back toward Jake, his legs blocking her view.

Jake! Where was he? Mike still stood in front of her. She couldn't see through the darkness. Cautiously, she started to get up. When she was on her hands and knees, she paused, listening for some clue what was going on between the two men in that deadly, silent standoff.

Suddenly, something crashed into her side and fell across her, knocking her flat to the floor. The sound of the gun deafened her, drowning out the screams she could only feel coming from her throat. All she knew was darkness, the echoing of that explosion and the terrible weight pinning her down.

Then the weight was being lifted from her, roughly. The lights flickered on, almost blinding in their sudden, cold harshness. Four uniformed policemen wrestled with Mike but his hands were empty. Where was the gun? Where was Jake? Oh, God! Had Mike shot Jake?

"Jake?" she called frantically.

"Right here, Sophie," he answered beside her. Sinking down to the floor, he took her in his strong arms and rocked her as she clutched at him and sobs of relief shook her. "Don't cry, sweetheart. It's all over and we're both safe."

She clung to him to reassure herself he was real and safe. His big hands stroked over her hair and her back, absorbing her fear. Finally she tipped back her head and gazed up through her tears. "Oh, Jake! I love you!"

Her words melted the last of the cold core of fear deep inside. He kissed her cheek, tasting the salt of her tears. "I know."

She sat up and glared. "You *know*? Then why did you leave me?"

He could almost hear Wilde answering: *Because he's pretty stupid for a genius.* "I didn't really leave. I needed to go somewhere to cool my heels. I, uh, I was thinking about you and me and Dean."

"I could have died without telling you I love you."

The way Dean had, he thought. He pulled her close again, unable to control the trembling that gripped him all over again. "This wasn't supposed to happen. You weren't supposed to be here."

She shivered in his arms. "That's what Mike said. Jake, what brought you here tonight?"

Love, he wanted to tell her. Instead, he said, "We knew Riordan had to come soon. He was running out of time. As soon as the cops discovered Larry is red color-blind, we showed him video clips of Dennis making service calls. Larry identified him right away. And that was that."

He bent to kiss her, hoping she would accept his brief explanation and let him move on to what was really important: the two of them. But Sophie dodged his kiss. He should have known it wouldn't be easy.

Sophie gaped at Jake. "You knew it was Mike? And who's 'we'?" she demanded, indignant that so many strings had been pulled behind her back.

"The West Hartford police and us. The Feds and me. They picked up Dennis this afternoon."

"That's probably a good thing. I'm afraid Mike was planning to kill him to protect himself."

Jake nodded. "Dennis was just a gofer. Riordan was the brains of the pair. Bank security is pretty sophisticated, so we knew there had to be an inside man, and Dennis is just too dumb."

"How did you know Mike would break into the safe?"

"We gambled that he'd play on your trust and get you to tell him." Surprise made her jaw drop, but anger robbed her of words. Jake placed a gentle fingertip on her lips. "We had this place wired with bells and whistles, but you put a hell of a glitch in things by staying late. I've never been so scared in my life."

Sophie gazed into his eyes and read regret in their brilliant depths. She kissed the finger against her lips, then clasped his wrist in her hand. He tightened his arm around her. She snuggled closer, feeling his heartbeat reverberate through her.

"I should have known you'd figure out a way to stall him." Jake murmured. She smiled into his chest at the compliment. "In his own way, Riordan loves you. He was totally freaked by the idea of hurting you," he added grudgingly. The truth of his insight saddened her.

"Poor Mike."

"Hey, don't feel too sorry for him. He was willing to kill three people to cover his tracks."

It was a sobering thought that made her tighten her hold on Jake's solid, reassuring body. She heard heavy footsteps approaching, but didn't bother to look up past Jake. He was all she wanted to see.

"You folks ready to come out?" one of the policemen asked.

"Yeah," Jake answered. "Soon."

Embarrassed at the policeman's amused tone, she reluctantly started to pull away from Jake's embrace.

"Wait. There's something I have to—" He stopped abruptly, then swallowed. "Sophie, I love you. I know you'll always love Dean, but—"

"Oh, Jake!" She turned so she could look up into his eyes. There was vulnerability in their depths. "That night, I dreamed Dean came back to say goodbye, and it seemed so real. It was as if my subconscious was telling me I was free to love you. But when the storm woke me, I guess I thought I was still dreaming. In the dark, I thought you were Dean. All I really could see were your eyes. Dean's eyes were the same bright blue. . . ." His grimace made her words trail off.

She smiled hesitantly. "I really do know the difference between you and Dean, you know," she told him, her voice husky with emotions she could barely contain. "Dean is in my past, and I really have let him go."

Jake regarded her so solemnly that she wondered if he believed her. She stroked her fingertips over his smooth, warm cheek. His eyes closed, his long lashes casting shadows under the harsh fluorescent lights.

"Sophie?" he whispered, his eyes still closed. "Will you marry me?"

He looked at her then, and she saw herself reflected in his brilliant blue eyes. Her heart swelled with love, and her own eyes filled with tears of happiness.

"Yes." A single word, carried on a sigh, but it expressed all the hope and trust shimmering within her.

Pulling her close, Jake let his breath escape in a sigh of pure relief. Reluctantly, aware that the police were waiting for them, he released Sophie and helped her up. She looked up at him, a slight frown creasing her brow. He brushed his fingers over her forehead, wanting to smooth away all her worries.

He tipped up her head so he could look into the steady depths of her smoky eyes, smiling to see himself reflected back. It was a sign, he thought whimsically, that she had finally let go of Dean—and that Dean had released her, too.

Before he bent to seal their love with a long kiss, he grinned up at the ceiling. He didn't think Wilde was around, wasn't sure he'd ever been there.

But, just in case, he wanted to thank his guardian angel.

Epilogue

Sophie knelt by a mound of fresh earth, gently patting a small plant with tiny blue flowers into place. Months had passed since he'd seen her, and she was even more beautiful. As he watched her, Dean swiped at his face with the back of his hand.

"Something wrong, Dean?" a familiar voice asked.

"Nah." He sniffed a little. "Got something in my eye. How're you doing, Adviser?"

The Adviser's smug little smile didn't irritate him at all anymore. "You know what they say, Dean. No rest for the weary."

He grinned to cover his concern for the old guy. "Thought that was no rest for the wicked."

The Adviser's smile broadened just a touch. "Speaking of wicked, you did bend the rules again."

"Hey, all I did was give Riordan a little push. Warren's fast and strong, but that gun could have killed someone."

The Adviser nodded in that wise way he had. "Timing, as the comedians say."

Just then, Warren roared up the driveway on the Harley. Sophie stood up slowly, a sweet smile lighting her beautiful face. Jake ran across the lawn of the house that used to belong to bank president Eames and took Sophie in his arms. Dean felt his face heating up. Warren was doing fine without any coaching.

"Good thing Warren didn't lose his virginity in an abandoned railroad car, or they wouldn't be living in such fancy digs, huh?" he said to the Adviser.

For the first time, he heard the old guy laugh out loud.

"What did the doctor say?" Jake asked Sophie after—finally—breaking the kiss.

"Doctor?" Dean glared at the Adviser. "What's wrong with Sophie?"

"Shh! Listen."

"She says you'll be changing your first diaper around the end of October."

Jake whooped loudly, then picked her up and whirled her around, both of them laughing. Dean felt himself smile like an idiot.

"A baby, huh?" Dean pondered that. "They'll be good parents."

From the side of the house, a young golden retriever bounded toward them, tail waving joyfully. Jake threw a tennis ball for the dog to chase.

"Look at that," he said, using the diversion to wipe at his eyes again. "I told you they'd be good parents. They got him a dog already."

"Her."

"Huh?"

"Their daughter."

He let that sink in. "A girl, huh? She'll be beautiful and sweet, like her mother, and brainy, like her old man. Probably much too trusting. I guess she'll need some kind of guardian angel."

The Adviser smiled. "I think that can be arranged."

"You mean . . . ?" It would be a chance to repay Sophie—and Jake—for teaching him the meaning of love.

"No, my boy. I have something quite different in mind for you."

"Uh-oh. I know that tone." He was a little disappointed, but he wasn't really worried about getting stuck with a dud assignment. It was just fun to tease the Adviser.

"Precisely," the old guy said, reminding him that his thoughts were an open book. The Adviser slung his arm over Dean's shoulder in that fatherly way that he kind of liked.

"Will there be a beautiful girl?"

"Woman."

"Okay. A beautiful woman. I can deal with that. Will I get to use what I learned about computers? I got to be a pretty good hacker—"

The Adviser actually snorted. "No, quite the opposite."

He could deal with that, too. "Will I remember what happened with Sophie and Jake?"

"Not the facts, only the wisdom."

That wasn't what he wanted to hear. He paused for a moment, sorry to have to let go of good friends. But Jake and Sophie had each other. Their love was strong. And a little part of him would always live in Sophie's memory. And in Jake's heart. The best part of him.

He grinned at his Adviser, suddenly feeling very, *very* good. "You know, it's kind of a kick helping people. I could get into this."

"Yes, my boy. You certainly could."

* * * * *

SPECIAL EDITION

COMING NEXT MONTH

MYSTERY WIFE Annette Broadrick

That Special Woman!

Since the accident that had taken her memory Raoul DuBois scarcely knew his wife. What was this cruel game of fate?

SHADOWS AND LIGHT Lindsay McKenna

Men of Courage

Craig Taggart had tried to forget nurse Susan Evans's tender touch and tempting lips now that she'd married another. He thought he'd succeeded…

LOVING AND GIVING Gina Ferris

Family Found

Outrunning danger Ryan Kent switched identities so often sometimes *he* lost track of who he really was. But he couldn't forget the long-lost family now searching for him or Taylor Simmons, a woman he reminded of her tragic past.

MY BABY, YOUR CHILD Nikki Benjamin

Will Landon had to ask Tess McGuire if she was prepared to save the life of the child to whom she had given birth. How could she say no?

WALK IN BEAUTY Ruth Wind

Luke Bernali had let Jessie down when she was pregnant with their child, but now he was determined to recapture that fierce, desperate long-ago love.

THE PRINCESS OF COLDWATER FLATS Natalie Bishop

Who would marry Samantha Whalen to help her save her impoverished ranch, when everybody for miles around knew she was the most stubborn, tempestuous woman west of the Rockies?